The outside  in infinite
empty darkness It opened
baleful red ey wn voice,
magnified so t nes of his
skull.

'Garth, why do you resist me?'

Uncertain what was happening, Garth did not answer.
And now he could see that the god had Garth's own face,
distorted into a thing of terror.

'It does you no good to defy me, Garth. You are my chosen vehicle. I created you in my image, shaped your body to house me. You are designed to wield my sword and wreak my will. I have waited since the beginning of time for my age of dominion, and you cannot deny it to me. You will serve me willingly in the joy of destruction or unwillingly in bondage. But you will serve me, for you are mine.'

By the same author

LAWRENCE WATT-EVANS

The Sword of Bheleu

Book Three of The Lords of Dûs

GRAFTON BOOKS

A Division of the Collins Publishing Group

LONDON GLASGOW
TORONTO SYDNEY AUCKLAND

Grafton Books
A Division of the Collins Publishing Group
8 Grafton Street, London W1X 3LA

A Grafton UK Paperback Original 1987

ISBN 0-586-07151-2

Printed and bound in Great Britain by
Collins, Glasgow

Set in Times

AUTHOR'S NOTE
Since many readers may be unfamiliar with the complex
pantheon of gods and goddesses known to the characters in this
novel, a glossary is provided at the back, listing those mentioned
in the text. This is not a complete listing, by any means, but
covers only those whose names appear, in one form or another,
in the course of the story.

This one's dedicated to my wife,
Julie Frances McKenna Evans
. . . but they all are, really.

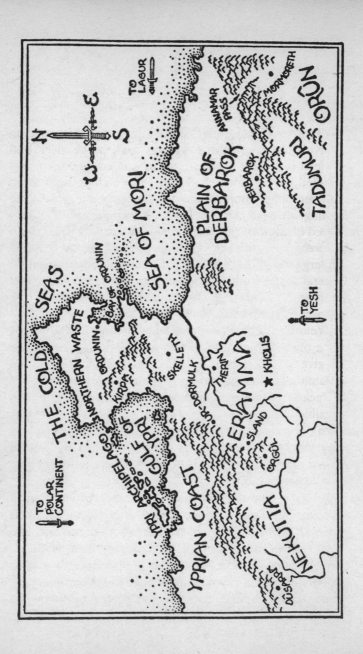

1

Galt, the overman trader, shifted uncomfortably, sending a rivulet of cold rain down the back of his neck and under his mail; it soaked into his quilted gambeson and trickled slowly down his furry back, chilly and damp and thoroughly unpleasant. He suppressed a growl. The itching of the armor was quite bad enough without this added discomfort. He wondered how warriors could stand to wear the stuff day after day. Despite the padded undergarment, he was quite sure that he had acquired several scrapes and scratches from the metal links, and nothing he had tried had alleviated the itching. He suspected that he was allergic to the quilting.

Wearing the mail was bad enough; the added annoyance of drenching rain during his watch had him ready to give up the whole venture. And what was he, the commander, doing standing watch in the first place?

Packing up and going home would undoubtedly be the sensible thing to do, he told himself; Kyrith, however, didn't see it that way. She had insisted on this ridiculous siege, and that meant he was stuck here. The City Council would never forgive him if he left her here unsupervised, in sole command.

In truth, though, he knew he didn't provide much supervision; there was no doubt that, whatever their nominal status, Kyrith was in charge and he was not. She was all fire and drive and fury, despite her handicap, while he had been restrained and reasonable. It was no wonder at all that anyone fool enough to have volunteered for this all-volunteer force would prefer to follow an aggressive idiot, a warrior and the wife of a warrior prince, rather than a quiet, calm trader.

He blinked rainwater out of his great golden eyes and pulled his cloak more closely about him; with his free hand he removed his broad-brimmed hat, shook off what he could of the accumulated rain, then jammed it back on his head. He glanced behind him at the dark shapes of the camp tents, black humps against the gray-black sky. The rain had put out the last trace of the campfires, and the last lantern had been extinguished hours ago. The old Wasteland Road was invisible in the darkness, and the northern hills too distant to see through the falling rain. A gust of wind swept water into his face, and he snorted, blowing the moisture out of his slit nostrils. Those ugly noses the humans had apparently had some use after all; they kept out the rain. There were plenty of advantages to being an overman, though, and on balance he felt his species came out ahead. The very word for his kind implied as much, of course. He looked about, peering through the rain and the darkness.

Immediately to his right waited the warbeast he had been assigned, its flank less than a yard away; its eyes were closed, either in sleep or to keep out the rain, he was unsure which. Its glossy black fur blended with the night sky and the darkened plain, so that it seemed almost a phantom, its edges indistinct, as if it were only a vague outline of an animal. Its triangular ears were laid back against its skull, smoothing its already sleek shape still further; its pantherlike tail lashed silently from side to side. Galt knew that most cats disliked water – very few overmen kept pets, but he had seen them aboard the trading vessels out of Lagur – and he wondered if the creature was as miserable as its feline forebears would have been if forced to stand in pouring rain for hours on end. He was not familiar with warbeasts, and could not tell from its face or its actions; to him it seemed as calm and impassive as ever, save for the motion of its tail.

To his left was empty plain; several yards away a dark shape rose up against the night sky where some human farmer had built his home. Somewhere beyond that, lost in the gloom, he knew there was another overman standing watch with a warbeast ready at his side.

Ahead of him, perhaps a hundred yards away, stood the ruined wall of the town of Skelleth, and the fallen towers that marked its North Gate. A pale flicker of light reminded him that some unfortunate human was also stuck with watch duty, but that man, whoever he was, at least had the comfort of a fire and whatever shelter was provided by the one tower wall that still stood.

Galt envied the man his fire. Even if he had had enough dry fuel to keep a fire going, he would not have dared to light one; it went against policy and good sense in so underequipped a siege as this one. The enemy forces could use such fires to locate the sentries, making it that much easier to send spies out between them, and to smuggle supplies in.

The firelight flickered oddly, and Galt's attention was drawn to it briefly, but he dismissed it as unimportant. The guard had probably walked in front of it, stretching his legs, no doubt.

The light flickered again, and then seemed to brighten. Galt blinked rain away and peered at it more closely.

It *was* brighter; in fact, there were now two lights, and one was moving. The watch fire remained where it was; the increase in brightness had been the addition of this new light, whatever it was. He watched and listened carefully.

The new, smaller light was slowly approaching. Galt stirred uneasily, sending another trickle down his back, and his right hand closed on his sword hilt. The light was definitely coming closer. Although it was hard to be sure

9

through the hissing rain, he thought he heard boots sloshing through the mud. He patted the warbeast's side, then returned his hand to his sword and loosened the blade in its scabbard. The warbeast's eyes opened, gleaming a ghostly pale green in the dimness as they caught the faint light; its tail stopped lashing. Galt took a step forward.

He had forgotten the added weight of his armor and that he had been standing in mud for several long minutes without moving his feet; there was a soft sucking sound as his boot came free, though the motion required little more effort than it would have ordinarily.

The light suddenly stopped moving, still at least a dozen yards away; there was an instant of silence, save for the pattering of the rain, and then a voice called softly, 'Overman?'

Galt made no reply, but slapped the warbeast's neck in the signal meaning 'separate and surround'; the monster obediently slipped silently away in the darkness. Galt spared a second to wonder how anything that large could move so quietly in the rain and mud.

'Overman? Please, if you're there, I come in peace, I want to talk to your leader.' The voice was speaking in little more than a loud whisper, but Galt had no trouble in making out the words. Aware that the warbeast was circling around and that a shouted command would bring it leaping upon the intruder, Galt decided he could risk replying.

'Who are you?' he asked.

There was a pause; the light swung, and slogging footsteps approached a few paces. Galt could see that the glow came from a lantern held by a human, but could make out no details.

'My name is Saram. I used to be a lieutenant in the Baron's guard. I want to speak with your leader.'

'Saram?' Galt was startled; he knew the man very

slightly, having met him in the course of the trading expedition that had started this whole silly mess. Garth, the leader of that expedition, had spoken with Saram at length. Since Garth's disappearance was more or less the cause of the siege, conversation with the man might prove worthwhile.

'Where are you?' the human asked.

'Never mind where I am. Hold the lantern up so I can see your face.'

The man obeyed; although he was still too far away for Galt to be certain, his face could well have been Saram's.

'What do you want?' Galt asked.

'I want to talk to the leader of your expedition.'

'About what?'

'About Garth.'

'Speak to me, then. I will decide whether what you say is worth bringing to the attention of our commanders.'

'But . . . who are you? I can't even be sure you're an overman. Come where I can see you.'

Galt considered. The man was merely human, and it was plain that he was alone; unskilled as he was in fighting, Galt was sure he could handle a lone human – particularly with the warbeast lurking somewhere close by.

'As you wish.' He walked carefully forward until he stood at the outer edge of the lantern's circle of light. His left hand dropped from holding his cloak closed and fell instead upon the hilt of his dagger; his sword was drawn and ready in his right. 'Speak,' he commanded.

Saram hesitated. 'Who are you? You look familiar.'

'I was unaware that humans could tell one overman from another.'

'I may be mistaken.'

There was no harm in admitting his identity. 'No; we've met before. I am Galt.'

'Oh, of course; the trader.'

11

'The master trader, yes.' There was a moment of silence as each considered the other; then Galt demanded, 'Speak. What have you to say regarding Garth?'

'I know where he is.'

'Do you know when he will return?'

'No. But what difference does that make? He is not in Skelleth. I will swear to that.'

Galt smiled humorlessly. 'I am afraid it will take more than the word of a single human to convince our leaders of that. If he is not in Skelleth, then where is he? As a matter of fact, Saram, I know as well as you that the Baron of Skelleth banished Garth; I was there, after all. Unfortunately, there are those who prefer to view that entire scene as a fraud, a drama to convince me that Garth was not in Skelleth while the Baron laid subtle plans for his capture.'

Saram snorted, a sound barely audible above the drumming rain. 'That's absurd.'

'To you, it may seem so. To overmen and overwomen who know nothing of humankind, it seems perfectly plausible. The treachery of mankind is legendary among my people.'

'But if I say where Garth has gone?'

'Merely another lie. However, I admit to a certain curiosity; where *has* he gone? He told me only that he would be back before the start of the new year.'

'I had hoped to have some assurance of peace before revealing what I know.'

'I'm afraid that we'll just have to forget about it then. A pity. I would very much like to know.'

Saram considered for a moment, looking up at Galt's inhuman face, and then said, 'He has gone to Dûsarra on an errand for the Forgotten King.'

Galt did not reply immediately; this brief answer raised so many further questions that he preferred to tally them up in his head before asking any.

When he had thought it over, he asked, 'Who is the Forgotten King?'

'An old man who lives in a tavern in Skelleth; more than that is hard to say. He claims that his kingdom is also forgotten and that he has lived here in Skelleth for centuries. There is good reason to believe him a wizard of some sort.'

'Why would Garth be running errands for him?'

Saram shrugged, and the lantern bobbed, its light dancing and spattering. 'Garth is not, perhaps, the least gullible of beings. Apparently, some oracle told him that the old man could grant him wishes, and he believes it. I think that his current quest is supposed to be rewarded with immortality.'

'An oracle, you say?'

'I believe he mentioned one.'

'The Wise Women of Ordunin, perhaps?'

'I don't know; it could be.'

This began to make sense. Garth was one of the privileged few the Wise Women would speak to, and he had consulted them on several occasions. No one had ever yet known the Wise Women to be wrong, or actually to lie; however, they took a perverse delight in misleading their questioners. Undoubtedly Garth had misinterpreted some deliberately vague answer and betaken himself to this mysterious old man on the basis of that misinterpretation.

'Why, then, did this so-called King send Garth to Dûsarra?'

'I'm not sure. He has some complicated magic he's planning, but he lacks some of the necessary ingredients, it seems, and I think Garth was supposed to bring back something he needed.'

'Where and what is Dûsarra?'

'I believe it is a city far to the west, in Nekutta.'

'How far?'

13

'I don't know.'

Galt contemplated this. 'Could it be so far that he has not yet had time to return? It was a month or more ago that he vanished.'

'Certainly it could. The world is a very big place.'

'We overmen wouldn't know. These past three centuries we have had little opportunity to see it.'

Saram ignored the sarcasm. 'I haven't seen much of it, either, but I've heard that the land extends for hundreds of leagues to the west and south.'

'So it is your belief that Garth is off adventuring in this Dûsarra and will return in due time?'

'Unless he gets himself killed, yes.'

'Why have you told me this? Why come here, alone, in the middle of the night, in the pouring rain, to tell us that our missing comrade is running some fool's errand for a crazy old man?'

Saram was momentarily taken aback. 'It's the truth!'

'Quite possibly it is, but why have you told me?'

'To end the siege!'

'You think this information will end the siege?'

'Why not? You came to rescue Garth; Garth isn't here.'

'It would be more pleasant for all of us if things were that simple. Unfortunately, they are not. Garth is not the *reason* for our presence so much as the *excuse*. We are here at the behest of his wife Kyrith – who has come seeking her husband, true. But do you think sixty of Ordunin's warriors and a dozen of the best and most valuable warbeasts would be out here solely to please a lone overwoman who prefers not to believe that Garth would rather go off adventuring than come home to her? I was there when the Baron sentenced Garth to exile and I do not think the man was dissembling. Further, I know Garth reasonably well, and I am well aware that in his resentment of his exile he would be disinclined to go meekly home to his wives and children. I know that he might well be impulsive enough to undertake this mission you mention, yet here I am, wearing armor in this miserable rain, watching the North Gate of your stinking village in the middle of the night.

'No, I will be frank. Garth's disappearance was only an excuse. This expedition was intended as a show of force. Our intent was to ride into the market square, confront the Baron, and renegotiate the terms of our existence. For three hundred years overmen have lived a lean and bitter life in a harsh wasteland because your ancestors defeated ours in the Racial Wars and drove us into the barren north. We believed that the defeat was final and irreversible. Our legends taught us that Skelleth stood at the border, a mighty fortress, ready to oppose any attempt on our part to renew our acquaintance with the rest of the world. Your people were reputed to be our implacable and deadly foes. Rather than confront you, we sailed the full width of the Sea of Mori and traded with the smugglers of Lagur for the necessities our land could not provide, paying whatever they asked because we had no choice and knew no better.

'Then Garth came south on some quest of his own invention and discovered that Skelleth was a pitiful ruin, three-fourths abandoned and on the edge of starvation, worse off than we were ourselves. He returned with me and two others to establish trade and, in accordance with our long tradition of bowing to human demands, we allowed your Baron to set the terms of that trade, including Garth's banishment and a dishonorable oath.

'However, this is not just. We saw, we four, just how low Skelleth had sunk. There is no longer any reason for us to cower. It is not fitting for us to do so. Therefore, we shall not. The time has come when the overmen of the Northern Waste are going to assert themselves once again.'

'Have you then decided to start the Racial Wars anew?' The harsh sarcasm in Saram's tone was unmistakable.

Galt chose to ignore it. 'No. We have no wish to commit mass suicide, either slowly by starvation or quickly by a disastrous war. We had planned to ride into the market and confront your Baron; we would present our demands, and he would have no choice but to agree as completely as possible. He would, of course, be unable to produce Garth. His failure to do so would allow us to maintain a position of moral superiority in what would otherwise be a case of outright aggression, and from that position we would dictate terms – the revocation of Garth's exile, the elimination of all tariffs and restrictions on trade, and free passage throughout his domain.'

'It's a lovely theory.'

'Yes, it is. It would have worked, too, had your Baron done his part and met us in the marketplace yesterday morning. He is no fool; he would have given in rather than risk a war he could not win.'

Saram paused before replying. 'It's hard to know,' he said, 'just what the Baron would do. He is mad, after all. You have only seen him during a lucid period. It's his madness that fouled up your whole plan.'

'It is?'

'Of course!'

'Your captain swore by all the gods that the Baron was ill in bed and could not move or speak. That put us in a very awkward position; we had no choice but to leave the town and begin our siege. Was he lying?'

'No, he spoke truly, but this is a regular occurrence. Every fortnight or so the Baron's madness overtakes him, and he sinks into a state of depression so intense that he cannot speak, cannot stand, cannot feed himself. Such an attack occurred when word arrived that your company was approaching Skelleth.'

Galt digested this information. 'How long will this last?'

'Who knows? It varies. This looks like a bad one; it could be days.'

There was a moment of silence, save for the pattering rain, as each considered his position. Saram was the first to break it.

'Then you will stay until the Baron recovers and meets your demands?'

'Yes. For myself, I was tempted to abandon the whole thing and try again later, but Kyrith would have none of that. She is quite convinced that her mate is somewhere within your walls and she has no intention of departing without him. Most of the warriors are overeager young hotheads who did not care to give up their chance for glory so easily, and they supported her. This is the first time in more than three hundred years that the warriors of Ordunin have been on the offensive, and they like the feel of it.'

'I am . . .' Saram paused, as if reconsidering what he had to say, then went on, 'I am surprised that you have merely besieged us. Why not take Skelleth by storm?'

Galt snorted. 'And start the Racial Wars again? I know little of human politics; but, while I doubt the High King at Kholis will interfere with trade negotiations no matter how we carry them out, he can scarcely be expected to ignore the capture of one of his baronies.'

'It would seem we have a stalemate, then.'

'Only temporarily; sooner or later your Baron will recover and face us. It should be a simple matter to resolve everything when that happens.'

'I hope you're right.'

'In the meanwhile, of course, I must stand watch in this miserable rain. There is no need for you to be here, though; go home and dry off. I appreciate your efforts at peacemaking, but there's little you can do.'

17

'So it would seem. Farewell, then, Galt, and I wish you luck.' He turned, and began slogging back toward the ruined gate. The overman watched as the lantern light receded and finally merged once again with the light of the flickering watch fire.

2

The rain stopped shortly after dawn. Garth mounted his warbeast – which had been named Koros after the Arkhein god of war by a captured bandit a few months earlier – for the last leg of his long journey back to Skelleth from the black-walled city of Dûsarra. The clouds lingered in the sky, hiding the sun, making the day gray and gloomy, allowing the road to remain a soggy, muddy mess. Garth's supplies and clothing and the clothing of his human captive had all been thoroughly drenched when Garth had found no shelter from the downpour the evening before, and they remained uncomfortably damp for hours. Even Koros' fur was soaked, and the captive, a Dûsarran girl who called herself Frima, complained about the smell.

It didn't bother Garth particularly, though he couldn't deny its presence. He ignored her monologue; in the last two weeks, spent mostly in the saddle, he had grown accustomed to Frima's fondness for complaining.

When she had exhausted her first topic, the smell of wet warbeast fur, she went on to others – her own sopping garments, the unsuitability of her attire for a respectable person, the length of the journey, and all the other things that displeased her about the world and her place in it.

The overman didn't really blame her. He wasn't particularly happy about being caught in the rain; the water had soaked into the garments he wore under his mail, and the armor was holding the moisture in. His own fur was as wet as the warbeast's, though not as odorous.

Even Koros seemed to be irritated, and it was usually

the most tranquil of beasts as long as it was properly and promptly fed and not attacked. The mud of the highway stuck to its great padded paws, slightly impeding its usual smooth, silent, gliding walk, so that its footsteps were audible as faint splashings.

Frima was still complaining when Garth first caught sight of Skelleth, a low line of sagging rooftops and jagged broken ramparts along the horizon.

He pointed it out to her, and she immediately forgot her complaints. 'You mean we're finally there?'

'Almost.'

'I can't see any domes or towers.'

'There aren't any.'

'There aren't?'

'No.' Garth had long ago gotten over his annoyance at the girl's habit of asking questions over again and simply answered each one however many times it might be asked. They had been together more than a fortnight, and he had grown accustomed to queries and complaints. She was only human, after all; he couldn't expect much from her.

'What are their temples like, then?' she asked.

'To the best of my knowledge, there are no temples in Skelleth,' he replied.

'There aren't?'

'No.'

'Really?'

'Really.'

'Are they all atheists, then?'

'No. At least, I think not.'

'Are you an atheist?'

'I used to be; I am no longer certain.'

'Why aren't you certain?'

'Because I saw and felt and did things in Dûsarra that have convinced me that at least some of your seven gods

20

exist – though I am not certain they are truly gods, rather than some lesser sort of magical being.'

'They're not *my* seven gods; I worship only Tema!'

Garth did not bother to answer. Instead, he studied the horizon carefully. Skelleth looked different from this angle; he had never approached from this direction before. Even when he had left on this expedition, he had done so by way of the West Gate, and then circled southward on to the highway he now rode.

He wondered briefly if it might be wise to enter by another gate. After all, he was still an exile by order of the Baron of Skelleth. It might well be advisable to use caution until such time as a proper opportunity for vengeance presented itself.

But no, that was not what he wanted; he would ride directly into town, defying the Baron to stop him. He had previously acquiesced to his banishment to avoid damaging the prospects for trade, but his trip to Dûsarra had proven very educational indeed; besides learning more about the gods humans worshipped, he had become convinced that Skelleth was by no means the only possible overland trade route between the Northern Waste and the rich lands of the south. It should be possible, he thought, to circle around Skelleth and trade directly with southern cities; he no longer believed that the old hatred between men and overmen would be strong enough to prevent commerce from flourishing once the southerners saw the gold his people mined in the Waste. Furthermore, he had learned that the Northern Waste was not the only surviving colony of overmen; Dûsarra traded with overmen who lived on the Yprian Coast, and though he knew nothing about these people beyond the simple fact of their existence, he saw no reason that his own people couldn't trade with them as well.

With all these opportunities, he had no intention of

being pushed around by the mad baron of a filthy little border town.

He had no intention of cowering before the Baron of Skelleth; he would ride straight into town, straight into the market square. If the Baron objected, then Garth would laugh at him. Better still, Garth would kill him! He would take the great sword he had brought from Dûsarra, hack the Baron into pieces, and spill his blood across the dirt of his village . . .

'The ruby's glowing again,' Frima said, interrupting his chain of thought.

Garth looked down at the hilt of the immense two-handed broadsword that was strapped along the war-beast's side. Sure enough, the large red jewel that was set in its pommel sparkled with more light than the morning sun could account for.

The thing had been at him again, he realized; it was the sword's influence that had made him think of killing the Baron. He forced thoughts of blood and destruction out of his mind, concentrating instead on his knowledge that the sword he had taken from the burning altar of Bheleu, god of destruction, was trying to warp his personality again. It had tried to do so several times on the journey from Dûsarra to Skelleth, but so far he had been successful in resisting its influence. He had avoided killing Frima several times, and kept himself from killing three farmers, two innkeepers, a drunkard, four travelers, and a blacksmith encountered along the way. The fact that both Frima and Koros remained calm and sensible had helped, and the glowing of the red stone served as a warning signal, allowing him to become aware of the insidious effects before they became irresistible.

He would be glad when he got rid of the thing. Along with the rest of his loot, including Frima, it was to be turned over to the Forgotten King. He would be reluctant to turn the sword over to anyone else; he knew how dangerous it could be. The Forgotten King, however, was a feeble old man and a wizard, presumably well able to resist such spells.

Of course, he was also the lost high priest of The God Whose Name Is Not Spoken, the god of death, according to the caretaker of that god's temple in Dûsarra. And it was a magnificent weapon, beautiful and deadly; it was a sword a warrior could be proud of indeed! With a blade like that he could slaughter any foe . . .

The red glow caught his eye, and he fought the blood-lust down again. He would have to discuss various matters with the King before he turned over the sword – or the other loot, for that matter; just because none of it had affected him significantly didn't mean it didn't have magical power – but one way or another he was going to have to get rid of the thing. He could not keep fighting off its domination forever.

The warbeast growled faintly, a noise he couldn't interpret; it was not the growl that meant danger ahead, nor was it a growl of displeasure. He looked away from the stone, but could tell nothing more from the back of the great beast's head than from its growl.

'Are you all right?' Frima asked.

'I think so,' he replied. 'It hasn't gotten a good hold on me yet.'

'That's good. I think there's someone on the road ahead.'

Garth peered into the distance; the girl was right. That, then, must have been what Koros was growling about. There was a mounted figure ahead in the middle of the highway, perhaps a hundred yards from Skelleth's ruined gate.

Had the Baron posted guards on this road, too? Previously only the North Gate had been guarded. The figure was quite large for a human. Garth tried to identify the mount; it did not appear to be an ox, a yacker, or even a horse. He had never seen any of the Baron's soldiers mounted.

Koros growled again and this time was answered by a roar from ahead. The animal was another warbeast, which meant that its rider was almost certainly an overman.

What, Garth asked himself, was an overman doing on the highway southwest of Skelleth? And with a warbeast? There was something strange going on.

Koros was making a hissing whine that was its noise to express frustration; Garth told it, 'Go ahead.'

The warbeast let loose with a roar in answer to its fellow and quickened its pace slightly.

Frima shifted behind him. He looked back to see that she had clapped her hands over her ears. He had not, and regretted it; Koros' friendly greeting left his ears ringing.

The other warbeast was moving now, approaching them. When Garth judged that he was within earshot, he called, 'Ho, there! Who are you?'

The reply was faint, but distinct. 'I am Thord of Ordunin! Who are you?'

'I am Garth, also of Ordunin!' He began to call another question, but thought better of it; he could wait until they were closer and save his breath.

A moment later the two came together; their warbeasts began to snuffle and growl at each other in the ritual greetings of their kind. Koros was by far the larger of the two, clean and sleek from nose to tail, every inch of its hide glossy black, while the other beast was slightly scruffy about the lower jaw, with its left fang broken off short and a patch of tawny brown fur on its belly. Both had great golden eyes.

Thord was the larger of the two overmen by about an inch in height and perhaps twenty pounds in weight; his black hair was hacked off just below the ear, while Garth's reached his shoulders. Other than that, the two

24

were quite similar. Both had the noseless, sunken-cheeked, lipless faces of typical overmen, and the leathery brown hide, beardless, but with a thin coat of fur from the neck down. Each had eyes of a baleful red. Thord wore full armor: mail coat, breastplate, helmet, gauntlets, greaves, and metal-clad boots. Garth wore a wide-brimmed trader's hat, battered mail shirt, soft leather breeches, and ragged, worn-out boots. Thord bore a sword and dagger on his belt and had a battle-axe slung on his back. Garth's only weapons were a stiletto in one boot and the two-handed broadsword thrust through the warbeast's harness.

Thord was alone; Garth had Frima perched behind him on Koros' back. The Dûsarran girl was in her late teens, with black, curling hair and brown eyes; her skin was a shade or two darker than that of the pale people of Skelleth, though lighter than any overman's. She was barefoot and clad only in an embroidered tunic that would have reached her knees were it not bunched up higher as she sat astride the warbeast – hardly respectable garb for a human female, as she had told her captor repeatedly. Though she was fully grown, particularly in the bust, and not especially thin, it was a safe wager that she weighed less than half as much as either of the overmen.

Thord spoke first. 'So it really is you, Garth! Where have you been?'

'I have been travelling in Nekutta, on business of my own. What are you doing here on human land with this warbeast?'

'We have Skelleth under siege; I am assigned to guard this road.' There was a note of pride in his tone.

'Siege?' Garth looked out across the empty plain stretching away in all directions, broken only in the northeast where Skelleth stood. There was no sign of an army, siege engines, or even other guards.

'Oh, yes. We have insufficient numbers to surround the town completely, so we are using sentries such as myself in a ring around the walls, with orders to summon others wherever they might be needed. The humans are so weak that they haven't even attempted to break out yet.'

Garth suppressed a derisive smile; he did not care to insult a fellow overman, but the inadequacy of such a 'siege' was very obvious to him. If the humans had not yet broken out, it was not due to weakness, but either because they had not yet gotten around to it – probably because of poor organization – or did not choose to do so. He wondered what fool had contrived such a strategy even more than he wondered why his people had suddenly seen fit to take military action. 'Who devised this scheme?' he asked.

Thord smiled. 'Your wife, Kyrith.'

'What? Kyrith?' All mockery was forgotten in Garth's astonishment.

'Yes. She and Galt the master trader are our co-commanders, appointed by the City Council.'

Garth was momentarily dumbfounded. When he could speak coherently again, ignoring the plaintive questions Frima was asking, he demanded, 'What is going on here? Explain this!'

Thord was taken aback at Garth's flat and dangerous tone, but replied, 'Kyrith was concerned about your safety, Garth. She thought that the Baron of Skelleth must have abducted you when you did not return with the others from your trading mission. Galt told her that you had been exiled and had gone off on your own rather than return home ignominiously, but she didn't believe it. She petitioned the Council for permission to raise a company of volunteers to march down here, confront the Baron, and demand your safe return. The Council agreed; the story is that, though they believed what Galt said,

26

they thought such a threat might frighten the Baron of Skelleth and the other humans into treating us better in future. They insisted, though, that Galt share the command, since Kyrith knew nothing of Skelleth or of human ways and might behave rashly in her anger.'

Garth interrupted. 'They might have done well to include a commander who knew something of military matters. This so-called siege cannot possibly have cut off communications between Skelleth and the rest of Eramma, and we can only hope that no one in town has seen fit to summon reinforcements from the south as yet.'

It was Thord's turn to be struck dumb. 'Reinforcements?' he asked at last.

'Yes, reinforcements! Decayed as it may be, Skelleth is still an outpost of the Kingdom of Eramma, the nation that defeated ours in the last of the Racial Wars. They could probably have ten thousand men here within a week, to flay us all alive.' He had no real idea how large a force Eramma's High King could muster, or how quickly it could reach Skelleth; his figures were sheer guesswork. He had no doubt at all, however, that the Erammans would have no trouble in obliterating a force of overmen too small to lay a proper siege.

'Oh.' Thord's face remained impassive, but his discomfiture was plain in his stiff silence. Garth heard Frima suppress a giggle. He hoped that Thord hadn't noticed. He would undoubtedly be mortally offended to know that a human was laughing at him. Garth himself was slightly irritated at the girl's lack of respect and was equally annoyed at the stupidity of Thord and his comrades who had volunteered for so asinine and dangerous a scheme.

'Go on, then; you just explained how the Council came to grant their permission for this venture.'

'Oh, yes. Well, Kyrith had no trouble in finding sixty volunteers, and was allowed a dozen warbeasts as well.

27

We marched down and arrived yesterday morning, but the Baron refused to see us; one of his guards told us he was sick in bed. Galt thought that we should just set up camp somewhere to the north, in the hills, and wait, but Kyrith didn't want to do that; she was afraid that the Baron might slip out unnoticed, I think. There was a vote, and Kyrith won, and we laid siege to the town yesterday afternoon.'

That was a relief, Garth thought; it was too soon for any messages to have reached the cities of Eramma. It was possible that Skelleth's people had not yet even noticed that they were besieged; things could still be handled peacefully.

'All right,' he said, 'you've done your duty, but I'm relieving you now. You go back and tell my wife to call off this ridiculous siege. I'm safe and well and I'll come and find her as soon as I've finished a little business of my own in town. Where is she camped?'

'The main encampment is on the Wasteland Road to the north, but I can't leave my post yet.'

'Nonsense. You go tell her I'm here.' Garth was in no mood to argue; if he left Thord standing guard here on the main highway, the fool might attack a caravan or an innocent traveler, should one happen along.

'I have my orders, my lord.'

'Forget your orders. I outrank whoever gave them and I'm countermanding them. This siege will end immediately; as a member of the City Council, the Prince of Ordunin, and a lord of the overmen of the Northern Waste, I am assuming command. Now, go tell that to Kyrith and tell her to wait for me and do nothing hostile toward the humans until I arrive. Is that clear?' Without his intending it, his right hand crept down toward the hilt of the great two-handed broadsword; the gem in the pommel gleamed blood-red.

Thord hesitated a moment longer, trying to decide

28

whether Garth did in fact have the authority to overrule a commander appointed by a quorum of the City Council. Garth was here and annoyed; the Council was not. That decided him. 'As you wish,' he said, as he turned his warbeast's head northward.

Garth watched him go; he was growing angrier as he thought about the stupidity of the overmen who could plan and execute such an inept maneuver – his own chief wife among them! A siege was a delicate and sometimes dangerous operation, not a casual lark. It would serve the lot of them right if someone did happen along and take them in the rear. It would be only just and fitting if the entire sixty were slaughtered. For half a silver bit he'd go up there himself and teach them all something about war – teach them at swordpoint!

'Garth?' Frima's voice was not entirely steady.

The human had interrupted his chain of thought – the insolent creature! He almost snarled as he asked, 'What do you want?'

'The jewel's glowing again.' She pointed.

It was, indeed, and glowing relatively brightly. He looked at it and told himself that the anger he felt was not his own. There was no reason to be angry with the girl, who had acted as she thought best. There was no reason to be angry with Kyrith and her volunteers – at least, not reason enough for him to take action. They didn't know any better.

It took several minutes of effort to force himself back to a state of comparative calm. When he had managed it, he told himself that he would really have to get rid of the sword as soon as he possibly could.

Well, that was part of the personal business he wanted to attend to here in Skelleth; he intended either to deliver the loot he had brought from Dûsarra to the Forgotten King or dispose of it someplace where it wouldn't endanger anyone in the future.

With that in mind, he urged Koros forward toward the town's southwestern gate.

There was no guard; had the townspeople realized they were besieged, there almost certainly would have been, he told himself. Therefore, they apparently hadn't noticed. That was good; it meant that no act of war had yet taken place as far as the humans were concerned.

It struck him as curious that the only gate the Baron saw fit to guard was the one leading north. True, the other four all faced nominally friendly territory, and there was no real threat in any direction – except perhaps from his own people. Duty at the North Gate was a convenient punishment for guardsmen who had displeased the Baron; Saram had told him that, months ago. The other gates were less suitable, since they were more sheltered from the cold winds and more likely to have traffic disrupting the boredom.

Whatever the reasoning behind it, he was glad that the Baron did guard only the north. It meant he could enter the town unseen.

The gate before him was actually merely a gap in the wall where the road wound its way through the rubble of long-fallen towers; there was no trace left of the actual gate that had once been there. Koros had no trouble in making his way through it. The road through the West Gate was partially blocked by debris, but this one was not; it was kept clear for the caravans that provided Skelleth's only real contact with civilization.

Inside the wall, Garth found himself surrounded by ruins. The town had once been a fair-sized city, in the days when it was humanity's main bulwark against the overmen in the final years of the Racial Wars three centuries earlier; but when the fighting stopped, so did the flow of supplies and men from the south. Skelleth had withered, shrinking inward, until now it was mostly abandoned. The remaining village was clustered about

30

the market square and the Baron's mansion, surrounded by acres of crumbling, empty buildings.

His goal was the King's Inn, the tavern where the Forgotten King lived. It stood on a narrow, filthy alley behind the Baron's mansion, right near the center of town, so there was no way he could hope to reach it undetected. That being the case, he saw little point in trying; skulking about through the ruins would just slow him down, and he wanted to get to Kyrith's encampment before she had time to do anything else stupid.

Therefore, he rode straight onward, ignoring the astonished pedestrians and householders who stared as he passed.

It was quite likely that word would reach the Baron, which was unfortunate; Garth was still, after all, under sentence of exile, forbidden to enter Skelleth without the Baron's express permission. He might have to kill a few guardsmen in order to convince the humans that he would come and go as he pleased, with or without their permission.

It might be fun to kill a few guardsmen; he would use the sword, of course, and hack at them until . . .

He caught himself and glanced down at the glowing ruby before Frima had time to say anything.

It would *not* be fun to kill anyone. Humans had just as much right to live as he himself did. If he were forced into a confrontation with the Baron's soldiers, he would just have to hope that he could bluff them out of attacking, as he had done once before. He would not kill anyone if he could help it.

He didn't want to harm anyone, he told himself.

He had to repeat it over and over as he rode through the streets, watching the townspeople scatter at his approach. He had to resist the temptation to order Koros to charge, to ride them down like so many goats, to

31

snatch the great sword from the warbeast's harness and swing it among them.

By the time he reached the King's Inn he was muttering aloud, 'I mustn't harm them, I mustn't kill anyone.'

Far to the west, in the city of Dûsarra, in a room draped in black and deep red and lit by a single huge candle, a pudgy, balding man in a flowing black robe held a clear crystal globe and stared into its depths. Constant use of the scrying glass was tiring and it seemed to age him, but it was one of his greatest pleasures. His abilities grew stronger with practice, and of late he had practiced much.

He had not, however, practiced as much as he might have liked; he had other duties now, many of them. A month ago he had been under orders that severely limited his use of the glass, but when his special abilities were not needed his time had been entirely his own. Now he had no restraints upon him, no one who could tell him what to do or not to do; but with this freedom had come responsibility for all the affairs of his sect. He, Haggat, was the new high priest of Aghad, god of fear and hatred, and it was his job to keep the cult healthy and active. He could not do that merely by studying his glass; he had to sit in judgement on disputes, choose what course the cult would take, and sift through and consider all the information gathered by means both magical and mundane.

He had delegated many tasks, as many as he thought he could without weakening his authority, but he still found much of his time being spent on administrative trivia. It was a relief and a joy when he could return to his first love, spying.

Unfortunately, his time was running out; he had to go and tend to business, choosing a candidate for the night's sacrifice. He could not put it off if the victim was to be readied in time.

That was a great pity; he had been watching his favorite subject, the overman who had made him high priest by slaying his predecessor. Garth's image had been hard to summon of late, and Haggat did not think it was entirely due to increasing distance. Something was interfering, some magical force of great power. It was probably the Sword of Bheleu that was responsible.

The overman was not doing anything of great interest at the moment; he had apparently arrived in Skelleth and was making his way through the streets. Now he seemed to be stopping at a small tavern. He was muttering something, but the glass showed images only, without sound, and the scene was not sufficiently clear for lip-reading.

Haggat had better ways to spend his time than watching an overman take his noon meal, which was undoubtedly Garth's intent. The image was blurring, and the sacrifice had to be chosen. He lowered the sphere, letting the vision fade out of existence.

He would return, however, when time allowed. Garth had defied and defiled the cult of Aghad, and it was Haggat's duty to make sure that he suffered for that.

The cult of Aghad was quite expert in such matters.

3

'Where are we?' Frima asked.

'This,' Garth answered, 'is the King's Inn, where the Forgotten King may be found.'

'Does he own it? Is that why it's called the King's?'

'I don't know; it doesn't matter.'

'Are you really going to give me to him?' Her tone was wistful; Garth could not precisely identify the emotion, wistfulness being more or less alien to overmen, but he realized she was not pleased.

'Yes, I am; that is why I took you from the altar of Sai and brought you to Skelleth. I have no other use for you. It may well be that he will have no more need for you than I do, though, in which case you will most likely be free to go your way.'

'Oh.' That single syllable carried many mingled emotions; Garth was aware of none, and even Frima herself did not fully understand her feelings at that moment. There was trepidation as she faced an unknown fate, mingled with anticipation of meeting a wizard, hope that she might be freed, regret that her association with Garth was apparently about to end – a maze of confused and confusing sentiments.

They were in the alley behind the Baron's mansion, surrounded by filthy mire and an appalling stench. A few paces ahead, on their left, was the open door of a tavern, and its broad, many-paned window of ancient purpling glass was just beyond. The day was still gray and cloudy, so that the alleyway was full of shadows and the lanterns gleaming inside the King's Inn made the door and window into welcoming oblongs of light.

34

No one had dared interfere with the warbeast's smooth, silent progress through the town, but any number of villagers had seen it pass, and it was possible that some had recognized which overman it was carrying. Word had probably already reached the Baron of Garth's arrival; he could not afford to waste any time. He hoped that he would be able to speak with the old man and be gone before any opposition could be sent to stop him.

There was a stable just past the inn, but he ignored it and left Koros standing in the alley while he gathered together the booty he had brought from Dûsarra in fulfillment of the Forgotten King's task.

Most of it was contained in a single good-sized sack, which he slung over his shoulder. Frima was another part; he lifted her to the ground and ordered her to accompany him and remain silent. Finally, there was the bewitched sword; he was hesitant to handle it directly, since he well knew that, even when he was not actually touching it, it was able to exert considerable control over his emotions and actions. There seemed no good alternative, however, so at last he pulled it from the warbeast's harness, using only one hand and keeping a layer of cloth wrapped about the hilt so that his flesh was never in direct contact with the metal or the black covering of the grip.

At Garth's command, Frima led the way into the bright, clean interior of the tavern; she was less able to run away with him immediately behind her. He carried the sack in his left hand and the sword in his right; but had she made any suspicious move, he could have dropped them quickly and grabbed her.

The inn's main room was a pleasant contrast to the noisome alley; it was just as Garth remembered it, warm and clean and worn. The walls were panelled in dark woods, and light came from several oil lamps on tables and overhead beams, as well as from an immense fireplace that occupied much of the right-hand wall. Glassware and pewter sparkled faintly on shelves. The wall to the left was lined with great barrels of ale and wine, bound and tapped with shining, polished brass. At the rear, a wooden stair led to an upper floor. To the right lay the broad slate hearth that spread before the gaping stone fireplace.

The oaken floor was worn into strange, smooth shapes that showed that the furniture had not been rearranged in centuries. Shallow troughs led between and around the tables, where the feet of countless patrons had scuffed along; slight grooves marked where each chair had been dragged to and from its table over and over again. The tables themselves stood atop low hills, their legs perched on the only parts of the floor that had not been worn down.

Half a dozen humans were present. There was the portly, middle-aged innkeeper, a trayful of ale-filled mugs in his hands. There were two unkempt villagers in dirty tunics who had been calling for their ale when the girl and the overman entered; they fell suddenly silent as they caught sight of the newcomers. There was a guardsman in mail shirt and leather helmet, speaking to a black-haired man with a neatly trimmed beard; Garth recognized the civilian as Saram, formerly a lieutenant in the Baron's service, and a man who had sometimes been of service to both Garth and the Forgotten King.

And finally, there was the King himself. He was an old man wrapped tightly in his tattered yellow cloak and cowl, sitting at a small table in the back corner beneath the stairs. He might once have been tall, by human standards, but was now ancient, bent, and withered. The cowl hid much of his face, so that all that could be seen was the tip of his bony nose and the wispy white beard that trailed from his chin.

Garth pointed him out to Frima; she stared in open

astonishment. '*That's* the king you want to deliver me to?'

'Yes,' Garth replied. He fought down annoyance at the girl's surprise; he was very much aware of the sword he held in his right hand and the faintly glowing red gem set in its pommel.

The innkeeper and the other four patrons watched silently as the pair made their way to the corner table. The innkeeper stood still, not daring to move, lest he block their path accidentally, until they had passed him; then he hurried to deliver the ale he carried, before his customers had a chance to react to the overman's presence by leaving without paying.

The pair of civilians muttered quietly to one another. The guardsman, with no pretense of stealth, told Saram, 'I think I had better go and tell the captain.'

'You do that,' Saram answered. 'I'll stay here and watch.' His eyes followed Frima across the room.

The soldier nodded, rose, and departed, as Garth seated himself across from the yellow-garbed figure. Frima nervously sat at the nearest unoccupied table; there was something about the old man she found disturbing. She realized that even when she looked directly at him – or as nearly as she could – she could not see his eyes, but only darkness. His face was dry and wrinkled, drawn tight across the bone, and no matter how much she adjusted her position or her gaze, she could not make out his forehead or his eyes through the shadows of the over-hanging cowl. They must, she decided, be sunken back into his head; he did not seem to be blind. There must be more there than empty sockets.

Garth paid no attention to the shadows; he had seen the old man before and knew that he always appeared thus. He was not certain why the King's eyes could not be seen or how the trick was managed, but it had become familiar. He knew that the old man could see, and that sometimes a glint of light could be seen, as if reflected from an eye, so he was sure it was just a trick of some kind.

'I have brought you what I found upon six of the altars in Dûsarra,' he said without preamble.

The old man shifted slightly and placed his thin mummylike hand atop the table. 'Show me,' he said.

His voice was a dry, croaking whisper. Frima shuddered. The voice sounded of age and imminent death. It reminded her of the stories she had heard of P'hul, the goddess of decay. It was said that where the goddess walked, the ground turned to dust, plants fell to powder, pools dried up, and trees withered and died; the Forgotten King's voice would have fitted such a deity to perfection.

Garth dropped the sack he still held to the floor beside him and gripped the sword with both hands. 'First,' he said, 'there are matters to be settled.'

'What matters?'

The voice was the same; somehow Frima had thought that it would change, that the old man's throat would moisten.

'I want to know why you want these things. I want to know why you have refused to tell me what you plan to do. I want you to explain who and what you are and what you are doing in this run-down tavern in a stinking, half-deserted border town.'

'Why?'

Garth made an inarticulate noise of surprise and frustration. 'Why?' he said. 'You ask why? I have reasons, old man. If you want these things you sent me after, you will have to answer me.'

The yellow-draped shoulders lifted slightly, then dropped.

'Don't shrug it off! I want to know what you think you're doing.' Garth lifted the sword, and Frima saw that

38

the red stone was glowing brightly, a fiery blood-hued light.

The old man lifted his hand from the table and made a gesture with one long, bony finger; abruptly, the glow was gone. The red stone had turned black and now resembled obsidian more than ruby.

Garth and Frima both stared at it in silent amazement. The overman had half-risen; now he sank slowly back into his chair. There was a moment of silence.

It seemed to Garth that a fog had lifted from his mind. He felt curiously empty, as if a moment before his skull had been packed with cotton that had just now vanished, leaving it darkly hollow. His vision seemed preternaturally clear and pure, as if it had somehow been washed clean of an obscuring haze of blood and red light. The anger he had felt was gone, wiped away in an instant, taking with it the irritability and confusion that had seemed to color his every thought for the last two weeks.

Perhaps oddest of all was that, though he was still among the same people as he had been among before, he felt alone for the first time since he had seen the sword glowing red-hot in the ruined temple.

He knew with crystalline clarity and utter certainty that he was himself again – and only himself – where he had been something else minutes earlier. He felt clean, and it was a very good feeling indeed.

He wondered how long it could last. The sword was supposed to be a link to the god Bheleu; whatever the Forgotten King might be, could he defy a god? Was it truly the god of destruction who had influenced Garth? If so, how long would it be before he reasserted his authority? Garth looked apprehensively at the sword's pommel.

The stone remained dead black. At last, somewhat reassured, Garth said, 'I want to know how you are able to do such things. I apologize for the anger; as you obviously are aware, the sword has – had – a hold on me, and caused me to behave irrationally at times. However, it is not the sword, but my own will that forces me to insist upon an explanation before I give you these things I stole. What are you? What is it you hope to achieve?'

'You are troubled,' the old man said, 'because you have been told that I am the high priest of The God Whose Name Is Not Spoken and you do not want to aid one who serves Death.'

'You do not deny it, then?'

The Forgotten King did not answer.

'You understand, then, why I am reluctant. I know that at least one of these objects has magical power – I would have said very great power, had I not seen you deal with it just now. I suspect that some of the others are also magical, though subtler. I know that you sent me on this errand in the hope of acquiring items necessary for some great feat you hope to perform, but you have consistently refused to tell me anything of the nature of this feat. Is it any surprise that, when I learned your identity, I feared that this purpose must be dire indeed? The tasks you have set me are hardly comforting; you asked me to bring you the basilisk from Mormoreth, the deadliest creature I have ever encountered in fact or legend, and to rob for you the altars of the dark gods. Everything would seem to indicate that you plan some truly ghastly act of mass death in the service of your god.'

The old man sat silently for a moment, apparently considering this; as he did, Frima was distracted momentarily. Saram had crossed the room and now stood beside her.

'Do you mind if I join you?' he asked softly, indicating one of the other chairs at her table.

'No,' she replied without thinking; then she added, 'Garth might object, though.'

'Oh, I don't think he will,' Saram whispered. 'Those

two are too involved with each other to pay any attention to us.' He seated himself across from the girl, and together they watched and listened as the Forgotten King answered.

'I care nothing for any god's service. I seek only to die.'

After a brief pause, Garth answered, 'I had suspected as much. I could see no use for a basilisk except to kill. When you swore you meant to harm no other, I guessed that you wanted it to slay yourself. Later, though, I doubted my conclusions, for you said that what you sought would have some great significance to the rest of the world, and the death of one old man did not seem to fit. I thought that you might perhaps be lying, that in fact you did want only to die, and that all your other claims were merely to entice me to aid you – but the Wise Women of Ordunin told me that if I served you, my name could live until the end of time, which did not fit such a hypothesis.

'Now, you say that you seek simply your own death; how can this have such mighty repercussions? How can my aiding you ensure my eternal fame? I do not understand. Further, you say that you care nothing for the gods, yet there was no mistaking the Dûsarran priest's description; you *are* the one he described as the high priest of the Final God.'

'I was,' the Forgotten King answered.

'Were? Have you forsaken the service of the death-god?'

The old man did not answer.

Garth sat silently for a moment, then said slowly, 'I think I begin to see. The Dûsarran said that it was in the nature of your service to the god of death that you, yourself, cannot die. You wish to die, though; you have lived more than four ages, he said, and now you grow weary. Yet you cannot die so long as you serve The

41

God Whose Name Is Not Spoken. You have therefore forsaken your service – or sought to. You did not die when you met the gaze of the basilisk; your immortality is still strong. Death has not accepted you, the god has not accepted your renunciation of him.'

The old man nodded very slightly.

'Then is it that you mean to force the gods to acknowledge your resignation, so that you may die? Do you intend to invoke the gods themselves?'

The Forgotten King did not answer.

'That must be it; you will bring The God Whose Name Is Not Spoken into our own world, so that you may end your pact with him. Such a conjuring would indeed be a feat worthy of eternal fame, a thing unequalled in history.'

The yellow-robed figure shifted slightly. 'Not "unequalled in history," Garth. I did it once, when I first made my pact.'

'I can see, too, how you could offer me immortality; I could be presented to the god as your replacement. Such an eternal life does not appeal to me.'

The King shrugged.

'This conjuring – how is it to be done?'

'I have not said that I plan any such thing,' the old man answered.

'You keep up your air of mystery, but what else can you intend? You do not deny it, do you?'

Again, the sagging shoulders rose and dropped.

Garth sat back and considered. His chair creaked beneath his weight. The Forgotten King would not confirm it, but his theory made sense; it hung together neatly and fit all the known facts, as well as the old man's previous statements. Why, then, did the King not admit it? There must be possible consequences that he thought would displease Garth and discourage any further aid. Such consequences must be fairly easy to discover, too; if they were in the least esoteric, it would be simple enough to keep Garth from learning them.

He thought the matter over. Bringing The God Whose Name Is Not Spoken into the mortal realm – what would that entail? The god sometimes demanded human sacrifices; could that be it? It could, indeed. Further, the invocation itself surely would involve the speaking aloud of the unspeakable name, whatever it was – that was supposed to mean certain death. Obviously, it would not kill the Forgotten King, but what of those around him? What of Garth himself? What would the presence of personified Death do to the surrounding area?

He had no way of knowing what would be involved. Probably no one knew except the Forgotten King.

'What will happen to those around you, if you are successful in whatever magic you intend to perform in order that you may die?'

The old man shrugged once again.

'Do you mean that you do not know, or is it merely a matter of indifference to you?'

'I do not know exactly.'

Garth paused, phrasing his next question carefully.

'Have you reason to believe that the magic which will permit you to die will also bring about other deaths?'

After a moment of silence, the King replied, 'Yes.'

'How many other deaths?'

'I don't know.'

'One? A few? Many?'

'Many.'

That was it, then; that was why the old man had been so reluctant to say what he was after. Furthermore, it was the reason Garth would not serve him any longer and would not turn over the booty he had brought from Dûsarra.

At least, that was what Garth told himself. Then he reconsidered and asked, 'Is it possible that there might be some other way in which you could die, some way that would harm no one else?'

The old man answered, 'I do not know of any such possibility; I have sought one for centuries without success. The basilisk was very nearly my last hope for such a death.'

Very nearly his last hope, Garth thought – not absolutely. There was a chance, then. He would not aid in the Forgotten King's scheme to loose The God Whose Name Is Not Spoken, but he might be willing to help out in other ways. He might not win eternal glory by helping the old man to die, but it would be something worth doing. He would not assist in bringing the gods down from the heavens, but he would put an end to an immortal and kill the high priest of Death. That was something that would be noteworthy and significant. He did not feel that he owed the King anything, but there was no reason he shouldn't take pity on him.

That being the case, he did not wish to antagonize the ancient wizard-priest. However, he also was hesitant to turn over the Dûsarran loot. He sat, debating with himself what he should do next.

'You said you had brought me things; let me see them.' The dry, deathly voice cut through his meditating.

'Forgive me, O King, but I am reluctant to give you what I brought, lest you perform your magic and cause these many deaths we spoke of.'

'I ask only to see them.'

He could hardly refuse such a request, under the circumstances. Perhaps the old wizard could tell him what some of the items were, what magic they possessed.

'First,' he said, 'there is the sword. I pulled it from a burning altar in a ruined temple, apparently dedicated to Bheleu, god of destruction. It appears to have great power – or at least, some power.' He remembered the

44

seeming ease with which the King had turned the blood-red gem black and decided to forgo guesses as to relative magical might.

'It is the Sword of Bheleu, true token of the god,' the Forgotten King said.

Garth was startled; the old man rarely volunteered information. He looked at the shadowed eyes and thought he might have seen a glint. Was the ancient actually showing signs of excitement?

Interested now himself, the overman reached down and lifted the sack on to the table, then thrust a hand into it.

The first item he brought out was wrapped in cloth. 'This is the gem from the altar of Tema, the goddess of the night,' he explained. 'I keep it concealed because it has hypnotic properties that can snare the unwary.' He placed the head-sized bundle on the table beside the sword.

At the other table, Frima sucked in her breath.

'What is it?' Saram whispered.

'He robbed Tema! That's sacrilege!'

'Is it?'

'Of course it is!'

Saram would have said something further, but Garth was bringing a second stone out of the bag. This one was unwrapped and gleaming black, apparently a faceted and polished chunk of obsidian.

'This,' the overman said, 'came from the altar of the god of darkness and of the blind; I don't recall his names offhand.' He plunged his hand in again and pulled out a small pouch.

'The altar of P'hul was empty, save for dust; I brought you some of the dust.' He tossed the pouch beside the two stones and dragged out a larger and obviously much heavier pouch. He opened it and poured coins out on the table top. They were all gold, but encrusted with something dark brown and powdery.

'This is what I found on the altar of Aghad; the stains are dried blood.' A bitter note crept into his voice as he added, 'At least two people died while I visited that temple, for no reason but to amuse the Aghadites.'

Frima interjected, 'You slew their high priest, though.'

He turned, reminded of her presence. 'I would prefer that I had slain the entire cult, as I did Bheleu's. Come here, girl.' He beckoned.

Hesitantly, Frima got to her feet and stepped up beside the Forgotten King's table. Garth placed a hand on her shoulder. 'This,' he said, 'is what I found on the altar of Sai, goddess of pain. However, lest she not be what you had in mind, I also took what I was told the pain-worshippers customarily kept on their altar.' He dumped the almost-empty sack out, revealing a coiled whip and a narrow-bladed dagger.

'Was there nothing else?' the King asked.

'I am afraid I didn't think to bring the ropes they used to bind their sacrifice.'

'That is not what I meant. This is junk for the most part, Garth. The stones are the true pieces, but their power was largely spent long ago. The sword – that is worthwhile. The rest is nothing, mere trash. This whip is a false imitation; the true token of Sai is shod with silver. The token of Aghad is a golden dagger. P'hul's tool is a ring in the possession of a council of wizards.'

'This is what I found on the altars,' Garth replied. He was amazed at the King's loquaciousness.

'What of the seventh altar?'

Garth hesitated. 'I took nothing from the altar of Death,' he replied.

'Why?'

'I did not trust you; I feared what you might do should

46

it prove as powerful a force for death as the sword is a force of destruction.'

'The book was there, though?'

Startled, Garth stared at the King. 'What book?' he asked.

'There was no book?'

'No.'

'Then what was on the altar?'

He could see no harm in telling the truth. 'There was a horned skull, from no species I have ever heard of.'

There was a moment of silence. Then the King said, 'Did you move it?'

'No, I left it there. It was attached to the altar, and I thought better of separating it.'

'Of course it was attached, you idiot! It's part of the altar! Was there nothing else?'

It was the first time Garth had ever heard the old man raise his voice; it was not a pleasant experience. Though still not loud, the sound seemed to bite through him.

'No, nothing else. The top of the altar was empty. Oh, there was slime all over it, from the monster . . .'

'I care nothing about slime! I need that book!'

'There was no book there, I am quite certain.'

'Begone with you, then! Keep your trinkets and leave me in peace; I must consider this.' With that, the old man rose, wrapped his cloak more tightly about him, and moved around the table and up the stairs.

Garth watched him go in open-mouthed astonishment; then a glimmer of light caught his eye, and he turned to see that the stone in the pommel of the Sword of Bheleu was red once more and flickering with a fitful, uneven glow. He felt a moment of horror as the familiar suffocating blur of anger and confusion closed on him; the horror faded with the death of the mental clarity sufficient to recall what he had lost.

4

Saram was the first to speak after the Forgotten King's abrupt departure. 'What was that all about?' he asked.

'I don't know,' Garth replied. His thoughts seemed muddy and vague and laced with a lingering annoyance.

'What happens now?' Frima asked.

The overman had been staring at the steps the old man had just ascended; at the sound of the girl's voice he turned to face her.

'It would seem,' he said, 'that you're free now. As I told you, I have no use for you; I brought you here only because the old man told me to bring whatever I found on the altars, and you were on Sai's altar. I thought that my taking him literally might convince him to be less cryptic in the future. It appears it hasn't quite worked – but that's not your concern. I delivered you to him, and he rejected you, so I have no further need for you. You're free to do as you please.'

'Will you take me back to Dûsarra, then?'

'I hadn't planned to.'

'Oh, but you have to! I can't go back myself; it's not safe, and I don't know the way!'

'Do you really want to go back? When we left, there was a plague loose in the city.'

'Oh.' She was immediately less enthusiastic. 'That's right, the White Death was in the marketplace, and the city was on fire. Maybe I don't want to go back. What should I do, then?'

'That's up to you.' Garth rose. 'I have affairs of my own to attend to, and I want to get out of here before the

48

Baron sends his soldiers after me – if he hasn't done so already.'

'You can't leave me all alone in a strange town!'

Garth hesitated. 'I can't very well take you to a military camp either. How would I explain a human's presence? Besides, I can't keep looking after you forever. At least here in Skelleth you're among your own species.'

Saram interjected, 'I could look after her for a while, I suppose.'

The overman was startled. 'It is not necessary; she's not your concern.'

'I don't mind.'

Garth looked from Saram to Frima and back. Was he missing something here? Had the former guardsman taken some sort of interest in the girl? He had noticed them speaking to each other, though he had not heard what had been said.

What sort of an interest could it be, though? He knew that he didn't understand humans very well, but what sort of attachment could have been formed so quickly? No, more likely the man was just curious about the Dûsarran, or wanted to do Garth a favour – doubtless expecting the debt to be repaid later. There was nothing wrong with that; Garth already felt he owed Saram something, as the man had been of assistance in the past.

'Very well, then. Perhaps you can find her some more suitable clothing; she's been complaining about what I gave her, and I would like to have my tunic back.'

'Don't worry; I'll take good care of her.' There was something odd about the man's smile, Garth thought, but he dismissed it.

The sword and other items were still strewn across the table; though he was eager to be on his way to straighten out the mess Kyrith and Galt seemed to have gotten themselves into, Garth paused to gather them up. It would not do to leave magical objects lying around where any casual tavern patron might pick them up. He knew from personal experience that the white stone and the sword were dangerous, and the black stone might be as well. The rest the King had dismissed as junk, but gold was gold, and not to be thrown away, while the whip and dagger were decent enough weapons. The pouch of dust he almost left, but an instinct for tidiness overcame him, and he threw it into the sack with the rest.

The sword, of course, didn't fit in the sack; he kept it clutched in his right hand while his left hefted the bag up on to his shoulder. The gem flickered dimly.

A final glance assured him that he had left nothing behind except Frima. The Baron's guards could appear at any moment, he knew. He turned and strode out the door.

Saram and Frima watched him go. When he was out of sight, the former guardsman turned and looked his new companion over carefully, then said, 'Sit down, girl, and tell me about yourself.'

Frima saw the obvious appreciation in Saram's eyes and noticed that the man's hair and beard were as dark as any Dûsarran's, and they neatly framed a strong, attractive face. With a shy smile she sat and said, 'My name is Frima. What would you like to know?'

Outside the King's Inn, Garth slid the Sword of Bheleu back into his warbeast's harness, then climbed on to the creature's back. Koros stood placidly, apparently paying no attention, until the command came to go; then instantly, it surged forward in its customary smooth, steady glide.

If guardsmen were coming, they had not yet arrived; there was no opposition as overman and warbeast made their way northward through the twisting streets. The ground had finally dried somewhat, though it was still soft underfoot, and the warbeast's great padded paws were able to move with catlike silence, no longer hampered by clinging mud.

As he rode, Garth found himself wondering at the Forgotten King's behavior. What had the old man expected him to bring back? He had spoken of a book; what book did he mean? There had been no book in the temple of Death. The temple had been a cave in the side of the volcano that towered above the black walls of Dûsarra, a cave that had been enlarged artificially, with elaborately carved walls. The altar had looked as if it were carved from a stalagmite; it was tall and narrow, he recalled, with a sloping top, rather like a lectern or reading stand, with the eerie horned skull where a candle or lamp would go on a reading stand. Other than the skull, it had been completely empty. There had been no book. There had been nowhere in the cave that a book could have been hidden where it would not have risked being consumed by the monstrous thing that lived in the depths below and behind the temple.

The altar was, he had to agree, the right shape to hold a book. Could the doddering old priest who tended the temple have taken the book and hidden it somewhere outside?

Why would the caretaker do such a thing? To protect it from the thing within, perhaps? That might be it. He would suggest such a possibility to the Forgotten King should he ever care to return to the old man's service.

What made this book so precious?

That, actually, was fairly easy to guess from what the King had said. The book must be necessary for the magic he intended to perform. Perhaps it was a book of spells, containing the needed instructions and incantations, or perhaps the book itself had some magic to it.

Whatever the exact situation, it didn't really matter. What mattered was that he had performed the errand he said he would perform for the King, keeping his word, and that the King was not able to perform his death-causing magic. That put his dealings with the old man at an end. Now he was free to do as he pleased with the loot from Dûsarra, to deal with the upstart Baron of Skelleth as he saw fit, and to straighten out the actions of Galt and Kyrith. When the Baron and his wife's war party had been taken care of, his time would be his own once again, and he could relax and figure out what to do with the magical sword and gem at his leisure.

He was approaching the North Gate now; as he had expected, there was a guard posted in the ruined watchtower beside the road. He expected no difficulty there; the man was supposed to keep the enemies out, not to prevent them from leaving.

Beyond the gate lay open plain, and perhaps two hundred yards along the Wasteland Road stood the encampment he was headed for. He could see warbeasts standing calmly in a group at one side and overmen milling about amid the tents. They appeared to be moving in an aimless muddle; he hoped they weren't as disorganized as they looked. How could the City Council have been so stupid as to send them out without a competent warrior in command?

The human guard had noticed him now, alerted by the jingling of armor and harness; Koros' soft footfalls were inaudible. The man rose to his feet, short sword drawn; even Garth, inhuman as he was, could read the confusion and nervousness on the young human's face.

'Halt!' the guardsman cried.

It was too soon for trouble; Garth spoke a word to his mount, and Koros halted a few feet from the soldier.

The man was obviously unsure what to do next, so Garth took the initiative. 'I think you are making a mistake in stopping me, man,' he said. 'I am leaving peacefully. You are here to warn of approaching enemies; I am not approaching, but departing.'

The soldier was still plainly uncertain.

When no response seemed forthcoming, Garth continued, 'Besides, you cannot very well stop me. You are a lone man on foot, while I am an overman with a warbeast and with many more of my kind within earshot.' He motioned toward the camp. 'I suggest you tell me I can go, before I become impatient.'

The logic of this was irrefutable. The guard sheathed his sword and waved Garth on. 'You . . . you can go.'

'Thank you,' Garth replied politely. He tapped a signal to Koros, and the warbeast moved onward. He didn't bother to look back.

Behind him, the guard considered for a long moment. He faced a difficult decision; should he leave his post to inform his superiors of this occurrence, or should he wait until his relief arrived?

His relief was due at sunrise the following morning, and it was now scarcely past midday. Anything could happen in so long a time. If he stayed where he was, the overman might have time to work some dreadful plan. He would be of little use where he was; his only purpose, really, was to run ahead of any attack that might come and give a warning, since a single man couldn't be expected to delay even a lone overman for more than a few minutes. For that purpose the two scouts Captain Herrenmer had posted in hiding on either side of the gate should be plenty; the gate had remained openly guarded only so that the overmen would not be certain that the men of Skelleth had taken any action at all.

Of course, if he left his post, the overmen would see that and know that action *had* been taken.

A third solution occurred to him, finally, one that was wholly satisfactory. He left his post for a few moments, as if answering a call of nature somewhere in the rubble of the crumbling walls, and found one of the hidden scouts. After informing the other man of what had happened, he returned to the gate and resumed his watch.

Meanwhile, the scout was on his way back into the center of town, staying always out of sight amid the ruins.

5

The encampment was fully as disorganized as Garth had feared. He was halfway from the wall to the camp before anyone even noticed his presence, and no effort was made to stop or slow him before he reached the cleared area in front of the tents, though he was obviously out of place in his battered mail and drooping trader's hat, his warbeast laden with bundles, so unlike the clean, sleek, new appearance of the other overmen.

There was no sign of Galt or Thord, but there were various overmen standing, sitting, or walking about, and Kyrith stood in front of one tent, listening to a young warrior Garth did not recognize. The two turned when someone called out a warning of Garth's approach.

The young overman started to demand an explanation, but Kyrith's hand on his arm stopped him. She scribbled something on the wax-coated tablet she carried. He glanced at it, then looked back at the new arrival.

'You're Garth?' he asked.

'I am Garth, Prince of Ordunin. Who are you?'

The warrior blinked his red eyes and replied, 'I am Thant, son of Sart and Shenit.'

'I never heard of you. Are you helping to run things here?'

'Yes.'

'Have the sentries been called back, as I told Thord to do?'

'Well, no. You see, we could not be certain . . .'

'I don't care why. If you want to make yourself useful, Thant, son of Sart and Shenit, then you can go run around the village and fetch back all the sentries that you fools have posted. I'm putting an end to this absurd siege before it brings the wrath of all humanity down on us.'

Thant blinked again, then looked at Kyrith. She nodded. He hesitated a moment longer, until Garth bellowed, 'Move!'

He moved. Garth called after him, 'And when you get back here with the sentries, we'll break camp! I want us out of here before sunset!'

When the warrior was well on his way, Garth dismounted, swinging himself easily to the ground, and strode toward Kyrith. She met him halfway, and they embraced briefly. There was no passion in their embrace, and they did not kiss; for overmen and overwomen, marriage was a matter of convenience and companionship; sex was an involuntary function that occurred when an overwoman was in heat. Their mouths were virtually lipless and hardly suited to kissing. Had Kyrith been in heat, Garth's attentions would not have been so perfunctory.

When they released each other Garth asked, 'Where are Myrith and Lurith and the children?'

Kyrith pointed northward. Garth asked, to be sure he was not misinterpreting her gesture, 'You left them to take care of the house?'

She nodded.

'That's all right, then. Why did *you* come here, though? What did you want to stir up trouble for? Didn't Galt tell you that I'd be back by the end of the year?'

She reached for her tablet. Garth stopped her. 'Never mind. We'll discuss it later.' Communicating with Kyrith was annoyingly slow and inconvenient ever since the accident that had put shards of ice through her throat and destroyed her voice. He knew that she found it as frustrating as he did, and she resented it when he let his irritation interfere with their conversations; ordinarily he would have been more tactful about declining to let her write out her answer, but he did not want any unnecessary delays now. The people of Skelleth might well have been stirred up by the siege or his own ride through town. He said, as a partial explanation, 'We have to straighten out the situation in Skelleth. Thord told me that Galt is your co-commander. Where is he?'

She pointed to one of the tents and made a sign indicating sleep.

'He's asleep? It's after noon!'

She scribbled on her tablet and showed him the words: 'Night Watch.'

'I need to talk to him.'

Kyrith signed for him to wait and headed for the tent.

Garth waited and looked about. There was no organization to the camp at all, it seemed. The warbeasts were off to one side, in a rope enclosure that obviously wouldn't stop them for more than five seconds should they decide to leave; there was no sign of any food supply for them, and a hungry warbeast was as dangerous to friend as to foe. Had the overmen been letting them hunt their own food? That was fine for one, two, or maybe three, but there were half a dozen in the pen, and more still out on sentry duty. A dozen warbeasts hunting in the same territory could strip it clean in a matter of days and might well start fighting amongst themselves over the game they found. Furthermore, most warbeasts weren't picky about what they ate so long as it was sufficiently large and fresh; they would hunt humans as readily as anything else, and that would hardly be good for inter-species relations.

He couldn't judge just how hungry the penned beasts were, but they did not look as if they had been fed in the last day or two; that was good, as it implied they had last hunted somewhere to the north, where humans were rare and uncivilized and wouldn't be missed by the people of

57

Skelleth. It was also bad, however, because it meant they would demand feeding soon.

The tents were apparently placed at random, wherever their owners' whims had chosen; most were clustered loosely about a large, square-framed one that Garth assumed must serve as a command post. Some were not set up properly; pegs were left hanging or lying on the ground.

There was no sign of any central supply; it appeared that each tent held its own stocks of food and water and its owner's own weapons and armor.

In short, the camp displayed all that was worst in the behaviour of overmen. Garth knew from his studies of the history of the Racial Wars that the humans had not won solely because they had never outnumbered his kind by less than five to one; they had superior organization, as well. Humans were naturally social animals; though they tended to be careless, sloppy, and stupid, they were able to function well in groups. A single competent military commander could organize a thousand humans and get them to fight with some semblance of efficient cooperation.

Overmen, unfortunately, were less gregarious. Each, when pressed, would invariably put his own well-being before that of anyone or anything else, including the very survival of the species. They resented taking orders, and, in fact, usually wouldn't obey even direct commands without an explanation of why they should. An army of overmen didn't function as a single unit, but as a collection of individual warriors, each ferocious enough in his own right, but with no sense of loyalty to his comrades, and prone to go off on solo adventures at the first opportunity.

What little cooperation overmen did display had been forced upon them by events, and its forms had usually been learned from the humans they despised. Marriage was a human invention that overmen had adopted because it simplified family responsibilities and inheritances. Cities facilitated trade and government – but even so, the overmen had only one in all the Northern Waste, and it sprawled over several square miles of coastline and hill with a population of less than five thousand, the houses strewn randomly about the countryside rather than laid along streets.

For that matter, nobody actually knew what the population of Ordunin or of the Waste was, as there had never been sufficient cooperation to conduct a census.

This camp, then, seemed typical of overmen when there was no strong organization and leader forcing them to behave. He knew from his military experiences in battling the pirates who occasionally raided Ordunin, that overmen *could* be made to form a coherent fighting unit – but it was extraordinarily difficult. Where one human officer might reasonably hope to manage a hundred soldiers in an emergency, each overman had commanded no more than ten, at the very most; three was better. Every two or three officers then needed a commander.

And here, sixty overmen were under two co-commanders with no intermediate organization apparent.

Had the expedition been set up properly, there would have been a supply train accompanying it, including a herd of goats to feed the warbeasts and a good stock of replacement armor and weaponry. There would be three captains, he thought, each with two lieutenants, each with two sergeants, each with three or four soldiers. The tents would have been set up in some pattern and the warbeasts tethered in a ring around the camp, to serve as the first line of defense.

Kyrith and Galt emerged from the tent, and he put aside his thoughts. Galt blinked at the daylight; the sky was finally beginning to clear. 'Greetings, Garth,' he said.

59

'Greetings, Galt. What are you doing here? What is this so-called siege supposed to do?'

'Don't blame me for the siege; that was Kyrith's idea, and I was overruled.'

'What are you doing here in the first place?'

'We came to speak with the Baron of Skelleth. Kyrith didn't believe that you had gone off on your own willingly; she thought that the Baron had you prisoner somewhere in Skelleth or had killed you, and she gathered these volunteers to come find you. The City Council sent me along. We had intended to ride into the village, confront the Baron, present our demands, and settle the matter on the spot, preferably by gracefully accepting his capitulation.'

'You needed sixty armed overmen for that?'

'As we both know, Garth, the Baron of Skelleth takes a great interest in military matters. Your disappearance gave us sufficient excuse for a show of force, which, it was felt, might serve to convince him where simple negotiations would not.'

Galt's smooth manner irritated Garth. He snapped, 'It didn't work?'

'It might have succeeded, had the Baron met with us. Unfortunately, we were told, with much sincere regret, that he was sick in bed and could not see us. We did not care to force the issue then and there, but Kyrith was unwilling to do nothing; hence the siege.'

'The Baron refused to see you, and you simply left town?'

'We set up the siege.'

'Siege! You call this farce a siege?'

Galt shrugged, and Garth's annoyance grew.

'You accepted the word of the humans that the Baron was ill? You did not insist upon seeing him?'

'No. The captain of the guard swore by half a dozen gods I never heard of and by various parts of his anatomy that the Baron was ill in bed. I spoke last night with the man called Saram, whom you know and whom I believe you trust, and he told me that the Baron's illness is legitimate – a side-effect of his madness.'

'Did it not occur to any of you that it would be far more effective to camp in the marketplace, where you could not be so easily ignored or put off, rather than to establish a siege you cannot possibly maintain? Furthermore, a single message slipped past your pitiful line of sentries could bring the wrath of the entire Kindom of Eramma down on you and on the Northern Waste, since a siege is undeniably an act of war. Had you camped peacefully in the square, you would have been honest petitioners, breaking no laws.'

Galt was slow to reply. 'Such an audacious action did not occur to me.'

'Audacious? The Baron of Skelleth is the audacious one! He dares to dictate terms to overmen as if we were mere peasants? To refuse your embassy an audience? It is time that we showed him the error of his ways. I propose that we march back into town; if he will still not speak with us, we will camp in the market until he does.'

'I am not sure that would be wise. I did not approve of the siege, but I think that your plan faces the same objections. We dare not push the Baron too far; we need this trade with Skelleth.'

'No, we don't. We can trade anywhere we please. The Racial Wars are over, Galt, whatever we may have believed while isolated in the Northern Waste, and regardless of what the Baron of Skelleth may have told us. I have just returned from a city called Dûsarra, where overmen are an everyday sight. The humans have forgotten their fear and hatred; remember how short their lives are! To them, three centuries are a dozen generations, almost five lifetimes.'

'How can overmen be a common sight anywhere outside the Northern Waste?'

'Ah, this is the best news of all! There are overmen living on the Yprian Coast. We are not the only survivors.'

'The Yprian Coast? That barren wasteland?'

'Is the Northern Waste any better?'

Galt did not answer that. Instead, he asked, 'Are you sure we could trade elsewhere?'

'At the very least, we could trade with the Yprians and with Dûsarra. I think we could probably go anywhere we pleased without interference; humans care more for gold than for ancient hatreds.'

'Still, any overland trade route would have to go through the Barony of Skelleth; it extends from the Yprian Gulf to the Sea of Mori.'

'What of it? Do you think the Baron's thirty-odd guardsmen can patrol the entire border?'

'It would still be preferable to have the Baron's permission.'

'Yes, it would be preferable, but it is not necessary, and it would also be preferable to make plain to all that overmen are not to be treated with the disrespect the Baron of Skelleth has displayed.'

While Galt digested this, Kyrith scribbled on her tablet, then handed it to Garth. It read, 'What disrespect? Why not go home?'

He handed it back. 'No, Kyrith, I can't go home yet. I can't go back to Ordunin until the Baron releases me from my oath.'

She made a questioning gesture.

Garth said, 'What are you asking?'

She wrote and handed him the tablet. It read: 'What oath?'

'Galt should have told you,' Garth replied. 'He was there. I swore an oath to the Baron of Skelleth when last I saw him. He proposed that in order to remove all legal impediments to trade between Skelleth and the Waste and to put a formal end to the war with Eramma, I, as Prince of Ordunin, should surrender and swear fealty to him, thereby making Ordunin and its territory – which is to say, the entire eastern half of the Northern Waste – part of the Barony of Skelleth. He called this a simple and reasonable thing, but we both knew he devised it to humiliate me, as I had humiliated him once before. He insisted that I swear to present this proposal to the City Council as soon as I returned to Ordunin. I was unarmed, on a peaceful trading mission, and caught off-guard; I swore the oath he demanded. I will not present any such disgraceful scheme to the City Council, however. Therefore, if I am not to break my sworn word, I cannot return to Ordunin until the Baron releases me from my vow. This is one reason we must confront him, quite aside from trading concessions or my exile from Skelleth; he must release me. He *will* release me, or I will kill him.'

Garth's voice had gone flat and toneless during this speech, which was a sign of mounting anger among overmen. Galt and Kyrith both noted it, and Kyrith put a hand on her husband's arm, attempting to calm him.

Galt noticed the gesture, and something else caught his eye as well. Koros stood behind its master, and an immense two-handed broadsword, easily six feet in length, was thrust horizontally through the warbeast's harness, along the creature's right flank. A huge red jewel was mounted in the weapon's pommel, and the gem was glowing with an eerie, bloody light of its own.

'Garth,' he said, 'that's an interesting sword there. Where did you get it?'

Garth turned to glance at the sword and froze when he saw the crimson glow. He had been working up to a murderous fury, imagining himself using the sword to impale a cowering, whimpering Baron of Skelleth; visions

63

of blood and fire had been flashing through his mind. Now he struggled to suppress those urges.

For a moment he regretted leaving Frima in Saram's care; had she been there, she would probably have warned him sooner.

When he thought he had himself more or less under control, he said, 'I found it in Dûsarra, in a ruined temple. It appears to have some sort of enchantment to it.' He found himself curiously reluctant to speak of it, and therefore did not explain the nature of its power over him and did not mention Bheleu or any other deities.

'It's magical? Is that why it's glowing?' Galt was fascinated; he had heard of magic, but had never before seen any at first hand. He looked more closely. The glow seemed to have dimmed somewhat, but it was still clearly visible.

'Yes.'

Galt stepped around the other two, to get a better view of the strange gem.

'Don't touch it!' Garth roared.

Startled, Galt stepped back. 'I wasn't going to.'

Garth was annoyed with himself; there had been no need to bellow at Galt. He was unreasonably touchy about anything having to do with the sword, it seemed; he told himself that he would have to keep that in check. He would also have to get rid of the sword, and quickly; its hold on his emotions seemed to be getting stronger and had been quite dangerous enough before. It would not do to go into a killing frenzy while negotiating with the Baron of Skelleth.

On the other hand, it was a beautiful weapon, a magnificent blade; it would be a very impressive thing to have along during negotiations. He would take it, he decided, and keep himself under careful control. After all, he could not safely leave it lying around untended and he would not trust it in the hands of any of these

64

idiotic volunteers. He would worry about disposing of it after he had settled with the Baron.

He had turned away as he reached this decision and therefore did not see the glow flare up brightly once more. Galt saw the increased brightness, but did not realize it had any significance and said nothing. His attention was distracted from the sword when Garth announced, 'I want the entire company packed up within an hour, so that we will have time to reach the market square and set up camp there before full dark.' Galt turned away to help in breaking camp and paid no more attention to the great sword or the shining jewel.

He had a curious feeling, however, that he was being watched.

Garth had lived with that feeling almost constantly for more than a fortnight and no longer noticed it, but he, too, was slightly troubled. He seemed to sense mingled amusement and triumph without actually feeling either emotion himself.

6

Herrenmer, captain of the guard, had wasted no time; within five minutes of hearing from the scout that an overman had ridden openly *out* of Skelleth to the encampment on the Wasteland Road, he had summoned his five lieutenants and told them to put every man on active duty immediately. He didn't know exactly what was going on, but he intended to take as few chances as possible. He was sure that the overman was Garth. Earlier, Shallen had reported that the self-proclaimed Prince of Ordunin had turned up at the King's Inn, and no other overman had been seen inside the walls since the whole company had been turned away the preceding morning.

When he heard that, Herrenmer had immediately sent someone to see if the Baron was able to take charge of affairs once again. The report had been negative; he was stirring, but not yet coherent.

Herrenmer had not dared to take action against Garth on his own authority; he was nervous about the overman's claims to nobility, since he didn't understand just what that might entail. Therefore he had just waited.

Now, however, Garth had gone to join his fellows. With their leader back, it was unclear just what action the overmen might take, but it seemed likely that they would do something. Garth's absence had been one of the things that had been mentioned by the leaders of the main group when Herrenmer had spoken with them yesterday.

They might be satisfied now that he was back and just go home peacefully – but Herrenmer didn't expect it. He thought that they would now probably march back into town and cause more trouble.

He intended to see that it was not that simple.

Once his lieutenants had gone to find and bring back all the men, he gave orders to those men who were already available that they were to proceed immediately to the north wall, with crossbows, moving under cover of the ruins and staying out of sight of the overmen. This time, the overmen would not be able just to walk in unhindered.

When reports began arriving that the ring of sentries that the overmen had set up around the town was being removed, he was sure that something was planned, and soon. It was still possible that they were simply going home, but he would be shirking his duty if he took no action because he made that assumption.

When he had sent twenty men northward, he gave orders that the rest of the guards were to serve as a second line of defense here in the village, in case the overmen did march in despite his efforts. That done, he himself headed toward the North Gate.

He had not yet reached it when the overmen began moving south.

When Garth had announced his intentions to the gathered volunteers, there had been no dissent; all present seemed to take it for granted that he had assumed command and had the right to do so. Many of the warriors cheered when he spoke of showing the Baron that overmen would not be pushed around any longer. They were obviously glad to be taking action, any action, rather than standing guard or sitting around doing nothing.

Camp had been broken quickly and with reasonable efficiency; while that was being done, someone had found Garth an over-the-shoulder sheath for a two-handed broadsword, so that he was able to carry the Sword of

Bheleu slung on his back, rather than strapped inaccessibly in his warbeast's harness.

When everything was packed away and stored on the back of warbeasts and overmen – Garth regretted again that no one had thought to bring a supply train; even a handful of wagons or yackers would have helped – the company was formed up into something resembling a military formation, rather than a mob. He placed himself front and center, with Kyrith on his right and Galt on his left, all mounted on warbeasts. Behind them came a second row of five warbeasts carrying the overmen Garth thought showed potential. The main body of troops followed, arranged in ten rows five abreast, and the remaining five warbeasts and overmen brought up the rear.

It would have pleased Garth to have the overmen march in step, perhaps to some rhythmic marching chant such as he had been taught by one of his great-grandfathers, but he decided it would take more time and effort than it was worth. If he had time, he thought, he would also have liked to set up a proper military organization with a command structure that might actually work, rather than the current loose arrangement. He hoped that such organization would not be needed. With luck, the troops would not be required to do anything but stand there looking formidable – and that they could do.

When he was satisfied with the formation, he took his place at the head and gave the order to advance.

Movement was ragged and uneven at first, but the warriors got the hang of it fairly quickly. By the time they were within fifty yards of the North Gate, they were moving more or less in unison, staying more or less in their places in the formation.

Ahead of them, Garth saw the guard at the North Gate turn and run as they approached. He smiled; it felt good to inspire such obvious fright. Of course, the guard was just doing his duty, running to alert the village, since one man could not possibly hope to stop more than sixty overmen, but it was still pleasant to see.

He glanced back and saw that other overmen were smiling as well.

Then he heard the slap of a bowstring and ducked instinctively. A crossbow quarrel whirred past his head.

He knew, in a vague and detached way, that he should get down, order his troops to do the same, and appraise the exact situation before taking any direct action, but a blinding wave of fury drowned all such logic. He reached up and grabbed the hilt of the great sword and pulled it from its sheath.

'Human scum!' he bellowed. 'You dare defy me?' The sword came free, and he swung it over his head.

The sun, low in the western sky, vanished behind a cloud at that moment, and the glow of the jewel was visible to friend and foe alike.

'I am Bheleu, bringer of destruction!' Garth cried. 'Who dares stand against me?'

Two dull snaps sounded, and two more bolts sped toward him; he spun the sword and somehow met both in mid-air, striking sparks as their barbed heads hit the steel of the sword's blade. The quarrels flew harmlessly aside; one left a trail of smoke in the air.

As it moved, the sword shone silver, then white, as if the blade were now glowing as well as the gem. Garth laughed. 'Flee, humans! Flee before the wrath of a god!'

Clouds had gathered overhead with incredible speed, and a distant roll of thunder answered him.

No more crossbows were fired. The guardsmen, already terrified at facing three times their number in overmen, did as they were told and fled. None of them cared to face this supernatural being who could knock arrows out of the air with his glowing sword. The cover provided by the crumbling wall and heaped rubble suddenly seemed hopelessly inadequate. When the last to arrive, who had not yet had time to conceal himself, turned and ran, the others were quick to follow.

The overmen watched in amazed confusion as their foe, who had appeared from nowhere, vanished with equal speed, while Garth raved and did mysterious things with his strange sword.

As suddenly as it had come, the spell departed, and Garth found himself holding the sword awkwardly above his head while men newly visible were running southward into the town. That was not what he wanted; he wanted to negotiate peacefully. The show of force was to have been just that, a show; he had no desire to risk starting the Racial Wars anew. 'No!' he called, 'they mustn't flee!'

Behind him, someone overheard him and misinterpreted his intent. 'After them!' he called.

Before Garth could recover sufficiently to countermand, his troops were surging forward, yelling and cheering. They poured over the broken remnants of the wall and into the town, pursuing the running guardsmen.

Galt and Garth were both shouting, trying to stop the forward rush, but neither could be heard above the clamor. The warriors of Ordunin were on the offensive for the first time in three hundred years and enjoying it.

Garth quickly realized that he could accomplish nothing where he was. The other overmen were getting further away and more scattered with each passing second. He would have to head them off. He ordered Koros forward, along the roadway and through the gate. Galt followed his lead; Kyrith trailed behind.

Garth reached one of his warriors, grabbed the overman by the shoulder, and bellowed in his ear, 'Let them go! Form upon the road!' Before the warrior could acknowledge the command, Garth was on to the next.

Moving in a straight line and mounted as he was, he quickly passed all the infantry; the warbeasts, fortunately, had not joined in the headlong dash after the fleeing humans. He had collared half a dozen of his troops, and they were now gathering on the road as he had ordered, but looking none too pleased about it. He turned and bellowed, 'Hold! Let them go!'

Another half dozen overmen stopped and looked at him.

'Get back in formation on the road!'

Reluctantly, those who heard him obeyed; the clump of warriors on the road grew. Galt, too, was gathering them in.

A few moments later Garth had to turn and head off a few who had wandered well off to one side. When he came back with them in tow, he found that Galt had managed to gather more than half the company into position. The rest, seeing what was happening, were now drifting back, one or two at a time.

It took perhaps fifteen minutes before they were all together, and Garth found himself again at the head of sixty overmen.

He was also, he discovered, apparently in command of four human soldiers who had been captured. He ordered their captors to release them and had them come to the front of the column where he could address them.

'Men,' he said, 'I wish to apologize for our part in this unfortunate incident. However, you brought it upon yourselves by firing on us. We are here as a peaceful embassy, whatever the appearances may be, and do not wish to harm anyone. Our people remember the Racial Wars, though, and remember that your ancestors stole our lands and goods and drove us into wastes; thus their eagerness in pursuing you. We know that our best hope lies in peaceful trade, but the desire for vengeance is strong. Do not provoke us in the future, and both sides will benefit. I am sending you back to your captain and to your lord, the Baron of Skelleth, and I want you to convey to them our intention to come and treat with them. We want only to speak peacefully with them, but we come prepared for whatever eventualities may arise. I will not be responsible for anything that may occur if we are again attacked without cause. Do you understand?'

The four heads bobbed up and down.

'Good. You may go then.' He waved a hand in dismissal.

The four men, hesitantly at first, moved down the road. With each step they moved a little faster; by the time they were lost to sight amid the ruins along the winding road, they were almost running.

When they were gone, Garth turned to look over his troops. They were slightly less impressive than before, as their armor was no longer spotless and shiny; the scramble across the rubble had left them spattered with mud.

There were fewer smiles in evidence than previously. A speech was probably needed, Garth decided. To give himself time to devise one, he called, 'Was anyone injured?'

The overmen shifted about, but no one answered.

'Did anybody injure any of the humans?'

Again, there was no reply.

'Good. Now, warriors of Ordunin, I have a few words to say. We are here on a peaceful mission, not to start a war. I am not sure whether you are all aware of it, but the Racial Wars are finished and we do not want to start them all over again. We cannot afford to. The humans outnumber us probably a hundred to one in the world as a whole and have every logistical advantage; that has not changed in the past three centuries. Therefore, whatever the temptations or provocations, we must not take any aggressive action unless driven to it. In the incident that just occurred, I know we were fired upon from ambush without warning or justification – but remember that the humans were probably terrified at the sight of us and acted without thinking, in defense of their home. You saw that the display I put on frightened them away almost immediately. I did not call for their pursuit; what I said was simply in surprise at the ease with which they were driven back, as I had wanted to speak to them. Someone among you – I did not recognize the voice – then called for pursuit and you obeyed. I ask that, in the future, you obey only orders given by your three commanders: Galt, Kyrith and me. Is that understood?'

There was a reluctant chorus of assent.

'Good. Then take a moment to brush yourselves off, so that we will look suitably impressive when we confront the Baron, and get back into formation.'

A moment later, again impressive in shining armor and neat formation, the company renewed its advance down the street toward the center of Skelleth. Garth regretted once again that he did not have time to teach the overmen to march in step and hold a properly tight formation; that, he thought, would really have provided a show!

Ahead of them, Herrenmer met his fleeing soldiers halfway between the wall and the square and gathered them together and brought them back into some semblance of discipline. He had to knock a few heads to do it, but he managed. Once that was done, he made his plans. He knew that his little force could not stop the overmen in open combat, and there wasn't time to set up a decent ambush along the road. Therefore, the best course of action would be to withdraw to the marketplace and meet them there. Accordingly, he formed his men up in a column and marched them back to the square.

Along the way he wondered just what magic the overmen actually possessed. The old legends of the Racial Wars made no mention of overmen using magic. The wizards had fought almost invariably on the human side; at least, so he had heard.

It wasn't really his concern; he was a simple soldier.

73

Magic was for others to worry about; he could only do the best he could with what he had.

As Garth passed the first houses that still had roofs, he was considering what he would say to the Baron. He glanced back over his shoulder at the hilt of the Sword of Bheleu; it would not do to go into a berserk rage while trying to negotiate trade concessions or have his oath renounced. The Baron of Skelleth seemed to have a special talent for annoying Garth, who had found the man difficult enough to deal with in the past without any supernatural interference. He hoped that he would be able to keep his anger down. Perhaps, he thought, the little display he had put on at the North Gate had used up the sword's power for a while; he had felt no particular anger since.

Its magical power aside, the sword was truly a beautiful and impressive weapon, and he would regret parting with it. The blade was six feet of gleaming steel; the hilt was made of some black, polished substance he couldn't identify, the pommel was a silver claw clutching that immense red jewel. It looked like a ruby, though it was hard to believe a ruby could be that large. Whatever it was, it was the color of fresh blood, and he was relieved to see, glancing back, that though it sparkled in the afternoon sun at the moment, it did not appear to be glowing.

He would definitely have to get rid of the thing. It might even have been wise to dispose of it before speaking with the Baron, but he could not bring himself to do so. That would have left him virtually unarmed, and he wanted every advantage when confronting Doran of Skelleth.

His first sight of the Baron had been as the man presided over the execution of the guardsman whose negligence had allowed Garth to enter Skelleth unannounced the first time he came south; the townspeople had blamed Garth for the man's death. The Baron had demanded at swordpoint that Garth turn over to him the basilisk that he had just gone to great trouble to fetch. Garth had come out ahead in that encounter by stealing the basilisk back and later killing it before the Baron could recover it – but that had so annoyed the Baron that, when Garth returned as a trader, he was systematically insulted, humiliated, and forced to swear the oath he now hoped to have revoked.

They were well into the inhabited area now, but there were no people to be seen; Garth guessed that they had been warned by the guards and had taken shelter. He caught sight of someone on the street ahead, making hand signals to someone else Garth could not see before the signaler vanished around a corner. Whatever other advantages the overmen might have, they would not have the element of surprise.

They didn't need it, Garth told himself. An overman could easily handle any two humans, and a warbeast half a dozen; and Skelleth's entire military was comprised of about three dozen guards – perhaps not quite that many, since the Baron had executed Arner and dismissed Saram as a result of Garth's earlier visits and might not have replaced them yet. His company could deal with the guards easily, should it become necessary.

If the civilian population were to attack them, though, there might be a real problem. Garth had no idea what Skelleth's population was; he doubted anyone knew. It didn't matter, he assured himself. This was to be a peaceful demonstration, not a battle.

The streets remained deserted, save for occasional figures ahead who vanished as soon as they signalled that the overmen were approaching. Garth spotted three of these before he led his party into the northwest corner of the marketplace.

The square was not deserted. There were no merchants,

no farmers, none of the ordinary villagers going about their business; instead, there were two dozen guardsmen lined up neatly in front of the Baron's mansion, along the north side of the market. They were divided into two equal groups, one on either side of the central door, with each group arranged three deep and four abreast. Every man wore a shoddy mail tunic and held a drawn short sword; every head wore a leather helmet, and every belt bore a dagger. Four of the helmets were studded with iron, indicating that their wearers were lieutenants; these men were located in the center of each block.

This pitiful squad, Garth realized, represented the armed might of Skelleth, the once-great fortress from which his people had cowered in fear for three hundred years. He suppressed an urge to laugh in their faces as he marched his own force into the center of the square, swinging around to the south to come to a halt in some semblance of formation, directly facing the human soldiers. In this half-circuit of the market, he and his troops got their first good look at the civilian population of Skelleth; the people were crowded into every street that entered the square, except for the one the overmen had marched on. They watched with varied emotions the arrival of their traditional foes. None stepped across the invisible line dividing the market from the rest of the village.

Whispers, rustles, and shuffling feet were audible, but no one spoke aloud until Garth bellowed, 'We have come to speak with the Baron of Skelleth!'

The sounds shifted subtly; fewer feet scraped the dirt, more voices whispered. From the corners of his eyes Garth could see the mouths of two streets; both were full of people, all ragged and dirty, and almost all thin and unhealthy. These were the invincible warriors his ancestors had feared. A surge of fury fountained up within him; how could he and his people have taken so long to discover their foe's weakness? It was not fitting that overmen should have feared such creatures.

The door of the Baron's mansion opened, and the whisperings faded in anticipation.

It was not the Baron who emerged; the whispering flourished anew as Garth recognized the man who stepped out into the square and stood between the two groups of guardsmen. Tall for a human, dark of hair and eye, wearing the steel helmet that was his badge of rank, Herrenmer, captain of the Baron's guard and Skelleth's military commander, faced the overmen.

'The Baron is not well,' Herrenmer said. 'I have just come from his bedside. Perhaps I can serve in his place.'

Only the Baron could free Garth from his oath, so Garth's reply was immediate. 'We have come to see the Baron on matters that cannot be left to underlings. We have come peacefully seeking an audience, despite the assault upon us by your men, and we will remain here in this square until that audience is granted.'

'Very well; I will inform the Baron of what you have said and see if he feels well enough to deal with you himself.' Herrenmer turned and re-entered the mansion.

Garth and the overmen waited, sitting astride their warbeasts or standing where they were. Garth remained as motionless as he could; the sinking sun was hot on his left cheek, and there was an unpleasant itch below his left arm. Even had he been able to scratch it through his armor, to do so would have ruined the dignity of his appearance. Instead he sat, waiting for Herrenmer's return or the Baron's emergence, growing steadily more irritated as the whispering in the watching crowd ebbed and flowed.

Beside him, Galt and Kyrith also sat still; but behind them the other overmen were less restrained. They were in unfamiliar territory and looked about themselves with interest.

The poverty and decay of the town were plain on all sides; the only building not in obvious need of repair was the Baron's mansion. Shutters were missing or broken, roofs sagged, doors failed to fit their twisted frames. It appeared that little had been done to maintain the town in the three centuries since overmen had last seen it. For the most part, the warriors thought very little of the place.

The mansion's door opened again, and again the whispers hushed; this time Herrenmer pushed the doors wide and latched them open, then stood to one side. A moment later the Baron of Skelleth emerged, shuffling forward uncertainly. He was clad in a black robe embroidered with red and wore a circlet of gold on his brow; his hair and sparse beard were black. He was small and thin and seemed even smaller as he was hunched over slightly; his right hand appeared to tremble slightly as he raised it and said, 'Greetings, overmen.'

'Greetings, Doran of Skelleth,' Garth replied.

'So you have come to torment me further? Is not the life the gods have cursed me with torment enough to please you?' His face twisted in a ghastly smile; he raised his head, struggling to stand upright, and looked directly at Garth. The overman met his gaze and was taken aback by the abject despair he saw there, the liquid sorrow of a dying animal.

He was slow in replying, 'We have come to ask you to reconsider some of your previous decisions. My people are not pleased by your actions in response to our attempts to establish peaceful and profitable trade between our two nations.'

'You have forced me to rise from my sickbed because I have allowed you insufficient opportunity to swindle my subjects?' The parody of a smile remained, perhaps broadened. Garth, already annoyed, felt his anger piling up within him; he began to wonder whether the Baron was exaggerating his illness. The question was not that of a man sunk in unbearable woe; it smacked rather of the cleverness that Garth had seen the Baron display when at the peak of his cycle.

'We do not swindle anyone. You have compelled me to swear an oath that is intended to humiliate me. You have exiled me from your realm for no reason other than your personal dislike for me. The trader Galt tells me that the tariffs and regulations you propose, should my people refuse to acknowledge you as our overlord, are prohibitive, making peaceful trade impossible, although we all know it would benefit Skelleth as much as Ordunin. We have come here to ask you to correct these injustices, to benefit the people of your village as well as ourselves.'

'What injustices? I ask nothing unreasonable!' The mocking smile was gone; the slouch and the trembling had lessened until they were almost imperceptible. The eyes were still desolate, though; Garth found that disturbing.

He did not understand this man at all. His failure to understand enraged him further. His answer was shouted, not spoken. 'Nothing unreasonable? Is it reasonable to prevent the enrichment of us all merely to feed your own bloated ego? Do you seriously think that any overman could swear fealty to a human?'

Beside him, Galt's red eyes shifted back and forth, scanning the crowd. He was not happy with what he saw; Garth's outburst was provoking fear and resentment in both soldiers and civilians; this was plainly visible in their faces. He upbraided himself mentally for allowing Garth to act as sole spokesman; Garth was not as stupid as some overmen, nor as ignorant or careless, but he did have a nasty temper at times, and was not trained at restraining it. Galt, on the other hand, had spent most of his apprenticeship learning to take in his stride the asinine behavior a trader was likely to encounter among humans;

he was sure that he could have handled this affair with greater tact.

It would have been difficult, he thought, to have shown *less* tact. He debated breaking into the conversation himself, trying to calm everyone. He was quite sure that, if Garth was not careful, this debate could lead to bloodshed and disaster. He cast a glance sideways at Garth, but could read nothing in his face; before he could reach a decision his gaze was caught by the hilt of the strange broadsword that Garth had acquired. The red gem set in it was gleaming brightly.

The Baron, too, seemed to notice the sword as he replied to Garth's outburst. 'Do your people need this trade so desperately? You come here armed, with a force twice the number Skelleth can muster, the least of you carrying weapons and armor better than I can afford for myself. Your leader has a sword set with gems. Every one of you is well-fed and healthy, as far as I can see. Yet you protest mightily that I have demanded more than you can give. My people are starving, overmen. Look around you; my people are dying of cold and hunger. Is it unfair that I ask tariffs of you before allowing you to come and frighten them into giving you what little they have in exchange for the worthless trinkets you bring them? Is it unfair that I have hoped to collect taxes from you, that I might relieve their suffering? Is it unfair that I have tried to keep away from them those of you known to have committed murder, such as you? Is it unfair that I have asked your people to come only in groups small enough to pose no threat to the safety and well-being of Skelleth? Our two nations have been at war for half a millennium, Garth; now you come here, defying the laws and edicts of this realm, and demand that you be treated as an honored friend and neighbor. Can you think that I will give in willingly?'

Garth's right hand had crept across his chest toward his

left shoulder and the hilt of the great sword during this speech; his fingers touched the weapon as Galt replied quickly, 'You are twisting the truth and playing with words, Baron. We would not protest reasonable tariffs, though they would go, not to your starving people, but into your own pocket. We have no wish to cheat or deceive your people. If you do not want what we can trade, we will pay in gold for what we need. We can abide by restrictions on our travel in your lands, but you have ordered that no party of more than three may come; how can we form caravans to pass the dangers of the road in safety? Your claimed reasons for distrusting us are nonsense; Garth has killed in self-defense, but is no wanton murderer, and the war between our peoples ended three hundred years ago. You have asked us to give up our independence as a nation simply to obtain the right to trade; would you be willing to surrender your barony to us were the situation reversed?'

Galt's intrusion into the conversation had come as a surprise to everyone present; Garth had thrown him a startled glance, but let him speak. The Baron continued to stare directly at Garth.

'I do not parley with servants,' the Baron said.

Galt fought back a reply; it was Garth's turn again.

'He speaks the truth, Baron, perhaps more eloquently than I could, while you lie. You say that you do not parley with servants, yet you seem willing enough to speak to one you call a murderer; where is the logic in that? Galt is no servant, as you well know; you seek to insult and enrage us. Why?'

There was a moment of silence; then the Baron turned and began walking back toward his home. 'I do not answer to murderers,' he said.

'Hold, man!' Garth bellowed; his right hand closed on the sword and snatched it out of its sheath. With a flourish, he swung it about and hoisted it crosswise above his head.

The Baron stopped on the threshold and turned back to face the overmen again. 'I have called your bluff, Garth,' he said. 'I hold all powers here, save what you take by strength of arms. You have that strength; we both know that. You could kill me, and destroy Skelleth – but to do so would start the Racial Wars anew, and this time humanity would not be satisfied to drive you filthy monsters into the wilderness. This time, Garth, they would wipe you out, to the last stinking freak. You have no other choice; accept my terms, or fight and die. I will not change my terms. I am neither fool nor coward to be impressed by this handful of would-be warriors. If your people want to trade here, then you, Garth, are exiled, and sworn to offer your City Council the opportunity to surrender to me. Any trade in Skelleth will be by *my* rules. I will forgive you this one intrusion, but the next time armed overmen come here, I will send word to the High King at Kholis. Now, put away that ridiculous sword and go, all of you; leave me in peace!'

Garth's mounting fury could no longer be contained; he spun the Sword of Bheleu over his head, screaming, and then hurled it at the Baron's back as the man stepped through the doorway.

With a roar, the sword burst into flame in mid-air, and plunged burning into the Baron's back; his embroidered robe blazed up immediately as two feet of fiery, blood-stained blade protruded from his chest.

Despite the obvious force of the blow which had so easily pierced him, the Baron staggered and remained upright. He turned one last time, to face out toward the marketplace; his clothes and hair were lost in red flame. For an instant it seemed to Garth that his eyes, too, were afire.

'Fool!' he said, then he toppled forward onto his face.

The sharp impact with the threshold drove the blade backward through his chest and out his back; as he twitched one final time it came free and fell forward across one shoulder, its hilt pointed directly at Garth.

7

There was a frozen moment of near-silence; the only sound was the crackling of the flames. For long seconds, no one moved.

Garth thought he heard soft, mocking laughter; he turned, but could not locate its source. The fury still boiled within him, but when he had thrown the sword its hold had loosened, and he was able to think again.

As he looked round, he saw shock and astonishment on every face; humans and overmen alike were staring at the burning corpse. No one was laughing; no one smiled; no one spoke. Then one of the guardsmen broke the silence, speaking in a harsh whisper that carried to every corner of the square. 'Black magic!'

Another voice, this from one of the crowded streets, shouted, 'Kill them! Kill the overmen!' Garth spun about and thought he saw the shouter, an old man wearing dark red who stood in the forefront of the crowd in the street that led to the West Gate. He had no chance to reply or to make certain of his identification before he heard the snap of a bowstring. Instinctively, he ducked.

For the second time that day, an arrow whisked over his head; it continued on, to scrape against Galt's breastplate before falling to the clear ground between the soldiers of Skelleth and the first row of warbeasts.

'Down! Get down!' Garth called; following his own advice, he slid from the saddle. As he reached the ground, a ragged volley of arrows followed, coming from all directions.

Immediately, he understood the entire situation and berated himself for not anticipating it. He had seen the twenty-five guardsmen in front of the mansion and considered them to be the entire force, even though he knew there were more than thirty men in the Baron's service. The others had been stationed in windows and on rooftops all around the square. The Baron had been a clever man, even in his madness. It was possible there were other dangers hidden in the crowds – and the crowds were themselves a problem, blocking every avenue of retreat save one, keeping the overmen bottled up in the market where they were easy targets.

More arrows flew, whistling and buzzing; the thumping of bowstrings was now coming in a steady, uneven rhythm. Around him, the overmen were shouting; he heard a cry of pain and the growling of a warbeast.

It was far too late now to prevent bloodshed; despite his good intentions, the sword had overcome him, and this peaceful mission had become a battle. That being so, Garth told himself, it was a battle he intended to win. The anger still seethed in him; it had been far too long since the overmen of the Northern Waste had won a battle, and this seemed a good place to start.

He looked around; the situation was bad. His troops, completely untrained, were milling about in confusion as arrows rained down on them from every side; half the mounted overmen had followed his example and dismounted, but the others were still on their warbeasts, looking about in dazed confusion. The villagers, soldiers and civilians alike, were staying well back, letting their archers deal with the invaders. None of the overmen had yet taken any action to remedy their vulnerable position.

'Ho, overmen of Ordunin!' Garth bellowed at the top of his lungs. 'The battle is begun, whether we want it or no! Advance, then, and kill the guardsmen!' He gave this order, not because he considered the soldiers a threat, but because the archers would be reluctant to shoot into a mêlée involving their own comrades. It was the simplest order he could think of that would serve a useful purpose at this point. Once he had his overmen acting together again and responding to his commands, he could worry about better tactics.

Confused and angry, the overmen were glad to obey; now that they had a direction, they charged forward around the warbeasts that blocked their way. The mounted warriors did not seem to hear Garth's order; they continued to look about in confusion. As Garth watched, an arrow caught one young overman in the throat; soundlessly, he slid sideways out of the saddle, blood welling in his mouth, his red eyes wide with shock.

The overmen who had dismounted joined their companions in the charge, leaving their beasts behind. Garth suddenly realized that none of them really knew how to control the great animals.

The best thing for morale, Garth knew, would be to join the charge himself; there were tactical considerations, however, that were more important. As he had hoped, the archers were slackening their fire for fear of hitting their townsmen; but when the overmen had wiped out the humans – as they inevitably would do – the archers would again have a clear field of fire. The bowmen remained, therefore, the biggest threat, and Garth knew his best weapon was the warbeasts. It was time to pit the two against each other. When the first overmen reached the human soldiers, Garth spotted the location of one archer as the man leaned out from behind a chimney to release another arrow. With a wordless growl, Garth pointed this out to Koros, then ordered the warbeast, 'Kill!'

The monstrous animal roared in response, a sound that drowned out the growing clamor of the battle for a moment, then turned and leaped on to the back of its neighboring kin. From there it sprang upward in a magnificent jump that landed it on the roof where the bowman lurked. Shards of splintered slate flew in every direction at the impact of the warbeast's weight; the man had time for one short scream before Koros smashed the chimney out of the way and ripped him apart.

Garth did not wait to watch the archer's death; he was already pointing out another to Kyrith's warbeast. When that animal had leaped for its target, he turned back to Galt's, and then started on the first row of five.

Not all the warbeasts were as successful as Koros; one missed the roof it was aiming for and tried to scramble up the wall, its claws tearing out chunks of wood and plaster. Another made its leap perfectly, but landed on a thatched roof that was unable to support its weight; the beast and the archer it pursued both vanished into the building's upper floor, amid growls and screams.

Not all the bowmen were on rooftops; some were behind upper-floor windows too small for the huge animals to fit through. The warbeasts, direct and simple creatures, dealt with this by ripping out the wall around each window.

When he had sent warbeasts after every archer he could locate, leaving four of the animals in the middle of the square, Garth turned his attention back to the fighting in front of the mansion. His troops appeared to have the situation in hand. Outnumbering the humans two to one, even after the casualties inflicted by the archers, the overmen seemed to have their main problem in avoiding their own fellows. The twenty-five guards had been reduced to a knot of half a dozen, clustered in front of the open doors around the burning body of their lord.

The civilian population of the town had done nothing yet except to produce a great deal of noise; no one had ventured into the square. The crowds seemed smaller; probably, Garth thought, many had fled and taken shelter wherever they could. Those who remained merely watched, yelling.

Garth dismissed them from consideration for the moment and strode forward to aid his warriors in dealing with the surviving guardsmen.

'Hold!' he called. 'Stand back!'

Reluctantly, the overmen obeyed. The remaining humans stood, swords bristling, and waited.

'There is no need to continue the fight! Surrender and we will allow you to live.'

Herrenmer was one of the survivors. It was he who answered, 'Never, monster! We saw how well we could trust you when you slew the Baron!'

Garth fought down a surge of anger. 'Have not enough of your men died, Herrenmer? We outnumber you now by almost ten to one and we have our warbeasts as well. You have fought bravely and well on behalf of your dead lord, but you have lost; give up and we will let you live. I swear it.'

'Hah! This for your sworn word!' He flung his short sword at Garth, much as Garth had flung the Sword of Bheleu at the Baron.

Garth, however, ducked; the sword flew over his head and landed rattling on the hard ground beyond.

Several of the overmen growled, but made no aggressive move; this was between Garth and the human.

'Herrenmer, don't be a fool. Now you've even lost your sword; you can't fight anymore. Say that you surrender, and no harm will come to you.'

Herrenmer did not answer; instead he looked about in desperation for a weapon to replace the one he had lost. He found one; whirling, he dove for the hilt of the Sword of Bheleu.

Garth could not allow that. He knew how dangerous the great sword could be. He could not let a human, particularly one already almost berserk, get hold of it. He dove after Herrenmer.

The guardsman was much closer; before Garth had

covered half the intervening distance, the man's hands closed on the hilt. He screamed and immediately released it again, his palms smoking; the stench of burning flesh reached Garth's nostrils. It was too late to halt his own lunge, however, and he, too, grabbed the hilt.

He felt no pain, though the hilt was hot in his grasp. Instead, a wave of strength surged through him, filling him with fiery exultation. The red gem glowed more brightly than the dying flames of the Baron's garments, more vividly red than the blood that was pooled on the mansion's threshold.

Garth stood, the sword clutched in both hands; around him were the five remaining guardsmen, while Herrenmer lay crying at Garth's feet, the man's scorched hands held out before him. A foot or two away lay the smoking remains of the Baron. The sight of the dead enemy seemed a very good thing to Garth at that moment. He laughed in triumph. He had conquered! He was master of the village and could do with it whatever he pleased. He could destroy it all if he chose – and that was exactly what he chose!

Still laughing, he whirled, sword held out before him, and cut down the remaining humans. The blade sheared through armor and flesh and bone as easily as through air, leaving a trail of sparks behind. When he had completed the circuit, slicing open all five bellies before anyone could react, he plunged the point through Herrenmer's chest.

The captain gasped and twitched, then lay still; the other five took a few seconds longer to die. Garth pulled the sword free and looked about him.

The overmen – *his* overmen – were staring at him open-mouthed with surprise. They did not understand who led them, he realized. He cried out to them, 'I am Bheleu, god of destruction! Death and desolation are my companions, woe and hatred my tools! Follow me now to glory such as you have never imagined!' Some of the overmen still seemed uncertain; he lifted the sword above his head, blood dripping from the blade, so that the light of the jewel could shine on them. 'Skelleth is ours,' he cried. 'Ours to destroy! These humans have fought us, defied us; let us teach them the consequences of their defiance!'

The uncertainties were fading; enthusiasm flickered in the circle of the overmen's red eyes.

'Burn the village!' Bheleu called through Garth's mouth.

'Burn the village!' a few of the warriors answered.

'Slaughter the humans!'

'Kill the humans!'

They were with him now; the overman-god laughed, and the sword flamed over his head. He plunged it down, slamming the point into the threshold of the Baron's mansion; the stone step exploded into red-hot splinters, spraying up around him, but leaving him unscathed. The shards that landed inside the building set a dozen small fires on the wooden floor.

'Go, then! Kill and burn!'

The answering shout was wordless; the overmen turned away and ran with drawn weapons at the dwindling crowds in the surrounding streets. Garth laughed again, raised the sword, and swept it in an arc through the air; wherever it pointed, flame erupted. In seconds every building around the marketplace was ablaze. He strode forward into the square; behind him, the mansion flared up suddenly. He turned and gestured with the sword; the Baron's home was lost in a roaring curtain of flame. In moments it collapsed inward, falling into its own cellars; behind it, through the flames, Garth could see the King's Inn, where the so-called Forgotten King dwelt. He flung the fiery might of the sword outward toward it, as he had

90

toward the other structures, but nothing happened. Again he tried, calling aloud, 'I am Bheleu!'

The inn remained unharmed. He made a third and final attempt, willing all the god's available power to flow along the blade and strike at this resistance.

The tavern still remained untouched. Reluctantly, Garth gave up. He turned back to the buildings around the square; those, at least, behaved properly, flaring up like lit torches at his slightest whim. He laughed, and marched out into the village, spreading fire and destruction, but his dark joy was marred by his strange failure with the King's Inn.

The villagers scattered and hid before the onslaught of the overmen. Most took refuge in their homes or in the ruins that ringed the village. A few fled into the wilderness beyond the walls. None managed to put up an organized defense. Some found weapons; many barricaded their doors and windows. None had the foresight and ability to gather the townsmen so that their greater numbers could be of use against the overmen.

The overmen marched in small parties from door to door, smashing in barricades and butchering those who resisted. Where the resistance was too strong to be dealt with easily, warbeasts were called in. In all of Skelleth the only weapons that might have been effective against the great hybrids were buried in the burning ruins of the Baron's mansion. The animals served the overmen as battering rams, as armor, and as instruments of terror.

The humans who surrendered were spared, in most cases, and taken prisoner; the prisoners were gathered in the market square, guarded by four overmen and four warbeasts. A few overmen were too full of bloodlust and fury to restrain themselves, and some villagers were slain whether they surrendered or not, but generally even those individuals calmed down after a single such incident apiece.

Garth was the exception. As darkness descended, he strode laughing and screaming through Skelleth, killing every human he saw, burning every building he passed with the unnatural flames from the sword. Even the other overmen kept well away from him. He needed no warbeast to batter down barricades; a single blow from the sword shattered any defense set up against him. He seemed to take delight in killing those who could not fight back; he left the burning, dismembered corpses of women and children behind him.

It was full night when he came to one house where the door and shutters had been reinforced with steel. He was unable to carry through his first intention of burning his way in; when the wood had crumbled to ash, the metal still held. With a cry of *'I'a bheluye!'* he struck at the steel with the sword. Sparks showered, but the blade did not penetrate. He struck again, and this time the door exploded inward in a shower of twisted fragments.

There was no one in the room beyond; he stepped in and looked about. Even to his hazy, berserk mind, it was obvious that someone had locked and barred the door he had just destroyed. That meant that there was a prospective victim somewhere in the house. He decided to find this person.

The kitchen was empty; the back door and rear windows were locked and bolted. That left the upper floors. Garth found no stairs, but a ladder led through a trap in the ceiling.

The second floor was a single large chamber, furnished in a style that was luxurious by the standards of Skelleth, if ordinary enough in more fortunate places. A single bed stood against one wall; furs covered part of the floor, and hangings were on each wall. Tables and chairs were scattered about. Like the rooms below, it was unoccupied. Another ladder led upward.

With a snort, Garth climbed the second ladder, awkward with the great sword in his hand, and found himself in an unfurnished garret. There was a window at each end. The window at the back stood wide open; on either side of the window were stacked cages that held cooing birds. In front of the window stood a dour old man garbed in dark red.

With an exclamation of delight, Garth recognized him. This was Darsen, the rabble rouser, the troublemaker! This was the old man who had blamed Garth for the death of Arner the guardsman months ago and almost incited a riot; this was the man who had begun the battle by shouting, 'Kill the overmen!'

This would be fun, the overman thought; this man would die slowly. Garth advanced upon him, the sword held ready in his hands.

Darsen had been facing the window, clutching something in his hands; now, as he turned to face the approaching overman, he flung the object out the window. Garth saw the bird flapping wildly, catching itself in mid-air. He paid it no attention; pigeons had nothing to do with him. If the old man chose to spend his last pain-free moments playing with birds, that was his privilege.

The human tried to duck under the sword and slip past Garth, but did not make it; the overman's left hand released the hilt and grabbed the collar of the red robe. The last thing Darsen saw before pain forced his eyes shut was Garth's face, grinning broadly, teeth gleaming red in the light of the glowing jewel.

Outside the window, the bird was flying westward, toward Dûsarra.

8

The nightly sacrifice was done; this had been a sunset ritual, simpler and quicker than the midnight ceremonies used on special days. The victim's death had been relatively easy, and there had been no elaboration.

Haggat wondered whether such sacrifices were actually worth doing; did Aghad take pleasure in *every* murder? There was little real hatred in such slayings, little of the pure, dark emotion the god fed upon. Some stranger dragged from his bed had been killed; how did that help the cause of fear, of hatred, and of loathing? It did not truly increase the worshippers' hatred of their fellow Dûsarrans; if anything, he suspected it helped assuage their anger. It probably did little to increase the city's fear; the people had long since become accustomed to such random deaths and were much more frightened at present by the White Death, the plague that was loose in the city.

The sacrifices were traditional, though, and there was no real reason to stop them. They were no great drain upon the cult's resources, and the worshippers did enjoy them. His personal acolyte certainly did; she had been quite enthusiastic tonight, he thought. It was amusing to see the change that had taken place in her over the recent weeks. She had been a timid little thing at first, awed by her close contact with the then high priest, frightened at being given to Haggat, the temple's seer.

She had reason to be frightened, since tales of Haggat's idea of pleasure were common among the cultists. But she had discovered that she could survive his amusements and even enjoy some of them. With the death of his former master and Haggat's elevation to high priest, she suddenly found herself second in the cult's hierarchy. That position she enjoyed completely.

Now, as he had expected, she had prepared his special chamber; the scrying glass was gleaming, freshly polished, and the candle was lighted. She knelt by the doorway, awaiting his appraisal of what she had done.

He saw nothing wrong and made a sign of dismissal; she prostrated herself, then backed stiffly out of the room, closing the door behind her. He knew she would be waiting in his bedchamber when he was done with the glass.

There was no hurry, however; he enjoyed using the glass as much as he enjoyed his less savory pursuits. He picked up the crystal globe and held it so that the image of the candle-flame distorted within it.

When last he had used the glass, he had seen the overman Garth entering a tavern in Skelleth. It would be interesting to see what had become of him in the hours since. He concentrated on the globe.

The image of the flame grew and twisted, and then reddened.

That was unexpected; Haggat knew of no reason the image should be red. He wondered if the interference he had become familiar with was taking some new form. He tried to clear and strengthen the contact.

The crystal sphere was flooded with blood-red light. Two faces appeared, both etched in black and crimson. One was inhuman, eyes gleaming brightly; the other was a man, his face twisted in pain and terror. Haggat recognized them both, Garth and Darsen.

The high priest was surprised and confused. What was going on in Skelleth? Why was Darsen frightened? Why were the two of them anywhere near each other? Darsen was one of the more competent agents of the cult of Aghad and he certainly knew better than to confront so dangerous an opponent directly. He had been instructed to observe the overman and to do what he could to annoy and inconvenience him, to stir up fear, anger, and hatred. Had he gotten careless and provoked the overman openly?

A moment later it was plain that Darsen's terror had been justified; Haggat could still see nothing but the two faces, but he knew death when he saw it. Darsen was dead. The cult had lost its only agent in Skelleth.

Garth dropped the corpse, and Darsen's dead face vanished from the image in the globe. Haggat could not make out the overman's surroundings, even now, but only his face, hellishly red.

Garth looked up, and it seemed as if those baleful eyes, almost glowing in the red light, met Haggat's. The Aghadite knew that was impossible; only the greatest of sorcerers could detect a scrying-spell. Still, those crimson eyes, seemed to be watching him. Disconcerted, he let his concentration slip and lost the image of the rest of Garth's hideous face. He saw only the eyes.

Then a third red glow joined them, and Haggat drew back in shock and horror. What was *that*? He seemed to sense something dark and brooding in it, something beyond his comprehension. The new glow grew, and Garth's eyes faded. The crystal was suddenly hot in Haggat's hands, intensely hot; he dropped it.

It did not merely shatter when it hit the floor; it exploded, showering sparks and red-hot gobbets of glass in every direction. Miraculously, nothing caught fire, but Haggat would not have noticed if it had; he was staring at the burns on his palms.

This was powerful magic indeed! Could the so-called Sword of Bheleu truly be linked to the god of destruction himself? He had not seriously considered that possibility before. He knew of no device linking its user to Aghad, and had seen no reason to think other gods would provide what his own did not. He had dismissed such claims as superstition, or boasting, or an intimidating bluff.

This overman, however, seemed to have power of an order only divine intervention could explain. In that case, it would not be safe to use ordinary measures against him. Garth had defied the cult of Aghad and slain its high priest. For that he must die horribly; that could not be altered. Methods could be changed, however, and where Haggat had previously planned to use the cult's own elaborate system of spies and assassins to torment and eventually kill Garth, he now thought that might be unwise. It would be better to turn another enemy against the overman and let the two destroy each other, allowing the Aghadites to assess their power, and leaving the survivor weakened so that the cult might then handle him directly.

Furthermore, he knew exactly the right enemy to use for this purpose, an enemy of his own, an enemy he had long sought vegeance upon.

The priesthood had not been his first choice for a career; as a youth he had set out to become a sorcerer and had served several years as a wizard's apprentice. His master, a very great magician, had mistreated him, insulted him, abused him, and withheld secrets from him. His frustration and anger had fed upon each other and grown in him until finally, one night, he had demonstrated decisively how well he had learned his lessons and how much his master had underestimated him. The demons he conjured took more than an hour to finish pulling the old wizard to pieces.

It was only after the demons had done their work and been sent away that he learned one of the facts his master had concealed from him – the existence of the Council of the Most High, a secret society of magicians of every kind that sought to limit and control the knowledge and use of the arcane arts. His late master had been a member and had carried a spell that alerted his fellow councillors the instant he died.

The killing of one of their number was something the Council did not condone under any circumstances. They destroyed or confiscated all Haggat's belongings, placed a geas upon him that severely limited his magical abilities, cut out his tongue to prevent him from revealing any of his forbidden knowledge or reciting incantations, and then dumped him before a temple of Aghad, the god of treachery and ingratitude, among other things.

Aghad was also, as Haggat had known even then, a vengeful god, and he had willingly entered the priesthood in the hope of eventually gaining the revenge he had sworn. Though he rose steadily in the cult's hierarchy, due largely to the little magic he still retained, vengeance had eluded him; he had been unable to convince the cult to take action against the Council. Even now, when he had become absolute ruler of the Aghadites, he had not yet attempted anything. He knew that the Council was too powerful and too well-informed to be attacked without much careful planning and preparation. Its members included virtually all the most powerful wizards of the northern lands, and to defeat such a confederation would require great stealth and skill – or equal power.

He had assumed that no equal power existed in the world, but now, he thought, this enchanted sword that the overman called Garth carried might be just such a power. It angered him to think that the weapon had lain unused in Dûsarra, a few hundred yards from his own temple, without his knowledge. It could well have been there, offering countless opportunities for theft, since he first came to the city. He had been unaware of it until this overman came along and blithely stole it, wiping out Bheleu's cult in the process, defiling Aghad's temple, and spreading the White Death in the marketplace.

Now, though, Garth and the Council of the Most High

would both pay for their temerity in defying him. He needed merely to turn one against the other. Certainly one or the other would be destroyed, and he could then deal with the survivor.

How, then, could this be accomplished? How could he convince the Council that Garth was a menace, or convince Garth to attack the Council?

There was a hesitant knock on the chamber's door; the voice of his chief acolyte called, 'Is all well, master?'

He turned, his chain of thought broken by this distraction, and noticed for the first time the damage done by the exploding glass. Glittering chips were strewn everywhere, and the draperies that lined the walls were spattered with smoking scorched spots where bits of hot debris had struck them. His own robe was similarly damaged, with several smoldering patches and half a dozen holes where the flying shards had penetrated. None had struck his flesh, though; the protective charms he carried, feeble as they were, had at least done that much.

His hands were another matter; when he snapped his fingers to summon the acolyte into the room he discovered that his fingertips were burned, as well as his palms. He winced with pain; when the acolyte limped into the chamber, he had his fingers in his mouth, a pose most unbecoming the dignity of his position as high priest.

The acolyte was not stupid enough to remark on it or to acknowledge in any way that anything was out of the ordinary. She said, 'Forgive me, master, but I heard a strange noise, and feared for you. How may I serve you?'

Haggat considered for a moment. He would want her back in his bed shortly, but wished to have a few minutes to think first, and he knew he might as well put her to use. He made a sweeping gesture, indicating the broken glass on the floor.

'Your scrying glass?' The girl tried to keep her voice emotionless, but it was clear that she was puzzled.

He did not deign to nod; the fact that he did not hit her was acknowledgement enough that she was correct.

'I'll have it cleaned up immediately.' She noticed the damaged hangings and added, 'I'll have the draperies replaced as well, and inquiries will be made toward acquiring a new crystal. Is there anything else, master?'

It was not worth explaining by sign or note what he was considering; he would think it out himself first, before consulting with the other priests. He dismissed her with a wave, then caught himself. He did not want her to think that her duties would be done for the night after the clean-up. He pointed in the direction of his bedchamber.

'Of course, master; I am yours to do with as you will.' She bowed low and backed out, favoring the leg and foot he had injured a few nights earlier.

He looked about at the scattered chips of glass. How could he turn the Council and the overman against each other?

When Darsen's carrier pigeon arrived three days later with the old man's report describing the destruction of Skelleth and the murder of the Baron, Haggat had his answer.

9

Garth awoke to find himself lying in the middle of a narrow alleyway; to one side was an old ruin, to the other side a burning building. Directly before him the Sword of Bheleu lay in the dirt, the gem in its pommel dark.

It was night; his only light came from the fire. Stiff and sore, he clambered to his feet and looked about.

He recognized the burning building; it was the house where he had found and killed that old man. He vaguely remembered the actual killing; he had spent a long time at it. There was blood on his hands, he noticed, but he could not be sure that it came from the old man; he had killed several people. It might even have come from a wound of his own, though he hadn't noticed any.

He tried to remember what he had done after the man in red had finally died, to explain why he had found himself unconscious in an alleyway, but it was all very hazy. There had been something watching him, and he had done something with the sword – not cut, nor set afire, but something very difficult, something that had tired him. He couldn't recall exactly what. After that he had staggered out, setting the house ablaze behind him, and that was all he could remember. He must have collapsed immediately afterward.

Whatever he had done, it might have drained the sword of its power temporarily, he thought. He could detect not the tiniest spark of light in the jewel; it hardly even had the glitter of a normal gemstone. That was well; it meant that, at least for the moment, he was in control of himself.

That being the case, he knew he should get rid of the

sword while he could. He had offered it to the Forgotten King, and it had been refused – or at least, it had not been accepted. That certainly discharged any obligation he might have had to the old man, so he was free to dispose of the weapon as he saw fit. He did not want to keep it. He wanted nothing further to do with it; it had made him do insane things, incredible things. It was the sword that had been responsible for the Baron's death and the burning of the village, and if he kept it, he knew he could not control the sword indefinitely; sooner or later the gem would glow anew, and he would again spread destruction and death.

What, then, was he to do with it? The simplest solution would be to let it lie where it was and leave, but that would not do; some passing human would doubtlessly find it and pick it up, and there was no telling what would happen then. It was true that Herrenmer had been unable to handle it, but he could not rely on such a thing happening again. He did not understand the nature of its magic, and it seemed wholly untrustworthy, one moment burning with supernatural power, the next seeming nothing but an ordinary blade.

He could not give it to anybody else; anyone but the Forgotten King would probably be overcome by it as he had been. The King seemed able to control it, but he did not trust the old man; besides, the King had rejected it.

He would have to find a safe place for it, someplace where no one could get at it – either that or destroy it.

Could he destroy it? That would put an end to the problem once and for all.

It would be a shame to destroy such a beautiful weapon, but it was probably the only final solution. There was no hiding place in the world where it could not eventually be recovered. He would make the attempt.

He coughed; smoke from the burning building was beginning to reach him, though so far flames were only visible through the windows. He realized he was warm, almost hot, though the night was cool. It was time he moved away from the fire.

He reached down and reluctantly picked up the sword, keeping a wary eye on the gem. It remained dark.

He found his way out of the alley and debated briefly which way to turn. He wanted privacy for his attempt to destroy the sword. He turned left, which he was fairly certain would take him out of the inhabited portion of Skelleth and into the surrounding ruins.

Though it was a moonless night, he had no trouble at all seeing his way; burning buildings lighted the sky behind him a smoky, lurid orange. The breeze was following him, carrying smoke and ash with it; his eyes stung, and he had to blink often.

He wondered what was happening around the marketplace. Had the overmen suffered many casualties? Had they butchered the villagers? How many survived on each side? Had any of the humans fled south, to gain the aid of their kin and bring the wrath of the High King at Kholis down upon the invaders?

Had he started the Racial Wars all over again?

Whatever happened, it would take time before any human reinforcements could arrive. He wanted to use that time to destroy the sword, so that he could deal with any new threats rationally.

He came to a place where a wall of heavy blocks of cut stone had been tumbled into the street, to lie in scattered chunks. For the first time it occurred to him to wonder what could have brought down such a wall; was Skelleth prone to earthquakes?

There were too many questions, far too many questions.

Whatever had knocked down the wall, the blocks of stone were well suited to his purpose. He laid the sword across a large slab, its quillons and hilt extending to one

103

side, the last foot or so of its blade on the other. He placed another stone atop it, so that it was held firmly between the two smooth, solid surfaces. That done, he located another large, heavy block – one that he could lift, though it strained his inhuman strength near to its limit. He was not in the best of condition, after waking up in an alley after a messy battle, but he could still haul about three hundred pounds of stone up to chest level.

He then climbed atop the other two stones, so that his own weight was added to that on the sword, holding it motionless. Taking careful aim, he then dropped the stone he carried on to the sword's hilt, planning to snap it off the blade at the edge of the bottom stone.

He had gone to this amount of trouble because he was quite sure that this sword could not be broken simply by slamming it against a rock or bending it over his knee. Even a magic sword, though, could hardly survive his arrangement of stone, he thought. The finest sword ever forged could not withstand the shearing force of a three-hundred-pound stone block dropped on its hilt while it was held motionless.

The block fell, struck the hilt – and shattered. Garth could not see in detail what had happened, because he was too busy trying to keep his balance; the stone on which he stood had cracked, its two halves sliding to either side. He found himself falling, and dove off the stone, landing on his hands and knees. Slightly dazed, he got to his feet and turned to look at the blocks.

The sword lay gleaming, unharmed, on the stone he had used as a base; the block he had used as a cover lay in two jagged fragments on either side. The stone he had dropped had been reduced to scattered pebbles.

That approach obviously wouldn't work.

He thought he heard mocking laughter. He whirled trying to locate it, but saw nothing. He turned back and saw that the gem was now glowing brightly.

He resolved not to touch the thing. If he did, he was sure he would be possessed once more by whatever malign force the sword served.

It shone, red and beautiful, before him.

He would not touch it.

It seemed to beckon; the blade gleamed red, as if washed in blood, and the stone beneath was lighted as well. His hands suddenly itched. He knew that the itching would stop if he held the sword, which seemed to be drawing him. He wanted to pick it up, to hold it before him, to wield it in berserk fury.

He fought down the urge and stepped back.

The movement seemed to lessen the pull slightly, and he remembered that the spell of the basilisk and of Tema's gem was broken if the victim could look away in time. He forced himself to turn his head and look away.

The pull was still there, but not as strong. He heard laughter again. Anger surged through him. Who dared laugh at him? He would skewer whoever it was! He took a step toward the sword, then stopped.

The anger was not his; it was the sword's influence. The laughter was familiar, and he remembered that he had heard it before. He had heard it when he slew the Baron; he had heard it in Dûsarra, when the sword had used him there. He listened closely, then shuddered.

It was his own voice, his own laughter, the same maniacal sound he had made when possessed by the sword's power. Now, however, it came from somewhere outside him.

This was beyond him; he knew he was dealing here with forces he could not comprehend. The lure of the sword still drew him, but a stronger, more basic urge was also at work. He was afraid.

With a final brief glance at the glowing gem, he turned and ran.

A hundred yards from the fallen stones, he slowed;

fifty yards further along the street, he stopped. His sudden fear had subsided, and the compulsion drawing him to the sword had faded with each step, until it was now no harder to handle than a mild hunger in the presence of poisoned food.

He had to consider all this rationally, he told himself. He had to think it all through logically and follow the logical course of action.

The sword had some unholy power to it. It could steal control of his mind and body and turn him into a berserk monster. It could burn without taking harm, and set fire to anything in sight – or almost anything; he remembered the King's Inn. That had probably been protected by the Forgotten King's spells.

The sword could shatter stone and cut its way through solid metal as well. It resisted his attempt to destroy it and tried to draw him to it, as if it wanted him to carry and use it – but when Herrenmer tried to touch it, it had burned him. Was there some mystic link between the sword and himself?

He remembered how he had pulled it from the burning altar of Bheleu. Had that created a connection somehow? But even then, he had been drawn to it as if hypnotized, though he had not yet touched it. None of the worshippers of Bheleu had been affected by any such compulsion, so far as he could recall. Perhaps it had an affinity for overmen; he knew that the idols of Bheleu always took the form of an overman, though the god's worshippers had all been human.

That connection could explain a great deal. It made clear how the sword had existed before his arrival without having captured anyone until he came to rob the ruined temple. He had no idea when the blade had been forged, but he was sure it was not new.

But then, could he be sure? The blade had no nicks or scratches and bore no sign of ever having been used. The hilt was not worn. On the other hand, the blade showed no smithing marks, and the hilt did not have the rough feel of new work not yet smoothed by use.

The age of the sword was a mystery, he admitted.

Still, it seemed unlikely that it had been newly forged just in time to be placed in the altar the night he arrived to steal it. It had almost certainly been in the cult's possession for some time previous to his acquisition of it, and there was no evidence that it had ever before usurped anyone's will or caused widespread destruction.

Perhaps it was indeed attuned to overmen, and could not be used by humans. There were overmen in Dûsarra on occasion, he knew, traders from the Yprian Coast, but none of them would have any reason to visit the Street of the Temples. It was possible that none before himself had ever come within range of the sword's spell.

Its call did seem to be limited by distance.

Was there, perhaps, another explanation? Was he constructing his theory on insufficient evidence?

He felt that he could be sure that no one before him had wielded the sword to any great effect in Dûsarra, at least not within the past several years. If any such event had occurred, it would almost certainly have been mentioned to him by Frima or by Mernalla, the tavern wench he spoke with – or perhaps by the high priest of Aghad or the caretaker of the temple of The God Whose Name Is Not Spoken. None of them had made any significant comment about the temple or cult of Bheleu.

The god of destruction had been mentioned, however. Tiris, the ancient priest of P'hul, had told him that he, Garth, was either Bheleu himself or his representative. Garth had dismissed that as the babblings of a senile old man, but perhaps it had not been entirely that. Tiris might have known something of the magic sword and somehow recognized Garth as the one who would wield it. There was nothing particularly distinctive about Garth, except the fact that he was an overman.

That was evidence, then.

No other theory seemed to fit very well. Therefore, he would act on the assumption that the sword's magic was somehow geared so that only overmen could use it – or more accurately, it could use only overmen.

If that was in fact correct, then he need not worry about leaving it where it was. Wandering humans might come across it, but they would not be able to handle it. He would order the overmen to stay away from it, or perhaps even post guards around it.

Whatever became of it, he did not want to touch it again. He wanted to retain his own mind and will. The sword was insidious and unpredictable; he had managed to restrain it on the journey back from Dûsarra, when violence would have been nothing but an unfortunate incident, but had completely lost control here in Skelleth, where the resulting battle might have been the opening engagement of a new Racial War. Its magic had seemed to fluctuate randomly in strength, but Garth was beginning to suspect that it was not random at all.

Perhaps he could wall off this part of the village to keep out the curious. Some way to destroy or control the sword might eventually be found, or perhaps he could persuade the Forgotten King to do something with it, since the old wizard was plainly able to handle it.

That could all wait. He was rid of it for the moment and could turn his attention to other matters.

He and his troops had sacked and burned Skelleth with little or no justification. He had personally murdered the Baron, stabbing him dishonorably from behind. The people of Eramma would have to find out eventually; so major an event could not be kept secret. There would be much careful negotiating to be done if full-scale war was to be prevented, and only a near-miracle could restore the possibility of the peaceful trade he had hoped to establish.

Other trade routes were possible, though. There were overmen on the Yprian Coast, and a route might be found to Dûsarra or other cities in Nekutta. So far, the overmen of the Northern Waste had acted only against the people of Eramma; the other human nations would have no grievance. If overland routes could not be found, the sea trade need no longer be limited to Lagur; there were other seaports in Orûn, he was sure, though he knew no names. There might well be other lands of which his people knew nothing, lying beyond Orûn to the east and south, or beyond the Gulf of Ypri to the west. Expeditions would have to be sent out.

There was so very much to do!

The first thing to do was to gather together the survivors of both sides of the battle and set up some sort of organization. That could best be done from the marketplace; it was the one gathering place in town, the place where anyone seeking aid or leadership would go.

Garth knew he should return there immediately. He headed in that general direction, following the glow of the fires that were centered on the square. There was enough light for him to find his way, and within a few moments he found himself on a street he recognized. He followed it in the direction of the market.

He had been certain of the street's identity; but as he approached the market, he thought for a moment that he had made a wrong turn and become lost. The square and its surrounding buildings were unrecognizable; not a single one of the surrounding structures still stood. The smoldering ruins were more thoroughly destroyed than those on Skelleth's fringe. Only the fact that he knew there was no other large clear space in the center of town reassured him that it was indeed the familiar square.

The market was thronged with people and animals,

sitting, standing, or lying, clumped together at random. There were several overmen in sight, and a few warbeasts, but most of the crowd was made up of ragged humans and their pets and livestock. The majority were bunched tightly together in a mass that occupied most of the square, avoiding the hot and sooty rubble that surrounded it.

The overmen seemed to be distributed around the perimeter, Garth realized, acting as guards. It was obvious, though, that they were too few to have halted any concerted effort by the humans to leave. The warbeasts were posted in various streets, but the buildings had been so completely levelled that anyone with footwear adequate to protect him from heat and sharp edges could easily have walked out over the rubble between the streets. The humans stayed where they were because they had nowhere else to go.

He looked at the mob of sooty, filthy, ragged humans, at the sooty and bloodstained overmen, and at the smoldering ruins. This desolation was his own doing. He was appalled. How could he have done this?

No, he told himself, *he* hadn't done this. The Sword of Bheleu, or whatever power controlled it, was responsible. Garth's only fault had been overconfidence in believing that he could resist the weapon's magic. He was a reasonable being, with only good intentions; he would not willingly have contributed to such devastation. The sword's power had warped his thoughts and clouded his mind, subtly feeding the honest anger he had felt toward the Baron of Skelleth and using it to overcome his resistance.

He was rid of the thing now, and it was time to start making amends.

'Ho, there!' he called to the nearest overman. 'Who's in charge?'

The warrior had been facing away from him, watching

the milling humans; now he turned, and Garth recognized him as Tand, Galt's apprentice. His face was black with soot, but that did not quite conceal a line of blood on one sunken cheek. His breastplate was dented near the left shoulder, and a sword was ready in his hand.

When Tand saw who had spoken he lowered the sword. 'Oh, it's you,' he said. 'Galt and Kyrith are over there, talking to some of the humans.'

'Thank you.' Garth's gaze followed the younger overman's pointing finger, but he could not make out the two named with any certainty. He started to walk in the direction indicated.

'Garth?' Tand's voice was uncertain.

He stopped and turned back toward the apprentice. 'Yes?'

'What happened? I thought this was to be a peaceful expedition, but you slew that human, the Baron, and then everyone was fighting. How did it start? Why did you kill him?'

Garth did not reply immediately. After a moment's consideration, he said, 'It was as one of the guardsmen said; it was black magic. I was not myself. There was a spell upon me. I am sorry that it happened and I assure you I won't let it happen again.'

'Can you prevent it? How can you stop magic? If it could control you once, why not again?'

'I know what caused it and I have removed the cause.'

'Are you sure?'

Garth felt a moment of anger that the youth doubted him, and began a harsh reply. He stopped abruptly. The sword used and magnified anger, until his will was swallowed by his rage; could he be sure it was not still affecting him? He had left the sword in an empty street half a mile away, but he did not know how far its influence might extend. He could not give it any chance to gain control and lure him back. He suppressed his annoyance, fighting it down inside him. He did not answer the trader's apprentice, but turned and marched away.

Galt and Kyrith were in the northwestern corner of the square; Frima and Saram stood facing them. Koros stood, unattended, a few paces to one side. Garth noticed that Saram's arm was around Frima's waist, and hers was on his shoulder; the two of them, alone of all in sight, were clean, not smeared with dirt and soot.

Galt looked up as Garth approached and called, 'Ah, Garth! We missed you!'

'Greetings, Galt. Greetings to you all.'

'We were just discussing matters with these two humans. We're told you brought the female here from the city of Dûsarra.'

'I did.' Garth was not interested in talking about Frima.

'She tells us that you rescued her from a sacrificial altar in order to deliver her to the old man who lives in the tavern here.'

Garth did not want to discuss the Forgotten King either. 'Galt, you ask questions that do not concern you.'

'I ask on behalf of your wife, since she cannot speak for herself; she wishes to understand her husband's actions. I, too, am curious.'

'It seems foolish to me to waste time on such trivia when there are far more important concerns to be dealt with. We may have just started the Racial Wars again; surely you realize that.'

Galt's voice lost its normal lilt and turned flat as he replied, 'Of course I realize that. You and your temper may have consigned our entire species to extinction, and we must do everything we can to prevent this war from spreading. I saw no need to discuss that immediately, however, since there appears to be little we ourselves can do at present. Your behavior is something else entirely. You must guess, Garth, that all those who know you are curious about how you have acted these past few months.

112

I had hoped that we might come to understand your motives and perhaps learn what has brought about our present catastrophe, the better to prevent its recurrence. You are now inextricably involved in affairs of consequence, and your actions are therefore a matter of importance. Thus, we were attempting to understand them.'

'It was not my temper that did this,' Garth replied, gesturing to indicate the smoking ruins and ragged crowd. 'It was that enchanted sword I brought back from Dûsarra.'

Kyrith made a sign to Galt, who said, 'That was another subject that concerned us. Where did you get that sword? Why did the gem seem to glow? What sort of an enchantment does it bear? And where is it now? You were very vague about it before. And how did you make it burst into flame and spread fire about the way it did?'

'I didn't make it do anything. The sword has a will of its own, a very ferocious and destructive one, and it got out of control. It acted on its own.'

Galt was silent for a moment before replying, 'Are you serious?'

Garth suppressed his annoyance. 'Yes, I am serious. The sword is very powerfully enchanted and is either itself an independent entity or is magically linked to a spirit or wizard of some sort.'

'You said before that you found it in a temple someplace?'

'I pulled it from the altar in the temple of Bheleu, the god of destruction, in the city of Dûsarra.'

'The god of destruction? Is that what you were shouting about?'

'That was more of the sword's doing. The entity that controls it claims to be or represent Bheleu. It might be telling the truth. Enough of this, though; we have to straighten out the mess here and make peace with

113

Eramma before the High King at Kholis sends an army to destroy us.'

'A few moments will make no difference. Garth, you have been acting strangely for these past few months. You have gone off on mysterious expeditions with little or no notice, vanishing completely for weeks with no explanation, leaving your wives and family to worry. You have undertaken single-handedly to establish trade with the humans of Eramma. You have now returned unexpectedly from your latest venture and immediately started a disastrous battle . . .'

Garth interrupted, saying, 'The battle was not disastrous; we won easily. It's the consequences of the victory that may be disastrous.'

'I stand corrected. Let me finish, though. You started, then, a battle that could have disastrous consequences. You have acquired a sword with which you are able to perform destructive magic and you claim it has a mind and will of its own; after the battle the sword has mysteriously vanished. You have brought back with you a human female of no particular value, and then abandoned her. You have behaved oddly, perhaps even insanely, screaming a lot of nonsense about gods and death, while setting fires on all sides. I am told by this human, Saram, that you have made some sort of pact with a local wizard who has promised you immortality.

'Garth, surely you see that to all appearances you have become completely irrational, madder than the Baron you slew. We have all deferred to you, and let you go your way, so far as was practical, because you are a respected overman, an honored member of the City Council, an experienced military commander, the hereditary Prince of Ordunin, and generally as highly placed and well-considered as it is possible to be among our people. A great deal of eccentricity can be tolerated under such circumstances. There are limits, however, and until Kyrith and I, the legally appointed co-commanders of this force, have received some acceptable explanation of your behavior, we cannot allow you to go on as you have. The consequences could be too severe. If you refuse to explain yourself, we will be forced to consider you deranged – dangerously so, but perhaps only temporarily – and to exclude you from all authority. If you cause any further difficulty, we may have to disarm you and confiscate your goods and weapons, perhaps even place you under provisional arrest. Do you see our position?'

Garth listened to this speech with shifting emotions. At first he was annoyed, then astonished that Galt and Kyrith could think him to be mad. He was silent for a moment, considering.

He *had* behaved irrationally, he knew that. He had been under the sword's influence. He might even now be less than fully under his own control; he knew that the spell could be subtle and that he need not be touching the weapon to be affected, though he thought it must weaken with distance. He could not be trusted, either by himself or by others. Unpleasant as that consideration was, he knew he had to accept it.

Hesitantly, he said, 'You are correct, Galt and Kyrith. You are entitled to an explanation. I am not mad; I have reasons, reasons I think good and sufficient, for everything I have done. I can see, though, that from your viewpoint my behavior has been strange indeed. I will be glad to explain myself and let you decide for yourselves how to deal with me.'

Saram broke into the conversation. 'If I might make a suggestion,' he said, 'there is no need to stand about out here while explaining. The King's Inn, over there beyond the ruins of the mansion, was not damaged by the fighting. Frima and I were inside it the whole time, which is why we're unharmed. I suggest that we go there, where we can sit and speak more comfortably, and get some ale to keep tempers from fraying.'

Garth realized that he was, in fact, quite thirsty, his throat full of smoke. He nodded consent.

'An excellent idea,' Galt agreed.

Though the Baron's mansion was gone, the cellars remained, half-filled with rubble and not readily passable in the darkness, forcing the party to take a roundabout route to reach the street where the King's Inn stood. As they passed the ruins, Garth glanced down and noticed something pale in the wreckage. He looked more closely and saw that it was a statue. It had once been a human being, Garth knew; the Baron had used him as a test subject for the basilisk's legendary power. The overman suddenly no longer regretted killing the Baron, whatever the repercussions might be.

The street that ran behind the destroyed manor had been the town's filthiest alleyway, dark and forbidding; now, though, the destruction of the surrounding buildings had let in fresh air and firelight, so that it was no longer much worse than any other debris-strewn byway. Its most outstanding feature was the presence of an unburnt building, the King's Inn.

The three overpeople and two humans picked their way through the gloom, past broken stones and fallen timbers that littered their path, while Koros padded silently along a few paces behind, following its master.

Galt remarked, 'It's curious that this tavern should have survived unscathed, so close to the square.'

'It is more curious than you know,' Garth said. 'It alone, of all the buildings in Skelleth, withstood the power of the sword when I tried to set it ablaze.'

'I think that you and I, Garth, both suspect why this is,' Saram remarked.

'Tell me, then,' Galt said. 'Or is this some great secret that you two share?'

116

'No, hardly that,' Garth replied. 'This inn is the home of the Forgotten King, the wizard I first came to Skelleth to find. He seems to be capable of many amazing things; saving his home from the flames is simply the latest example of his power.'

'From what I know of the old man,' Saram added, 'he could probably have saved the entire village, but preferred not to take the trouble.'

Galt snorted in derision. 'If this man is such a mighty wizard, what is he doing in a pesthole like Skelleth?'

'That's one of the mysteries about him,' Saram answered.

They had reached the door of the tavern; it was closed, despite the relatively warm weather, the only sign that there was anything out of the ordinary. The broad front window was clean and unbroken, the half-timbered walls clean and smooth, with no sign of smoke or soot anywhere.

Saram opened the door and led the party inside; Koros, at a word from Garth, waited in the alleyway.

10

The interior of the tavern was crowded with people, all human. As the three overpeople entered a sudden quiet spread before them. Three dozen pairs of eyes watched them intently. In the silence Garth could hear the sound of a knife sliding from its sheath.

Saram muttered, 'I think you had better say something.'

'People of Skelleth!' Garth said. 'We have come in peace. The battle is over. We mean you no harm; we have come here to drink and talk, nothing more.'

The silence and tension remained; the crowd still watched.

'Innkeeper,' Galt called, 'five mugs of your best ale!' He sauntered into the room, found an empty chair, and seated himself. The table he had chosen was occupied by two grubby, middle-aged men in stained tunics. 'I hope you don't mind if we join you,' he said casually, 'but there don't appear to be any vacant tables.'

One of the men muttered a vague reply; the other sat and stared.

Galt waved to Garth and the others. 'Come and sit down!'

Hesitantly Garth obeyed, taking the remaining empty chair at the table. Kyrith followed, and stood awkwardly for a moment until Saram brought her a chair from a neighboring table.

'Uh . . . we were just going,' one of the villagers said. He rose and backed cautiously away. His companion sat and stared.

Saram escorted Frima into the vacated place, then

tapped the lingering human on the shoulder. 'Excuse me, friend, but would you mind moving to another table?'

The man looked up, startled. 'Hah? Oh . . . no, no, of course not.' He got awkwardly to his feet and followed his companion, backing away from the table and finding an empty chair elsewhere.

Saram seated himself and remarked, 'That's better.' He raised an arm and called, 'Innkeeper, where's that ale?'

Galt remarked, 'Garth, you really don't know much about dealing with humans. You don't want to make speeches to a crowd like this; just convince them that you belong. Actions are far more convincing than words.'

'A truth I had forgotten momentarily,' Saram agreed.

The other patrons were beginning to lose interest and turn away. The innkeeper was approaching with a tray bearing ale. Garth glanced around the room, realized the crisis was over, and allowed himself to relax. He also noted in passing that the Forgotten King was at his customary table, as if nothing had happened.

'Now, Garth,' Galt said, 'we would like to hear your explanation for your behavior.'

'One moment.' The ale had arrived, and Garth downed his in a few quick gulps. He handed back the empty mug and said, 'Keep refilling this until I tell you to stop.'

The innkeeper nodded. 'Yes, my lord.'

The other four were not hasty in their drinking; the man departed with Garth's mug while they sipped their ale.

'Where shall I begin?' Garth asked.

'Wherever you please,' Galt replied.

'At the beginning,' Saram said.

Kyrith nodded in agreement.

'What beginning?' Garth asked.

'We thought your behavior odd when you first ventured

119

south from the Northern Waste,' Galt replied. 'Why not begin by explaining how that came to pass?'

'I am not certain where the beginning of that was,' Garth said. 'Last winter, I suppose, though I cannot name a date; it seemed to grow gradually.'

'Start with that,' Galt told him.

'Very well. You all know how the winters in our lands can wear on one – save perhaps Frima, who is not from these northern realms. The shortness of the days, the paleness of the light, the cold, the snow, the ice – all oppress the mind and the senses. This past winter seemed to affect me more than usual, though it was not an especially harsh one. I found myself depressed and bored; each day I told myself that it would pass, but each day I seemed to sink further into gloom. I could think of nothing but death and despair, and the futility of our lives, struggling to live in the Waste, able to do little more than survive. Every event seemed to contribute to my melancholy; when the hundred and forty-fourth anniversary of my birth arrived, all I could think of was that I must now be more than halfway to my death. It seemed that I had done nothing of any importance in that half of my life. I had won a few inconsequential battles with pirates and raiders, I had fathered a few children, and I had spoken in the City Council on such matters as rebuilding wharves and buying arms. The pirates and raiders survived and will doubtlessly return; my children will grow old and die; my speeches will be forgotten. What was worse, I saw no prospect of anything better in the future. I would grow old and die without ever having done anything to make a mark upon the world. In a century or two, no one would remember that I had ever existed. I did not want that to come about, but I could think of no way to avoid it.'

'No one looks forward to death,' Galt said.

Garth glanced in the direction of the Forgotten King,

but did not deny Galt's statement. Instead, he said, 'I know, I know, it is the way of things. I was not satisfied with that, however, and resolved to change it, if it could be changed. I went to the Wise Women of Ordunin and asked, first, whether there was anything I could do that would alter the way of things, some act of cosmic significance I could perform that would change the nature of life. They told me that was beyond the power of mortals. I had expected that. I then asked if there was any way that I could be remembered forever, so that, if I had to die, at least my memory might survive.'

The innkeeper arrived with Garth's second ale; he drank it and handed back the mug. Before he could resume his narrative, Saram asked, 'Who are the Wise Women of Ordunin? You have mentioned an oracle of some sort, but you never told me much about them.'

'Ao and Ta are sisters who live in a cave near Ordunin; both are ancient and deformed overwomen,' Galt told him. 'They have been there at least since the city was built during the Racial Wars. They will speak with certain people, but avoid all others by hiding in the depths of their cave. They answer questions. Although no one has ever known them to lie or to be wrong, they are fond of evasive and confusing answers.'

'You trust them?'

'They have never been wrong and have never lied,' Garth said. 'I trusted them last winter. I am not certain I will trust them in the future.'

'Go on, then, with your story,' Galt said.

'When I asked the Wise Women how I might be remembered until the end of time, Ao told me that I must go to Skelleth, find the Forgotten King, and serve him without fail. She told me the name of this inn, and that he could be found here wearing yellow rags. I was sufficiently caught up in my search for eternal fame that I immediately gathered together supplies, armed myself,

121

and came south on Koros – though I had not yet named it then; it was simply my warbeast. I told no one what I planned because I considered it wholly my own affair and did not want it known that I was coming to Skelleth. I feared that the City Council might consider such a venture potentially dangerous, since at that time we all still believed Skelleth to be a mighty fortress, from whence the humans might attack us at any time. I could not then truly explain why I was suddenly so concerned with being remembered, why I was obsessed with death, or what had brought on my depression; I still cannot. Whatever the reason, knowing I would be remembered seemed the most important thing imaginable.

'I knew nothing about Skelleth, of course, save for the old tales from the wars, and not much more about humans. When I saw that the walls were in ruins, I thought that the fortress must be deserted; therefore, I rode directly in, making no attempt at stealth. When I came upon people, it was too late to change my approach, so I continued on openly and asked directions to the King's Inn.

'Here I found the Forgotten King, exactly matching the description I had been given; he told me he could, indeed, guarantee that my name would be known until the end of time if I were to serve him, and if he were successful in some great feat of magic he had planned. I agreed to undertake an errand for him as a trial of sorts; I was to go to the city of Mormoreth, southeast of here, and bring back the first living thing I found in the crypts beneath the city. I did as he asked, but I was not pleased with the outcome. The only living thing in the crypts was a basilisk, a magical and incredibly poisonous creature, so venomous that its slightest touch or even its gaze was fatal. To capture it, I had to kill several bandits and a wizard, which I had no wish to do.

'In the course of attempting to deliver it, I encountered

further difficulties; the Baron of Skelleth learned of the creature's existence, and desired it for use as a weapon of war. He took possession of it briefly, but I recaptured it and delivered it to the King. I didn't know what he wanted with it, or what he did with it, but it did not serve his purpose. When he had finished with it, I killed it, rather than let so dangerous a creature fall into the hands of the mad Baron.

'That enraged the Baron; he already disliked me because I had failed to cooperate with him, and being deprived of the basilisk seems to have caused him to hate me implacably.

'Meanwhile, I had reconsidered my bargain with the Forgotten King. I was dismayed at having accomplished nothing beyond several deaths in running his errand; when he pointed out that I would be remembered in Skelleth and Mormoreth for those deaths, I broke off our agreement, I was no longer so enamored of eternal fame as to wish to buy it through slaughter and servitude.

'The King, however, perhaps to soothe me, made a suggestion; he pointed out that, as I could see, Skelleth was no longer the unforgiving enemy of overmankind that it had once been, and that I might acquire some measure of fame and wealth by establishing trade between Skelleth and the Northern Waste. As you all know, I set out to do that. I found you, Galt, to handle the details of trade, that being outside my own knowledge, and brought you, Tand, and Larth back here to open up trade, only to learn that the Baron would not cooperate with the one who had deprived him of the basilisk and his hopes of becoming a mighty warlord. He set intolerable conditions on our trading in order to humiliate me. You know that, Galt; you were there. You know that he asked me to swear fealty to him, to become his vassal.

'Caught by surprise, I foolishly agreed to present his proposal to the City Council and, in fact, swore an oath to that effect. That was a bad mistake on my part; I concede that.'

A third mug of ale arrived; Garth paused to drink, but did not gulp it down as he had the first two. He waved the hovering innkeeper away.

'It is difficult for me to explain exactly why I acted as I did. I had it fixed in my mind that the establishment of trade was an absolute necessity, both for the good of our people and for my own aggrandizement. I wanted to accomplish something that would be an unmixed blessing, that would be beneficial to all concerned, and the opening of this trade route seemed to fit. No one would die; I would be serving no mysterious old man. Still, I would achieve renown which, if not eternal, would at least be of a positive nature. Convinced as I was of the value, to myself and to Ordunin, of trade, I was ready to agree unthinkingly to almost any terms. It took the shock of the Baron's insults and arrogance to jar me out of that.

'By the time I realized what I had done in swearing that oath and accepting banishment, it was too late to retract. To have gone to the Baron and asked him to reconsider at that point would have been humiliating in itself. I wanted time to think, to see if there were any way to arrange matters more to my satisfaction. The oath I had sworn had a loophole – I had agreed to speak to the Council immediately upon my return to Ordunin, but I had not said when I would return. I decided, therefore, that I would leave Skelleth as ordered, but would not return home. Galt told you this, Kyrith, or part of it, but you chose not to believe him. I have treated you badly in giving you no explanation before this and I apologize for my negligence.

'Having decided that I could be in neither Skelleth nor Ordunin, I had nowhere to go. I could have gone to Kirpa, I suppose, or Mormoreth, but I had no reason to. The Forgotten King had expressed an interest in renewing our bargain and had even offered to change the terms, promising me not merely eternal fame but actual immortality if I would return to his service. I was not eager to accept; I'm sure you know tales of how a long life can prove more a curse than a blessing, and I had begun to suspect that the old man was practicing deceit. I was wary. However, I had nothing better to do, and he promised me that running his new errand would provide me with the means of avenging the slights I had received from the Baron of Skelleth. Therefore, I agreed to attempt the task he set, though I made no promises that I would complete it. This task was to bring him whatever I found upon the altars of the seven temples of Dûsarra. I had no idea where Dûsarra was, or how long it would take me to rob the seven temples, or even whether I would truly go there; therefore I could not tell Galt when I would be back. I guessed that it would be by the end of the year and told him to tell you that, Kyrith. I should have told him more, explained the situation perhaps, but I was angry and slightly drunk at the time and in no mood to do so. I am sincerely sorry if I caused you worry.'

He finished his ale and put the mug to one side. Kyrith nodded, as if accepting his apology.

'You still haven't explained the sword or the girl,' Galt said.

'I'm coming to that. I did go to Dûsarra, you see; the task was an interesting challenge. I had a vague idea that if I found and brought back whatever it was the Forgotten King wanted, I could withhold it from him until he met whatever demands I might decide to make. He *is* a magician of some sort, there's no doubt of that.

'At any rate, I found Dûsarra and robbed six of the seven temples. Some were easy; others were not. I won't go into detail about what I found or what I did, but there are a few things worth mentioning.

125

'Dûsarra is the city of the dark gods, the seven gods of evil that humans believe in. Each of the seven has a temple and a cult – or had. One of the gods is Bheleu, the god of destruction; his temple was a ruin, his altar a pile of burning wood. The sword I brought back with me was on that altar. From the first moment I saw it, it seemed to have some sort of control over me; I felt a compulsion to take it from the altar, ignoring the flames, and to kill the worshippers of Bheleu with it. I did. It was involuntary on my part. As you have all seen at various times and in various ways, the sword is undeniably magical and powerful. It was also very useful; in the course of events in Dûsarra, I lost virtually all my other weapons, so that I needed it for my own protection. Therefore, dangerous as it was, I brought it back with me. That was obviously a mistake. I thought I had it under control, but I was completely wrong; it seized hold of me again and made me slay the Baron and start the battle. That did indeed gain me my vengeance upon the Baron, as the Forgotten King had promised, but the other results are less pleasant.

'After the battle, the sword had apparently exhausted its power temporarily; I awoke in an alleyway with it lying beside me, the red gem dark and no compulsion or anger working on me. I tried to break it, but could not. My attempt only caused it to glow again. Rather than permit it to dominate me anew, I fled and came here, leaving it where it lay.'

Having completed his tale, he sipped his ale.

'You claim, then, that your apparent insanity was the work of this magical sword?' Galt asked.

'Yes, exactly,' Garth answered.

'That alone?'

'I believe so – that is, if you refer to my actions since acquiring the sword. I have no good explanation for the depression that first drove me into venturing south after eternal fame.'

'No, I can accept that; I have heard of such emotions before. It's not uncommon for overmen of your age. It's the sword that worries me. If it is truly what you say, was it wise to leave it lying about unguarded?'

'Perhaps not, but I had little choice. I dared not touch it again; the brightness of the glow assured me that it would seize control immediately.'

'Would it not be better for you to handle it, now that you know of its dangers, than to leave it where any stranger happening along might pick it up?'

'Ah, but such a stranger could not pick it up. You saw, did you not, what happened when Herrenmer attempted to touch it?'

'My view was not clear,' Galt began.

'I was not there at all,' Saram said, interrupting. 'What happened?'

'The hilt grew hot to his touch and burned him so badly that he could not pick it up. Yet a second later, I used it without taking harm. I have thought this over, considering as well the circumstances under which I came into possession of the sword, and have concluded that it cannot be used by humans. Therefore, we need only keep our own troops away from it to ensure that it will not be used.'

'I am not sure, Garth. Perhaps we should test this.'

Garth shrugged. 'Perhaps we should, but to test it may be dangerous. If it worries you, then post a guard around the sword. That would ease my own mind as well.'

'I find it hard,' Galt said, 'to accept your claims about the sword's power. I admit that it has magic to it, but it is merely metal; how can it have a mind and will of its own?'

'I don't say that it does; it may merely be linked to some great power. I am tempted to believe that it is in

127

truth controlled by the actual god of destruction, whatever he may be. My experiences in Dûsarra have shaken my atheism; there are undoubtedly spirits and powers in the world beyond what we know.'

'Could it not be, Garth, that something – perhaps the sword, which plainly is magical, or perhaps something else you encountered in your journeying – has driven you mad and caused you to *imagine* this controlling power?'

Garth considered this. 'I suppose it could be,' he admitted. 'But I do not think it to be the case.'

'We will have to investigate the sword further and test out what you have said.'

'You are free to do so, but do not expect me to use it again. I ask only that you be very, very careful.'

'Whether you are correct in your belief in its power, or merely deluded by madness, it seems to me that we cannot wholly trust you.'

Garth shrugged. 'I will not argue with that. I think you will see, in time, that I am again as rational and sane as you.'

'That would seem to be settled, then.'

Galt was interrupted by Kyrith; she touched his arm and then pointed at Frima. 'Oh, yes,' Galt said. 'Who is this person, and why did you bring her here from Dûsarra?'

'Frima? That's simple. My task was to bring back whatever I found on the seven altars; at the time I arrived in the temple of Sai, the goddess of pain, her worshippers were in the process of sacrificing Frima. She was the only thing on the altar, so I took her and brought her back with me. Having done so, I had no further use for her and turned her free.'

'It would seem you have, as you said, an explanation for everything – bizarre as those explanations may be.'

'Yes. If you would like confirmation of some part of what I have said about the sword, Frima can attest to its effects upon my temper. She saw on the journey back here that, when the red jewel glowed, I became angry; when it dimmed, I remained calm.'

Frima spoke for the first time. 'That's right.'

'Another question occurs to me,' Galt said. 'You were sent to fetch these things by the so-called Forgotten King; why, then, did you not deliver them to him?'

'He refused them. You will recall I said I robbed six of the seven altars. The seventh held nothing but a skull that was apparently part of the altar and which I did not trouble to pry loose. The old man, however, claims that the altar should have held a book, which was the only item he really needed. My failure to deliver this book angered him so that he marched off and left the other things in my possession. I regret that, since his magic seemed able to control the sword; had he kept it, today's battle might not have taken place.'

'Curious.'

'Perhaps not. The caretaker of the seventh temple, the shrine of The God Whose Name Is Not Spoken, told me that the god's true high priest was a mysterious ancient called the Forgotten King. The description was unmistakably of the same man. The King has not denied it. It is not so strange, then, that he would know what might be found in his own god's temple, and that he might wish to make use of it.'

'I see. The underlying circumstances here remain unclear, but I begin to understand that they are in fact interrelated.'

'My own thoughts are similar,' Garth agreed, 'and I want no further part of it. I have done with magic and gods and priests, I hope. For the moment, since you feel I cannot yet be trusted, it appears I am done with politics and diplomacy as well.'

'Then we are agreed that Kyrith and I will retain command?'

'Yes. We cannot be sure that I am truly free of the sword's influence. From your point of view, we cannot be sure I am sane. I do hope, though, that you will permit me to advise you. I know more about Skelleth and the lands to the south from first-hand experience than any other overman living.'

'True. What, then, would you advise us to do in the current situation?'

'The most important consideration is to establish peace with Eramma, but it is not, perhaps, the most immediately pressing. The need to provide some organization here in Skelleth seems more urgent. A human should be appointed to take charge of the surviving human population, as a sort of interim baron, under your command; the humans would not take well to the direct rule of our people, and we in turn do not understand how humans think, so that direct rule would be inefficient and unnecessarily galling. I would recommend Saram here for the position, since as a former guardsman – and perhaps the only one surviving – he has some experience at organization. He was a lieutenant and therefore knows how to give orders. Furthermore, he is a human we are comfortable in dealing with, and one who seems comfortable with us, yet who is not outcast by his own kind.'

Saram protested, 'I don't want the job.'

'So much the better; you'll be less tempted to abuse it.'

'We can settle that later,' Galt said. 'What else?'

'Well, once some semblance of order is established, the human population should be set to rebuilding the town to suit themselves, while our people serve as garrison and administration and lend whatever aid we can. We now control Skelleth, but it remains essentially a human town and we should deal with it on that basis, allowing the humans to arrange it as they please.'

'You imply that we should retain possession of it, however.'

'Oh, yes; why give up a good bargaining point before we're even asked?'

'As a trader, I know that's sound. What else?'

'Word of events here must be sent to the City Council of Ordunin immediately, and their advice asked – but we must remember we are south of the border and outside their jurisdiction; and we are here on the spot and more knowledgeable than they, so that we must be willing to reject their advice, should it seem foolish.'

'Would you set Skelleth up as a new nation, then?'

'No, not necessarily, but I would keep every option open for as long as possible.'

'Is there anything more?'

'When the effort can be spared, an exploratory mission should be sent to the Yprian Coast. As well as establishing trade, such a mission should investigate the possibility that the overmen there will be willing to support us militarily against Eramma, should it become necessary.'

'Now there you have a very good point.'

'I envision that Skelleth may become a mixed community of humans and overmen permanently, equally part of Eramma and the Waste, serving as a center of trade between them and with the Yprians. I think such an outcome would be highly desirable. There is no reason that the memory of the Racial Wars should continue to blight all our lives.'

'You are ambitious, Garth.'

'I think such a scheme wholly practical, Galt.'

'It may be. We will try it and see. I will admit I have no better suggestions.'

'Good.' Garth downed the rest of his ale and signalled to the innkeeper. He was pleased; even though he himself was now to be excluded from the mainstream of events – and thereby freed of aggravating details – things seemed to be working out well. The Baron was dead and gone, Garth's commitment to the Forgotten King was at an end, he was free of the Sword of Bheleu, and it seemed quite likely that everything could be worked out peacefully.

Oh, there were still loose ends – the Forgotten King yet lived, the sword still existed, and peace was not yet made – but it looked good. It looked very good.

11

Dawn was breaking by the time Saram was convinced he should serve as acting baron until someone better could be found. Garth and the others decided that it was hardly worth trying to sleep before sunset. Garth had had his nap in the alleyway, but the others had not slept since before the battle. Galt had managed to sleep the previous morning, after standing the night watch, but his rest had been interrupted by Garth's return.

In short, all of them were exhausted, as were almost all the townspeople and overmen. As a result very little was accomplished beyond a good deal of bleary discussion.

At sunset nothing had been done about the Sword of Bheleu beyond posting two overmen to guard it – maintaining a safe distance at all times, since Garth insisted that, if they came close to the weapon, it might seize control of their actions. Nothing had been done toward the reconstruction of the village, except that the villagers had been divided into work parties of fifteen or twenty, each under the direction of a skilled craftsman. Ideally, each group would have been run by a master house builder, but the entire village had only a single journeyman in its surviving population; for decades there had been no need for new houses and few had bothered to repair the old ones.

The overmen had pitched their tents in the market-place, as they had planned, but did not enjoy the privilege of occupying them; instead, preference was given to women and children, followed by the wounded – including seven injured overmen – and finally by the feeble or elderly. That accounted for at least three people to a

133

tent. The remainder of the population was left to take shelter in the ruins or do without.

The warbeasts were gathered together; after carrying out their attacks on the archers, some of them had been left undirected during the remainder of the battle and had strayed aimlessly through the town. They were fed with unidentified corpses or those with no surviving kin; the recognized bodies were spared to avoid offending their families. Some protests arose when it first became known how the overmen proposed to feed their animals, but were quieted when it was pointed out that if the warbeasts weren't fed they would seek their own meals, and that they preferred to take their prey alive. It was suggested that the town's livestock would serve, but the proposal was rejected on the grounds of unnecessary squandering of available resources.

Garth refrained from taking any direct part in the day's activity, but watched carefully and offered occasional suggestions to Galt and Kyrith. Galt strove mightily to retain his civilized calm, but as the day wore on, it grew ever thinner, allowing flashes of temper to show. Kyrith, handicapped by her inability to speak, gave up trying to give orders by noon and instead sat sulking in the King's Inn deigning only to answer questions brought to her and allowing Galt and Saram to run the entire affair.

Saram, for his part, despite his show of reluctance, took to command immediately. He appointed temporary officials to ad hoc jobs at the slightest excuse, ordering each to fulfill a particular function without even once explaining how the job should be done. Whenever he thought of something that needed to be done or had some matter brought to his attention, he named the nearest willing human as the minister in charge of getting it done. By the time new tasks stopped appearing, around midafternoon, he had at least fifty ministers under him, making up a good part of the surviving population.

The new officials, unfortunately, were not coordinated and were as tired as anyone else, so that very little was actually done as well as it should have been. Food and water were found for all the survivors, and the tents were distributed, but rubble was not cleared, no construction was begun, and the remaining fires were left to die on their own.

Still, Galt saw quickly that Saram had the humans in hand; even though they were accomplishing little, they were being kept busy, and had no time to think about the fact that they were now virtually slaves to an alien species in their own village.

Once he was convinced that he need not worry about a rebellion, Galt turned his attention to making use of his own warriors. Of the sixty overmen who had accompanied Kyrith and himself from Ordunin, eleven had died in the fighting – almost all from arrow wounds – and seven had been wounded in varying degrees, not counting scrapes and bruises. That left him forty-two. Besides the two he had assigned to guard the Sword of Bheleu, he posted two at each of the five gates and assigned ten more as their relief. That left him twenty. Saram assigned humans, mostly male teenagers who were eager to help but not otherwise much use, to guard the gates as well, so that each entrance to the town had four guards, two of each species, at any given time.

Galt had objected at first, on the grounds that the duplication was an unnecessary waste of manpower, but gave in when Saram pointed out that if men and overmen were to live together they had best learn to work with one another. Furthermore, he pointed out that the humans approaching Skelleth might be alarmed at seeing only overmen and might flee, while they would be only confused and wary upon seeing men and overmen together.

From the twenty remaining overmen Galt chose his apprentice, Tand, and four others, and assigned them to journey to the Yprian Coast as an impromptu embassy and trade mission. They were to depart the following morning and they spent the rest of the day gathering supplies and resting. They were to have two warbeasts – enough to carry them all in an emergency and adequate to defend them against almost any peril of the road, but not enough to deplete the force in Skelleth seriously. Galt held the remaining overmen in reserve in case of an attack by humans angered by the overmen's capture of the town.

A mission was also to be sent to Ordunin. At first Galt considered going himself, but he quickly realized that the only person he could possibly leave in command in his absence was Garth, and he did not feel ready to do that. Kyrith volunteered to go, but hesitated when Garth refused to accompany her; he insisted he still had business to attend to in Skelleth, primarily finding some permanent solution to the problem of the magic sword. At last, after some debate, she did agree to go, leaving immediately and taking three overmen with her for escort.

That left twelve warriors, Galt and Garth. The warriors were put to work pitching tents and carrying water. Galt was busy every minute overseeing the work. Garth watched as well, but without the responsibility of command.

Frima, for her part, served as a messenger.

The King's Inn was used as a command post, but throughout the long, wearing day no one spoke with the old man in the back.

When at last the sun oozed down past the western horizon, the anger and fear of the battle were gone, replaced by fatigue and resolve. Garth, despite his weariness, felt peculiarly refreshed and clean as he settled down for the night on straw from the stable beside the King's Inn – which, like the tavern itself, had not burned. For more than a fortnight his dreams had been only of

136

destruction, but he had spent this day obsessed with rebuilding – a welcome and healthy change. He was very pleased that he had managed to escape the spell of the Sword of Bheleu.

He was almost cheerful when he fell asleep.

Within an hour, though, his dreams began to trouble him. Images of blood and pain began to appear, and everything seemed washed in a red haze. He saw again the image of the high priest of Aghad whom he had fought in Dûsarra and again saw the Sword of Bheleu splatter the priest's brains and blood across the dirt of the Dûsarran marketplace. He saw himself slaughtering the entire cult of Bheleu with manic glee while thunder pounded overhead. He relived the battle just past and recalled in detail what he had done to Darsen. Finally, he found himself standing alone on a barren plain, holding the Sword of Bheleu before him. He tried to cast it away, but his fingers would not release the hilt; he tried again and became aware suddenly that there was someone behind him. He knew, not knowing how he knew, that behind him was the sword's rightful owner, the one to whom he could give the weapon and be rid of it once and for all.

He turned around and saw himself, clad in a loose red robe over black armor, hand held out to receive the sword; his other self's face was twisted into a malign grin that suddenly poured forth mocking laughter.

With a grunt of surprise, he awoke.

He was no longer on his pile of straw but on his feet, facing the part of town where he had left the sword.

He shook his head to clear it and looked about. He had not gone far; his pile of straw lay a yard away. He settled down upon it once again and considered.

The dream did not seem wholly natural. It might, he thought, be a lingering remnant of the sword's influence. Or perhaps he was more vulnerable while asleep, and the

137

sword or its master had sent the dream to him for some reason. Or, of course, it might be an ordinary dream – perhaps a bit more vivid than most, but that could be attributed to exhaustion and the excitement of recent events.

The oddest feature was that he had started to sleep-walk; he did not recall ever having done that before. That, more than anything else, made him suspect a magical influence. Perhaps the sword was attempting to draw him back, and the dreams had been his own attempt to resist.

Whatever had caused the dream, it made him uneasy and ruined his earlier contentment. It appeared that he could not be really sure he was free of the sword until it was destroyed. He would have to see to its destruction as soon as possible. He decided not to go to sleep again, but to stay awake until he could discuss the situation with Galt. Fatigue overcame him, however, and he dozed off and slept uneasily.

He awoke again as the first light of dawn painted the eastern sky with faded pink and lay for a moment watching the stars go out. He had dreamt again, but only in vague and muddled images – all unpleasant. There had been none of the eerie clarity of the first series; perhaps whatever power was affecting him had tired itself.

He had to destroy the sword. He dared not undertake any of the other tasks that he hoped eventually to complete while its baleful influence lingered. He could not, however, do anything with the sword without Galt's cooperation, as the guards posted upon it had been told specifically to keep Garth away from it unless Galt was with him.

At the first opportunity, he would have to take Galt out to the sword, convince him of its power, and then find a way to dispose of it once and for all. Until then, he could do nothing.

He sat back, leaning against the wall of a burned-out house, and did nothing.

When Galt awoke, he was instantly besieged with decisions to be made, orders to be given, and work to be done; Garth waited patiently. The morning passed. Garth contrived to speak with the master trader turned commander as they ate their noon meal.

Galt agreed that the sword should be dealt with. He promised that at the first opportunity he would accompany Garth to deal with it. The organization and reconstruction of the village was of primary importance, however; he had to oversee that. When he could spare the time, he would.

Garth resigned himself to waiting. He waited through the afternoon and evening. That night he slept heavily and dreamed of death; he awoke to find himself standing amid the ruins a few dozen yards from the sword.

Galt was busy throughout the following day as well, as heavy rains came, flooding foundations, turning the streets to mire, and slowing down all work. Villagers jammed themselves into the tents and the few structures that still had roofs.

The rain was not wholly unwelcome, though; for the first time, the smell of wood smoke subsided, and some of the soot and filth was washed from the ruins. Supplies of drinking water, which had grown scant, were replenished.

Garth spent the day in the King's Inn, speaking to no one, sitting in the front corner by the window, watching the people who crowded the room. He did not approach the Forgotten King. He did not see Galt at all. He noticed that Saram and Frima were together almost constantly and that the girl was now more of an aide than a messenger. On several occasions he noticed her staring at him; he guessed she was wondering at his inactivity or perhaps hoping he would return her to Dûsarra.

139

The third night after the battle, recalling his experiences of the first two nights, he moved his bedding further from the sword, up into the abandoned northeastern portion of Skelleth. He slept covered by a sheet of oilcloth someone had found in the rubble and felt the rain gathering in pools atop it.

He awoke several times, each time finding himself upright and moving south, the rain on his face. It was obvious that the rain had awakened him each time, and that only that had kept him from moving further. His dreams were jumbled images in red and black; he relived repeatedly all the bloodier incidents of his life. In stark contrast to the tedious hours he had spent doing nothing while he waited on Galt's convenience, his nights were full of fury and violence. He fought pirates and raiders on the coasts of the Northern Waste, killed bandits on the Plain of Derbarok, and slaughtered priests and worshippers in Dûsarra. Throughout, whatever the actual circumstances had been, he found himself gleefully wielding the Sword of Bheleu, laughing as blood spattered about him, killing anything, friend or foe, that got in his path.

By dawn, he was resolved that he could not wait much longer. If Galt could not spare the time before sunset, he would leave Skelleth and try to get far enough away to escape the dreams.

12

The village of Weideth lay in a small valley in the foothills below Dûsarra and consisted of perhaps two dozen homes and a single combined tavern, inn, and meetinghouse, all arranged around a crossroads. The West Road led up the slope to Dûsarra; the North Road led through the mountains to the Yprian Coast; the South Road led to the rich farming villages along the upper branch of the Great River; and the East Road led through the heart of Nekutta to the civilized lands of Eramma, Orûn, Tadumuri, Amag, Mara, and Orgûl.

Of late there had been a great deal of traffic coming down the West Road and leaving by either the East or the South. Those who had bothered to stop at all reported that they were fleeing from an outbreak of the White Death. There were also stories of great fires, riots, and a heightening in the city's perpetual internal conflict among the seven cults.

There had also been more overmen leaving Dûsarra than usual; the Yprian traders had cut short their visits and were turning back their fellows from approaching Dûsarra. No more caravans came down the North Road, and all those that had come before had already returned. It seemed likely that there was not a single overman left in the city.

The people of Weideth had watched the refugees go through, had offered what aid and comfort they could, and had accepted whatever payment was offered in exchange. They were practical people and saw no reason to refuse good money. The village was wealthy with Dûsarran silver.

It was three weeks since the plague's outbreak, and the number of people coming from the West Road had dropped from more than a hundred a day to a mere handful, when the girl in the black robe arrived in the nameless village inn.

She was young and walked with a limp, the Seer of Weideth noticed when she entered the public room. Her face was hidden by her cowl – that was typical of the secretive Dûsarrans. She carried no personal belongings that he could see; that was unusual for a refugee at this late date. There had been plenty of time now for anyone planning to flee to have gathered a few things together. Perhaps, he guessed, she had converted everything to cash and had the money hidden somewhere beneath her robe.

She paused just inside the door and looked about. He knew that she was looking for someone specific – he did have the true talent of a seer, though only weakly. That was very odd; how would a Dûsarran know anyone in Weideth? There were no other city-folk in the tavern just then – only him and a dozen of his fellow villagers.

He was interested. Could it be that she was not a refugee after all?

The innkeeper had noticed her now and was coming over to speak to her. The Seer watched and had one of his erratic flashes of insight. She was looking for *him*, the Seer of Weideth. Before he could do anything about this sudden knowledge, she was asking the innkeeper, who pointed him out.

He put down his wine cup and considered her as she approached the table.

'I am looking for the Seer of Weideth,' she said.

'I am he,' he answered. 'Have a seat.'

Made awkward by her injured foot, she took a moment to arrange herself on the offered chair. The Seer looked her over.

142

She was olive-skinned, like most Dûsarrans, with thick, curling, black hair which she wore long; a few strands spilled out of her cowl, reaching down past her breast. She seemed pretty, but he could not see clearly the outline of her face. There was something out of the ordinary about her that he sensed rather than saw, an aura of perversity and twisted emotion.

'I am Aralûrê; I'm a wizard's apprentice. I was sent here with a message for you.'

She was lying about her identity, but had indeed been sent to him. He nodded. If it was important he could worry later about who she really was and why she was lying.

She hesitated. 'How can I be certain you're really a seer?' she asked.

He shrugged. 'Ask anyone in Weideth.' He knew her uncertainty was due partly to the ease with which he had accepted her lie. When she still seemed unsure, he added, 'Your name is not Aralûrê, and you are not a wizard's apprentice, but you do have a message for me. What is it?'

'How do you know who I am?'

'I don't, but I would be a very poor seer if I could not tell truth from falsehood.'

That seemed to satisfy her. 'I have been sent here to warn you and any other magicians I may find, of whatever discipline, of the actions of a certain overman.'

'You refer, I suppose, to Garth of Ordunin, who caused so much havoc in Dûsarra.'

'You know his name?'

The Seer was gratified by her surprise. 'Oh, yes,' he answered. 'Am I not the Seer of Weideth?'

The girl eyed him dubiously. 'How much do you know about him?'

'Tell me what you came to tell me.'

The Dûsarran considered for a moment, then said, 'As

you will. It was Garth who loosed the White Death upon the city, you know. He killed a great many people in other ways as well, including several priests. He was responsible for the burning of the market place.'

'I know all that, and I am sure you know that it is common knowledge. The refugees who have passed through Weideth have kept us well-informed, quite aside from my own abilities. We have an ancient prophecy here that when an overman comes out of the east to Dûsarra he will unleash chaos and disaster upon the world. It would appear that Garth is the overman described, and the White Death the prophesied disaster. What of it? Why have you come here to tell me what I already know?'

'You did not allow me to finish, my lord. Did you know that the overman is still spreading destruction? Three days ago he destroyed the fortress town of Skelleth, on the northern border of Eramma.'

The Seer studied the girl. 'How do you know that?' He could perceive beyond any doubt that she spoke the truth as she knew it. 'Skelleth is a fortnight's ride from here.'

'My master has methods of learning what goes on in the world.'

'Your master is the one who sent you to me?'

'Yes.'

'Who is he?'

'A wizard; he prefers not to give his name.'

'He's no wizard. Is he a priest, perhaps?' He read in her face that he had guessed correctly. 'A priest who seeks vengeance upon Garth?'

She nodded reluctantly.

He sat back. It seemed plain enough. One of the Dûsarran cults, unable to avenge itself directly, hoped to recruit his aid in pursuing the overman. He had little love for any of the vile cults of the black city, but if this Garth were in truth disturbing the peace of the world and

144

causing further destruction, then the overman had to be stopped.

He wondered why the priest had chosen him to contact. Were there no wizards left in Dûsarra?

Perhaps there weren't; the plague might well have depopulated much of the city. Reports were vague and inconsistent, since even those still healthy remained in isolation in their homes for the most part.

Or perhaps this priest had an inflated idea of the Seer's own power; perhaps the priest did not realize that the Seer's predecessor, a truly remarkable prophet of great vision, had died and been replaced by a much lesser seer.

Perhaps . . . but there was no need to wonder, when he could ask the girl. 'Why were you sent to me?' he asked. 'What can I do?'

'I don't know,' she admitted truthfully. 'My master did not say. He told me to seek you out, and to speak also to any and all other seers, or wizards or magicians I might encounter.'

Perhaps this priest thought that the Seer would spread the word, until eventually the news reached someone in a position to act upon it. That made sense, though he found himself resenting slightly the implication that he was a gossip. As a matter of fact, though there was no way the priest could know it, he would see that the news, once verified, did indeed reach those who could respond appropriately; he would send a message to the Council of the Most High, of which he was a very junior and peripheral member. No priest would know that the Council existed, though; it had been a lucky chance, he was sure, that brought this young woman – whoever she was – to one of the councillors.

Surely it could be nothing more than that.

'I see,' he said. 'Very well, then. You have done your duty.' He wondered if he should pursue the question of her identity, but decided against it. Every sect in the city was dedicated to darkness, in one way or another, and every sect apparently had been affronted by Garth. It mattered little, he thought, which one had chosen to take action.

There was the question, though, of how word had been received from Skelleth in a fourth the time it took a man with a good horse to cover the intervening distance. Perhaps one of the priests had a hireling wizard with a scrying glass. That might be dangerous.

It wasn't his concern, however. He would contact the Council, tell them everything he knew on the subject, and let them worry about it. His place was here in Weideth, tending to the needs of the villagers, guarding and interpreting the prophecies of his forebears.

He downed the rest of his wine and rose. The girl rose as well. He nodded politely to her and turned to go.

The Aghadite watched the gray-robed man leave with her contempt scarcely hidden. The fool had hardly questioned her at all! He had asked for no proof, no details of Skelleth's destruction. He had not questioned her motives nor divined her identity. He had not even taken the trouble to ask her to show her face!

He was probably a worthless drunkard, she decided, whatever talent he might possess.

It didn't matter; all that mattered was that she had done what Haggat had ordered and delivered the message. Her part was finished. She could not imagine what good it could do to inform this third-rate oracle of Garth's actions – but she was still a novice in the ways of intrigue. Haggat knew what he was doing, she was sure.

And if he didn't, if the whole thing turned bad, that was all right too; she would use the failure to ruin Haggat and enhance her own position in the cult. She could advance with equal ease, she knew, either by allowing herself to be pulled along in Haggat's wake or by stabbing him in the back.

And if the time came, she would enjoy stabbing the lecherous high priest in the back – either figuratively or literally.

13

It was midafternoon of the fourth day after the battle when Galt finally found himself with time to spare for Garth's obsession with the magic sword. As he had expected, he found the older overman in the King's Inn, sulking in a corner with a mug of ale.

'Greetings, Garth,' he said, standing beside the table.

'Greetings, Galt. I don't suppose you have time to sit down.'

'No, but I do have time to tend to the sword, if you like.'

'Good!' Garth rose, a trifle unsteadily; Galt realized, with considerable misgiving, that the overman had been doing nothing but drinking since early morning. He knew that Garth would be offended if he suggested putting off the matter of the sword, and he was not sure how long he would be free of other concerns, so he said nothing, but followed as Garth led the way out of the tavern.

The fresh air seemed to help, Galt saw; Garth's step steadied quickly.

'Have I mentioned,' Garth asked, 'that I've been having strange dreams lately?'

The question caught Galt by surprise. It was not customary to speak openly of dreams; it was widely believed among overmen that, if properly interpreted, they revealed the inner truths of the dreamer's personality, so that learning the nature of another's dreams was a serious breach of privacy.

Besides, overmen only rarely remembered their dreams, unlike humans, who seemed to think that dreams showed the future and who therefore cultivated the art of remembering and interpreting them. They seemed undeterred by the usual failure of reality to fulfill the prophecies that resulted.

Startled, Galt said nothing.

'I have,' Garth continued. 'I have dreamed of blood and death every night since I abandoned the sword and I often awake to find that I have arisen and moved toward it in my sleep. I think it's trying to draw me back.'

Galt glanced at his companion, but said nothing. Such talk worried him. Surely Garth knew that dreams were wholly internal, he told himself. Was the prince really going mad?

'Had you not found time today, I had thought I might leave Skelleth for a time, and go further from the sword, to see if the dreams were lessened by distance. At the very least, I would then be assured that I could not reach it before waking.'

'Garth, are you certain that the power that has influenced you is entirely in the sword? Perhaps some spell has affected you, some enchantment encountered in your travels, and this obsession with the sword is a mere after-effect.'

Garth considered this, then replied, 'It could be, I suppose; I have had spells put upon me in the past, and they can be very subtle. I honestly doubt it, though; I think you're overcomplicating a simple situation. Wait and see what you think when you've handled the sword yourself.'

'Speaking of the sword, would it not be useful for your demonstration to have other subjects besides ourselves? In particular, you claim that the sword behaves differently when handled by humans than when handled by overmen. Should we not take a human or two along to test this theory?'

'You have a good point. You run things here, Galt; where can we find a subject for such an experiment?'

The two had now reached the market. The square was still cluttered with tents, but the surrounding ruins had been cleared away, and low barriers erected to keep passersby from falling into the open cellars. Work crews were busy sorting out stones and fallen beams, dividing those that might be re-used from those that were nothing more than ballast or firewood.

'Humans are Saram's responsibility,' Galt replied.

'Then let us ask Saram.' Garth pointed.

Saram and Frima were leaning over the barrier that had replaced the threshold of the Baron's mansion, speaking quietly between themselves; Galt had not noticed them until Garth drew his attention to them.

Galt shrugged. 'As you please,' he replied.

The two overmen turned from their course and approached the two humans. Saram heard them coming and looked up as they drew near.

'Greetings, my lords,' he said.

They returned his salutation.

'What can I do for you?' Saram asked.

'We are going to deal with Garth's magic sword,' Galt replied, 'and it would be useful to have a human along to test Garth's theory that only overmen can use his weapon. Who can you spare for such a task?'

Saram glanced around the square, then shrugged. 'I'll come.'

'No, you have to stay here and supervise,' Galt protested.

'Do you see me supervising anything?' He waved to indicate the cellars he had been staring into. Garth smiled, amused by Galt's discomfiture.

'But . . .'

'Besides, I want to see this.'

Galt gave in. 'Very well, but do put someone in charge here.'

'Certainly. Frima?'

'No, I'm coming, too. I don't trust that sword.'

'All right. Ho, Findalan!'

A middle-aged man Garth recognized as one of the village's few carpenters looked up from assembling something.

'I'm going away for a little while; you're in charge until I get back!'

Findalan nodded.

'There. Let's go.'

Reluctantly, Galt followed as Garth and Saram led the way. Frima brought up the rear at first, then ran forward to be nearer Saram.

As they made their way through the village and into the encircling ruins, Saram said, 'We had an idea, Galt, that I wanted to discuss with you.'

Galt made a noncommittal noise.

'Did you know there's a statue in the dungeons under the Baron's mansion?'

'No,' Galt replied.

'It isn't a true statue,' Garth said.

'No, but it will serve as one. That was our idea. Might we not hoist it out and set it up somewhere as a monument?'

'What sort of a monument?' Galt asked.

'That statue is a petrified thief, Saram, a half-starved boy. What sort of a monument would that make?' Garth asked.

'It would serve as a reminder of the cruelty of the Baron you slew, Garth.'

'It would serve as a reminder of my stupidity in allowing a madman to gain possession of a basilisk, as well.'

'I think it would make a good monument,' Frima said. 'He has such a brave expression on his face! You can see that he was scared but trying not to let it show.'

Remembering what he had seen of the face in question,

Garth could not deny the truth of her words. 'Where would you put it?' he asked.

'We haven't decided yet,' Frima answered.

'I'll consider it,' Galt said, in a flat, conversation-killing tone.

A moment later, they reached the nearer of the two guards. Garth stopped.

'It's all right,' Galt said. 'Let them through.'

The guard nodded, but Garth still didn't move. 'I think we should take one of the guards with us,' he said.

'What? Why?'

'Because if the sword does take control of you or me, it will almost certainly require two overmen to restrain whichever of us it might chance to be. Saram may be strong for a human, but he would be of little help in handling a berserk overman.'

'Oh.' Galt considered that. 'Very well.' He motioned for the guard, a warrior named Fyrsh whom he knew only vaguely, to accompany them.

The five proceeded on. Galt found himself growing nervous. He felt as if he were being watched and criticized by someone.

Garth, for his part, felt an urge to run forward, to find the sword and snatch it up. The afternoon sunlight seemed to redden, and he found himself conjuring up mental images of blood and severed flesh, similar to those that had haunted his dreams.

'There it is!' Frima pointed.

The sword lay where he had left it, Garth saw, across the block of stone. The two halves of the broken stone that he had placed atop it lay to either side, and gravel was strewn about where the third stone had shattered. The hilt was toward him, and the gem was glowing vividly red.

'It's glowing,' Frima said unnecessarily.

152

Her words penetrated the gathering fog in Garth's mind. He stopped. 'Wait,' he said, 'don't go any closer.'

Galt stopped. He felt no attraction to the sword, but only the uncomfortable sensation of being watched. He wanted to get the whole affair over with, to convince Garth that he was ill and should go home and rest and not concern himself with Skelleth or the High King at Kholis or the Yprian overmen. 'Why?' he asked.

'This is close enough for now; from here, only the person who is going to try and use it should approach any nearer.'

'And if someone goes berserk, how are we to restrain him at this distance?' Galt demanded.

'I thought of that.' Garth reached under his tunic – Frima had finally returned it when Saram found her a tunic and skirt such as the local women wore – and brought out a coil of rope. 'We'll put a loop of this around the neck of whoever goes to touch the sword, with one of us overmen holding each end. If there's any danger, we can jerk it tight before whoever it is can reach us with the sword.'

'The person might choke to death.'

'We'll be careful. When the person drops the sword, we release the rope.'

Galt was still doubtful of the scheme's safety, but he was outvoted. Even Fyrsh sided with Garth. 'I've been nervous ever since you posted me here, Galt,' he said. 'There's something unhealthy about that sword. We shouldn't take chances.'

'Very well, then. Who is to make the first trial?' Galt asked.

'I will,' Saram said.

'All right. Now, as I understand it, Garth, it's your contention that Saram will be unable to pick up the sword?'

153

'Yes. It will feel hot, too hot to handle, to any human.'
He hesitated, and added, 'At least, I think it will.'

Saram was already on his way toward the sword as
Garth spoke. He slowed his pace as he drew near and
then stopped. 'We forgot the rope,' he called back.

'I don't think we'll need it,' Garth answered.

'It would be better to be cautious,' Galt replied.

Garth shrugged, found one end of the rope, and held it
while tossing the main coil to Saram. The man caught it,
unwound several yards, and threw a loose loop around
his neck. Making sure that it did not pull tight, he then
tossed the free end back. It fell short; Galt stepped
forward and picked it up. He and Garth each held one
end now, while the central portion was wrapped once
around Saram's throat.

Saram stooped and reached out for the hilt. His fingers
touched it. Immediately there was a loud hissing, plainly
audible to the four observers; smoke curled upward as he
snatched back his hand, thrust his fingers into his mouth,
and began sucking on them.

'It's hot!' he managed to say around his mouthful of
singed fingertips.

'It is?' Galt was genuinely surprised. 'Try it again.'

Reluctantly, Saram obeyed, reaching out toward the
sword.

The hiss was briefer this time; Saram had been better
prepared and was able to pull his hand back more quickly.
With his fingers in his mouth, he shook his head. 'I can't
touch it,' he called.

'All right, then. Come back here and I'll try,' Galt
said.

Saram returned, looking slightly embarrassed. Galt
handed his end of the rope to Fyrsh, then lifted the loop
from around the human's neck and lowered it down past
his own head onto his shoulders. That done, Saram

154

stepped aside into Frima's considerate attentions, while Galt walked forward toward the sword.

He stopped when he reached the blade's side and called back, 'As I understand it, Garth, you believe that I will be able to pick up the sword, but it will attempt to dominate me.'

'I think so,' Garth called back. 'It can be subtle, though; it may just make you more irritable at first, more prone to react with irrational anger.' He pulled in some of the slack in the rope he held.

Garth and the others watched intently; Saram, in particular, was curious as to whether Galt would be able to touch the sword without injury.

'I suspect that humans are merely over-sensitive to heat,' Galt said, hesitating.

'It did not burn me at all,' Garth replied, 'save for the first time, when I pulled it from a fire.'

Galt bent down and reached his hand slowly toward the hilt. As it neared, the black covering on the grip abruptly flared up in a burst of flame; as Saram had, Galt snatched back his hand. Unlike Saram, he immediately reached forward again. 'It caught me by surprise,' he called, 'but I think it must be an illusion of some sort.'

As the overman's hand neared it again, the flames died away to a yellow flickering. Galt ignored them and grasped the hilt firmly.

The smell of burning flesh filled the air and smoke poured from his hand; with a faint cry of pain he released his grip and looked at his scorched palm.

'I don't think it's an illusion,' Garth said, 'but I don't understand why it rejected you.'

For a moment the five stood silently considering. Then Saram asked, 'Guard, would you care to try?'

'I am called Fyrsh, human. Yes, I'll try it.'

Galt returned and exchanged portions of rope with

Fyrsh. The warrior had no better luck than his predecessors; like Saram, he touched the sword only lightly, with his fingertips, and received only slight burns. There was no flaring of flame, but the faint flickering remained.

'May I try?' Frima asked, when Fyrsh had rejoined the group.

There was a moment of surprised silence at this unexpected request. 'Why?' Galt asked at last.

'Perhaps it only burns males – or perhaps only those who have not been in Dûsarra.'

Galt looked at Garth, who shrugged. 'I don't know,' Garth said. 'She could be right. My theory that it was attuned to overmen obviously wasn't. Let her try.'

'Are you sure you want to?' Saram asked her.

She nodded.

'All right,' Galt said. 'Do you want the rope?'

'No.'

'I don't think we need it,' Saram said. 'She's outnumbered four to one and outweighed at least six to one.'

There was general agreement, and Frima approached the weapon unencumbered. She used only one finger for her experiment, and thereby escaped with the least injury of any.

She came running back into Saram's arms and held up her scorched finger for him to kiss.

'Perhaps,' Galt suggested, 'the sword has changed somehow – the time of year may have affected it, or some occurrence in the battle. Perhaps no one can now handle it.'

Garth nodded. 'I hope you're right; let us see if it will singe my fingers as it did yours.' He picked up the rope and threw a loop around his neck, handed the ends to Galt and Fyrsh, and then marched toward the sword.

Almost immediately he felt the familiar urge to grab it up, to use it on his enemies. The red glow of the jewel seemed to fill his vision and flood everything with crimson.

156

As he drew near, any caution he might have felt faded away. He reached down and picked up the sword, easily and naturally, as if it were an ordinary weapon. The flames that had glimmered about the hilt vanished as his hand approached; the grip was warm to his touch, as if it had been left in the bright sunlight for a few moments.

He lifted the sword, and the red haze vanished from his sight. The glow of the jewel faded. He felt none of the berserk fury that the sword had brought upon him in the past; instead he was strangely calm. He turned to face his companions. 'You see?' he called. 'It has a will of its own, and it has chosen me as its wielder.'

'I see,' Galt called back. 'Now put it down again.'

Garth nodded and tried to turn back.

The sword would not move; it hung in the air before him as if embedded in stone.

Garth tried to release his hold and drop it where it was; his fingers would not move.

'I think we have a problem,' he called.

Instantly, Galt jerked the rope tight; with equal speed, the sword twisted, feeling as if it were moving Garth's hands rather than the reverse, and cut the rope through. Before Fyrsh could take any action with his end it flashed back and severed that, as well. The two overmen found themselves holding useless fragments, while the loop around Garth's throat remained slack.

There was a moment of horrified silence; then Galt called, 'Now what?'

'I don't know!' Garth replied. 'I can't let go!' He struggled, trying to pry his fingers from the grip, but could not move them.

He attempted to move his arm and discovered that he could now move it freely. He lowered the sword from the upright display he had held it in; there was no reason to be unnecessarily uncomfortable.

He tried placing his other hand on the grip and then

157

removing it; there was no resistance. He then placed his left hand on the grip and tried removing his right.

It came away easily and naturally.

Now, however, his left hand was locked to the sword.

He switched back and forth a few times, and established to his own satisfaction that whatever power held him to the sword would be content with either hand or both, so long as he retained a hold suitable for wielding the thing. He could hold it with two fingers and one thumb, if he chose; that seemed to be the absolute minimum. Any one finger and both thumbs on the same hand would also work. A single finger and thumb, however, or just two thumbs, would not suffice; when he attempted to use such a grip, his other hand would not come free.

He was about to point this out to Galt as clear proof that there was a conscious power involved – after all, how could any spell, however complex, manage anything so subtle? Galt chose that moment to call, 'Garth, stay there; I will return shortly.'

For the first time Garth realized that while he had been playing with his fingers, the other four had been discussing his situation and had apparently arrived at some sort of a decision. Galt and Saram were leaving. Fyrsh and, oddly, Frima were staying. He called after the departing pair, 'See if you can find a sheath that would fit this thing! I have an idea!'

It had occurred to him that, if it were sheathed, the sword might behave differently; it was certainly worth trying.

He was frankly puzzled by this new difficulty. He had never before had any trouble in releasing the sword.

But then, he told himself, he had never tried to destroy it before, or tried to abandon it.

Perhaps he could still destroy it, he thought. His previous failure might have been because the sword held some special relationship to stone; after all, he knew almost nothing about it. The standard method for breaking a sword had always been to snap it across one's knee; he could try that.

He turned back toward the stone blocks – the sword seemed to have no objection now that the rope was cut. He placed one foot on a block, raising his knee to a convenient height.

Ordinarily he wouldn't have done something like this without armor. Metal splinters might fly, and the broken ends could snap back and gash his knee badly. He thought such injuries would be worthwhile, though, if he could be rid of this particular sword. He placed it across his knee, his right hand holding the hilt and his left gripping the blade, and pushed down.

Nothing happened. The sword bent not an inch.

He pressed harder. It still did not give.

He put his full strength into it, so that the pressure bruised his knee and the palms of his hands; had it snapped, he knew he would have been thrown forward on the fragments and probably seriously cut.

It did not snap. It did not yield at all.

He gave up in disgust and looked speculatively at the stone block.

Raising the sword above his head in a two-handed grip such as he would have used on an axe in chopping firewood, he swung the blade down at the stone with all the might he could muster.

The stone block shattered in a spectacular shower of sparks, dust, and gravel.

He studied the blade and ran a thumb along it carefully. It was as sharp as ever, with no sign of nick or waver.

Destroying this thing would be a real challenge, he realized. It might take days or even months to contrive an effective method.

It was very curious, though, that it was allowing him so much freedom to try. He knew that it could cloud his thoughts and turn him into a mindless engine of destruction or move in his hands without his cooperation, yet it was doing nothing of the kind. Instead it had displayed this new talent, this refusal to come free of his hold. Why had it not done so before?

Perhaps it had felt no need. He had cooperated with it readily, at first. Only after he realized how disastrous the consequences of the destruction of Skelleth might be had he seriously resisted. When he had actually managed to abandon it, perhaps it had become frightened, aware that it might lose its control of him.

Could a sword be frightened? Or, if the sword were only a tool, could a god be frightened?

Frightened might be too strong a word; 'cautious' would be better. If he could reassure the entity, whatever it was, perhaps he could contrive to slip away and abandon the sword for good. Once he was free of its hold, he would be certain never to touch it again.

If he could pick it up without touching it, with tongs perhaps, and transport it, he could find some way to get rid of it even if he couldn't destroy it. He could throw it in the ocean; no one would retrieve it from the bottom of the sea.

That assumed, however, that he would be able to get it out of his hands.

The Forgotten King would probably be able to make it let go. Judging by the ease with which the old man had darkened the gem and suppressed the sword's power before, he should have no trouble in doing so again. The only problem with that solution was that the King would almost certainly demand something in exchange, and Garth did not care to deal with him further.

Still, if he could not manage something else, sooner or later he might be forced to give in to the Forgotten King. Even that would be preferable to unleashing the sword again, he was sure. He had felt the sword's personality, if it could be called that, and he knew that it sought nothing but death and destruction. It was being canny now, biding its time, allowing him to think, but he was certain that soon its bloodlust would grow and more innocents would die, as they had died in Dûsarra and Skelleth.

Thinking of death, the sword, and the Forgotten King, he began to wonder at the exact nature of the King's immortality. What would happen if the old man were to have a blade thrust through him? Would he live on regardless? Could he bleed or feel pain? What if his head were to be severed? Surely, death-priest or no, he could not survive decapitation.

It might be, then, that he could not be decapitated, that any blade would break in the attempt. In that case, what would happen if he were to be struck by the unbreakable blade of the Sword of Bheleu?

This seemed a very interesting question. What would happen when the irresistible destructive power of the sword met the immortal body of the Forgotten King? One or the other would have to yield and perish.

If the sword were to break, then Garth would be rid of it.

If the King were to die – as seemed far more likely, more in keeping with the natural order of the world – then Garth would have performed an act of mercy, and would no longer need to worry about the old man's schemes. Unfortunately, he would also no longer have a means of last resort for disposing of the sword.

Perhaps both would be destroyed. That would really be the ideal solution.

He would have to consider this further, and perhaps attempt a few experiments. He might want to obtain some advice on the matter. He wondered if he could trust the old man to tell the truth; perhaps he would do better to go home and consult the Wise Women of Ordunin.

As he considered this, he saw Galt and Saram returning, leading a squad of half a dozen overmen and an equal number of humans. Someone was even leading a warbeast.

He wondered, out of a warrior's professional curiosity, whether the sword would be able to kill so many opponents before they could rip him apart. Without the warbeast, he suspected it would have no trouble. Warbeasts, however, were notoriously hard to kill and moved with a speed and ferocity that no overman could even approach, just as no human could equal an overman.

He hoped that he wouldn't have to put the matter to the test.

Several of the overmen, he saw, were carrying various ropes and restraints. Saram was carrying the same oversized, over-the-shoulder scabbard that had held the sword before.

That was encouraging, because it implied that they hoped to restrain him – and the sword – without harming him. Less pleasant was the fact that four of the humans carried crossbows. Galt apparently did not care to take too many chances. Garth hoped that those would be strictly a last resort and that the archers would not aim to kill.

The newcomers stopped where Fyrsh and Frima waited and spoke with them; Garth did not try to listen, but it was plain that Frima was protesting such extreme measures.

While the argument continued, Garth called, 'Ho, Saram! Toss me that scabbard!'

The acting baron looked up and thought for a moment before obeying.

Garth picked up the sheath with his free hand and flung it back across his left shoulder. He managed to catch the lower strap with the fingers of his right hand, despite the sword's encumbrance, and to bring it up to meet the shoulderpiece.

It took several minutes and much fumbling, but he contrived to tie a reasonably secure knot. He wished that the thing had a buckle; he was sure he could have managed that much more readily.

When he had the scabbard in place, he tipped it forward and slid the blade into it. Then, slowly, he removed his fingers, one by one, from the sword's hilt.

They came away easily, and the sword fell back into place, slapping his back. It felt peculiar to be wearing the scabbard without armor; a two-handed broadsword was strictly a weapon of war, not something to be carried casually about the streets.

'There, you see?' he called to the watching crowd. He held up his hands, showing that they were free and empty. 'All I needed was the scabbard.'

Galt called in reply, 'We see that you have released the sword, but has it released you? Can you remove the scabbard?'

'Of course I can, Galt, but I think I had best keep it with me for the moment. It's too dangerous to leave lying around.' He lifted the sheath's strap up from his shoulder, to show that it was not adhering unnaturally. He had no problem in doing so. 'See?' he said. 'And the gem is dark. It's quiescent right now.'

In truth, he did not believe that he could remove the sword and scabbard; he was sure that the knot would prove impossible to untie as long as the sword was sheathed. It was his own problem, though, and he did not want Galt and a bunch of ignorant helpers making matters worse. He was reasonably certain that the only way the sword would voluntarily let him go was if he were to be killed and that Galt's motley group would be unable to remove the sword against his will. He had no wish to die when they attempted to do so, nor to kill any of them.

He had some idea of how powerful the sword was, and they did not, as yet. He would be unable to convince them that the sword was more than they could handle without bloody experimentation. He therefore intended to convince them of the opposite, that the problem was already under control.

'Are you sure?' Galt asked.

'Yes, I'm sure. I've handled this sword for weeks, Galt. It's harmless right now.' He reached up and grasped and released the hilt a few times to show that it was not spitting flames or grabbing hold. It remained cooperatively inanimate.

He had it partly figured out now; it was determined to remain in his possession, but it was intelligent enough not to waste energy in holding him any more tightly than necessary. As long as he kept it on his person, it didn't care how it was carried.

He pulled it out, then sheathed it again, demonstrating that it was behaving like any ordinary sword. 'You see, Galt? I think it's worn itself out, at least temporarily.'

'Very well, Garth. Carry it, if you please. I warn you, though . . .'

'I know, I know. You cannot trust me while I bear it with me.'

'Exactly. I would ask, Garth, that henceforth you sleep well away from the center of town, lest it rouse in the night and drive you mad.'

Garth shrugged. 'As you please.'

Reluctantly, Galt dismissed his dozen supporters; they trailed off toward the market, returning to whatever they had been doing previously. After a final uneasy glance in Garth's direction, Galt followed them.

Garth, in turn, followed; Saram and Frima joined him.

164

Fyrsh turned, as if to accompany them, then stopped and said, 'We forgot Pandh.'

'Who?' Saram asked.

'Pandh. The other guard Galt posted here. If you're taking the sword, there's no need for him to stay here. He's still up the road; he probably hasn't noticed any of this.'

'You're right,' Garth agreed. 'Go relieve him, then.'

Fyrsh nodded and turned back down the street.

When he had gone, Garth remarked to the two humans, 'I'm bound for the King's Inn; all this shouting back and forth has made me thirsty.'

'We'll join you, if we're not needed elsewhere,' Saram said.

'I'll be glad of your company.' At least, Garth thought, they would be welcome while he quenched his thirst, which was quite genuine. His primary reason for visiting the King's Inn, however, was to speak with the Forgotten King, and he would prefer privacy for that. He hoped that Saram would be needed somewhere.

14

The Seer of Weideth had never acquired the knack of using a scrying glass and made do instead with an assortment of divining spells. Every spell he tried gave the same answer; the Dûsarran girl had indeed told the truth.

Garth of Ordunin had destroyed Skelleth for no reason. Furthermore, he had murdered the rightful baron of the village on only the slightest provocation, and killed a score of innocents with no cause at all. The girl had not mentioned that.

The overman had done this with the Sword of Bheleu, which was obviously an artifact of great power. The apparent level of arcane energy was, in fact, so great that no material force could possibly stand against it. There would be no point, therefore, in sending an army to Skelleth; only magic or stealth could hope to deal with such a menace.

The Seer wondered how so dangerous a weapon had been left lying about where any passing overman could pick it up in the first place; one of the Council's overseers must have been shirking his duties.

It was not, fortunately, his responsibility; he was only liable for the village and the surrounding hills. Since the matter had been brought to his attention, it was his duty to report it – and that was the entirety of his duty.

He gathered together the three village elders; his own powers were too feeble to reach more than a dozen leagues with a message-spell, and he judged that this matter was worthy of the immediate attention of the Chairman of the Council. That was old Shandiph, and a simple divination told the Seer that Shandiph was in

Kholis, the capital city of Eramma, which lay more than a hundred leagues to the east. Communicating over such a distance would require three other minds working in concert with his own. He had worked with the elders before, and they had become reasonably adept at this sort of thing.

By the time he returned to the tavern's common room after divining the Chairman's location, ready to make the attempt at contact, the messenger from the city was long gone and the elders were waiting for him.

In Kholis, Shandiph was visiting with Chalkara, court wizard to the High King. The two were alone in Chalkara's velvet-draped chambers, playing caravanserai with an ancient set of hand-carved jade and ivory, which the court wizard had inherited from her predecessor, and sampling a golden wine of unknown but venerable vintage that Shandiph had brought with him from a stay in Ur-Dormulk. Shandiph had had more than his share of the wine and was consequently a good sixty coins behind in the game when the image of the Seer of Weideth suddenly appeared on the tapestry Chalkara was leaning her back against.

Startled, the old man dropped his wine glass, scattering the green pieces in all directions and spilling yellow wine across the whites. For a moment both wizards were too busy picking up pieces and sopping up the spill with Shandiph's cloak to pay any heed to the message.

When some semblance of order had been restored, Shandiph demanded angrily, 'What do you want?'

The Seer's image mouthed something.

'Oh, Regvos, the damnable fool hasn't got a voice; I have to do everything myself!'

Chalkara said soothingly, 'I'll do it, Shandi.' She reached up to an ornate silk and silver box on a nearby table and pulled out a gleaming amulet, then recited a

167

brief incantation before slipping the golden trinket around her throat.

'Speak, image!' she commanded.

'I am the Seer of Weideth,' the image said, 'and I have an urgent and private message for Shandiph the wandering sorcerer.'

'I am listening,' Shandiph replied.

'Ah . . . it is not to be heard by any but Shandiph.'

'Never mind that, Seer, just give me the message. I have better things to do.'

'Oh, I'm sorry. Did I interrupt something?'

'Give me the damn message!'

With much hesitation and awkwardness, the Seer explained about the visit from the Dûsarran girl and reported what his divinations had told him.

When he had finished, he waited for a response. Shandiph sat silently for a long moment, then said, 'All right. You've delivered your message; you can go now.'

The Seer's image vanished immediately.

In Weideth, the Seer relaxed. The matter was out of his hands. He thanked the elders for their assistance, then ordered a final mug of ale before retiring.

In Kholis, Chalkara looked at Shandiph, who was staring at the floor. 'This could be serious,' she said. 'It could start the Racial Wars all over again.'

'We'll have to make sure it doesn't,' Shandiph replied. 'Listen, I'm having trouble thinking clearly; have you got something that counteracts wine? I left all my potions in my own rooms.'

'I think so.' She rose gracefully, crossed to a cabinet against the far wall, and began rummaging through it.

'Do you think he's right about how dangerous this overman is?' The elder wizard scratched his balding head.

'I don't know anything about it, Shandi. I have never even heard of Weideth or its Seer, nor Garth of Ordunin, nor of the Sword of Bheleu. The only name I know from

168

the whole affair is Skelleth; and even if Skelleth is a pesthole – it is, too – the High King won't be pleased to hear it's been destroyed. It's a bad precedent. Besides the Baron of Sland is bound to make trouble about it.' She pulled out a small brass bottle. 'I think this will do; it's a cure for drunkenness and senility.'

'I am neither drunk nor senile, woman, merely tipsy. Still, it should serve; pass it here.'

Chalkara complied and told him, 'The normal dose is three drops.'

'One should do, then, but I'll make it two to be safe.' He suited actions to words, then shut his eyes and mouth for a moment.

'It tastes awful,' he said a moment later.

'Potions usually do,' she replied.

'I know. You'd think something could be done about it.'

'Right now, I think there are other things more important to do.'

'You're right. I don't know anything about Garth of Ordunin or about Skelleth, and the Sword of Bheleu is legendary, which means the available information can't be trusted. I do, however, know the Seer of Weideth, albeit only slightly. It's a hereditary post, one of these odd little oracular talents that turn up here and there. Weideth is a village in the hills in the northwest of Nekutta, and its seers have certain undeniable gifts as long as they remain within the immediate area. The current Seer is no great prophet, but he can do a simple divination; I'm afraid there's no disputing his facts.'

'Then this sword really is too powerful to defeat by mundane methods?'

'Oh, we can't be sure of that; a clever assassin might manage something. There could be flaws in the Seer's detail work in that particular conclusion. I would certainly agree that an army won't work; he couldn't have missed the mark by that much.'

'Do you want to try an assassin, then?'

'Chala, my dear, *I'm* not going to try anything. I don't know enough about it. I'm going to get some expert advice first.'

'What sort of advice?'

'Oh, I think I had best consult an astrologer and a theurgist, since there may be a god involved, and experts on swords and overmen and perhaps an archivist or two. I'll find a really good diviner to study the entire affair; I'm no good at that sort of work myself.'

'Shandi, if you're going to do all that, wouldn't it be simpler just to convince the entire Council and turn the whole thing over to them at once? You know that you need approval from a quorum before you start commissioning assassinations or fooling with major arcana.'

Shandiph considered this silently for a moment. The pleasant glow he had felt earlier was almost wholly dissipated now, and he found himself slightly irritable in consequence.

'You're right, Chala. Aghad take this overman, you're right. I *hate* convening the Council; there's always argument, and I always have to break it up. There's no getting around it, though; this is important enough for the whole Council. A border has been violated and the invaders are using magic. That's exactly the sort of thing that the Council is supposed to prevent.'

'Well, at least if you turn it over to the Council, you won't have the entire responsibility.'

'Oh, I don't mind the responsibility. It's better than having to listen to that fool Deriam and his idiot theories about the natural supremacy of Ur-Dormulk or trying to keep peace between Karag of Sland and Thetheru of Amag. You know, I came down here early just to get

170

away from Deriam and now I'm going to have to invite him here.'

'I thought you came to see me!'

'I did, I did; after all, I could have gone anywhere from Ur-Dormulk, couldn't I?'

'I know, Shandi. I guess we won't be finishing the game, will we?'

Shandiph looked at the scattered caravanserai pieces. 'I suppose not. And just when my luck was changing!'

'Ha! You would have been lucky not to lose a hundred coins!'

'Would I? We'll see next time, then!' He smiled, then frowned. 'Right now, though, I had best go find the Charm of Convocation.' He clambered awkwardly to his feet.

Chalkara began gathering up the carved tokens. 'Shall I come with you?'

'You tempt me, but no. Only the Chairman is to see the Charm – another silly rule.'

'In that case, shall I go and tell the King to expect company?'

'Yes, I think so; it is his castle, after all. He might get upset if three dozen magicians were to turn up on his doorstep without warning.'

Chalkara nodded, and began placing the ivory pieces neatly into their places in the rosewood box.

Shandiph watched her for a moment, then said, 'Gau and Pria bless you, Chala.' He left, closing the door gently behind him.

That night each and every member of the Council of the Most High had the same dream, and each awoke knowing that he or she was to leave immediately for Kholis.

171

15

Saram was not called away immediately, but eventually, as Garth was beginning to feel rather soggy from the vast amount of ale he had consumed, someone came looking for the interim baron. A jurisdictional dispute had developed between two of his ad hoc ministers.

Garth watched him go, taking Frima with him, and marvelled that he could walk straight. The human had consumed ale mug for mug with him, and if Garth was feeling the effects, then surely, he thought, the much smaller human should be staggering drunk. It did not occur to him that he had been drinking earlier as well, before picking up the sword, while Saram had not.

It was the middle of the evening and the tavern was crowded; nonetheless, as usual, the Forgotten King was alone at his table in the corner beneath the stairs. Garth seated himself opposite the old man.

For a long moment neither spoke; Garth was unsure how to begin, and the Forgotten King preferred to let the other speak first.

'I have questions I would ask you,' Garth said at last.

The old man said nothing, but the yellow cowl dipped in a faint nod.

'You say that you cannot die by ordinary means. How can this be? What would happen if you were struck with a good blade? If your neck were to be severed, would you not die like any other mortal?'

'My neck cannot be severed by any ordinary blade,' the King replied.

The hideous dry voice caught Garth off-guard; he had

172

forgotten how unpleasant it was to hear. He hesitated before asking, 'How can that be?'

The yellow-draped shoulders rose, then sank.

Garth felt a flicker of annoyance and immediately looked at the hilt of the Sword of Bheleu. The gem was glowing very faintly.

That was not necessarily bad, he thought. Perhaps if he were to allow himself to become angry, the old wizard would douse the sword's power as he had done before, and Garth would be able to escape from the weapon's hold without making any sort of deal at all.

He turned back to the Forgotten King and asked, 'You say no ordinary blade can kill you; what of the sword I carry?'

'You are welcome to make the attempt,' the old man replied.

Garth considered that.

If the result were the destruction of the sword, then all would be well, and his problems would be at an end for the moment. If the result were the death of the King, then he would have performed an act of mercy, but he might be stuck with the sword indefinitely. If both were destroyed, that would be the best all around.

There was surely some other way of getting free of the sword. Perhaps, even if it were not destroyed, it would be sufficiently weakened by the effort to loose its hold.

One way or another, the odds appeared to be in his favor. He decided to risk it. He stood, reached up, and pulled the sword from its sheath, awkward in the confined space of the tavern. The tip of the up-ended scabbard scraped the ceiling as the blade came free. It was obvious that he would be unable to swing the blade up over his head; he would have to use a sweeping horizontal stroke instead.

There was a hush, and he looked about, realizing that the other patrons of the tavern had abruptly fallen silent.

They were staring at him and at the great broadsword, wearing expressions that ranged from vague curiosity to abject terror.

'Have no fear,' he called, 'I mean none of you any harm. The old man here has challenged me to strike off his head. Haven't you, old man?'

The yellow-garbed figure nodded, and Garth thought he caught a glint of light in one shadowed eye.

The overman looked along the path he planned for the sword and saw that it would pass uncomfortably close to the humans at a neighboring table. 'Excuse me, friends,' he said, 'but I would greatly appreciate it if you could step back for a moment, to give me room to swing.'

The humans quickly rose and backed away.

Satisfied that he would endanger no one but the King, Garth took a good two-handed grip on the sword and tried to swing it.

At first it moved normally, but as it approached the old man's neck it slowed, as if moving through water rather than air. From the corner of his eye Garth could see the red gem glowing fiercely, but he felt none of the roaring anger and exultant bloodlust that usually accompanied the glow.

Then the sword stopped, inches from the ragged yellow cloth, frozen in mid-air as it had been just before it severed the rope earlier that afternoon. He could force it no closer.

He strained, putting all the strength of his arms into driving the sword toward the old man's throat.

The blade did not move; instead it rang, like steel striking stone, and flashed silver. The hilt grew warm in his grasp.

That inspired him to push harder; perhaps he could force the sword to reject him.

The ringing sounded again, louder, like the sound made by running a moist finger along the rim of a fine crystal goblet, and this time it did not fade, but grew. The red glow of the jewel was brighter now than the lamps that lit the tavern, and the blade was unmistakably glowing as well. The hilt was hot, but there was no pain, no burning, and he knew that he could not release his hold any more than before he had swung.

The sword did not move, but remained stalled in mid-air, as if wedged in stone, a few short inches from the old man's neck.

Then, abruptly, it forced itself back, against his will.

Startled, he released his pressure and found the sword hanging loosely in his grasp, apparently quite normal. The ringing had stopped. The glow had vanished, and the hilt was cooling rapidly.

He was determined not to give in that easily. He swung the sword back and attempted another blow.

This time, as the blade approached its target, it veered upward, twisting in his hands, and cut through nothing but the air above the Forgotten King's head.

He stopped his useless swing and brought the weapon back for a third try. This time he found himself unable even to begin his swing; the sword was suddenly heavy in his grasp, impossibly heavy, and he could not lift it to the height of the old man's neck.

Annoyed, he applied his full strength and hauled the blade upward. It seemed to struggle, and he felt a pull, as if a great lodestone were tugging it away from the King.

He fought it, but could not bring the weapon to bear on the old man.

After several minutes of struggling, the Forgotten King's dead, dry voice called to him.

'Garth. Stop wasting time.'

Reluctantly, he gave up and let the tip of the sword fall to the floor. It lost its unnatural weight, and he picked it up as if to sheathe it.

Then, abruptly, trying to take it by surprise, he yanked it around into a thrust toward the King.

It stopped short a foot from the tattered yellow cloak.

He gave up in disgust and sheathed the sword. It did not resist.

He seated himself again and asked, 'Was any of that your doing?'

There was a pause before the King replied, 'Not willingly. None of it was my choosing, but it was as much my curse as the sword's power at work.'

'Then an ordinary blade would behave similarly?'

'Not quite. It would break if forced, rather than fighting back.'

Garth sat back, thinking.

He was unsure whether or not to believe that an ordinary blade would break. He was not even certain that he should believe the old man's claim not to have willingly interfered. Perhaps he had lied, lied throughout; perhaps he did not want to die. His claims might be camouflage for some deeper, more subtle scheme.

He could not be trusted.

He did, however, have the power to control the sword.

A vague, uneasy thought occurred to Garth; he considered it, let it grow and take form.

Perhaps it was in truth the Forgotten King who controlled the sword's actions entirely, and not the mythical god of destruction. Perhaps Garth's entire mission to Dûsarra had been an elaborate charade the old man had contrived for reasons that remained unclear.

Such a theory seemed unlikely, but could not be completely discounted.

Carrying his imagining a step further, Garth arrived at another possibility. What if the sword and the Forgotten King were both being controlled by some other unseen power? It might be Bheleu, The God Whose Name Is Not Spoken, or just some mighty wizard.

176

What if everything that had befallen him was part of some vast plot? Could his depression and resulting quest for eternal fame have been the result of some spell? Could the entire sequence of events that followed have been planned, his every action guided?

Had he ever had any choice at all in his actions?

He shook his head. This was all getting too complicated and farfetched; he doubted that there was any such conspiracy at work. If there were, it was obviously far beyond his own capabilities to do anything about it.

'O King,' he said, returning to the subject at hand, 'I would like to make you a gift of this sword. It was at your request that I brought it from Dûsarra, and I feel it right that you should have it.'

The Forgotten King said nothing.

'You will not refuse it?'

'I will not accept it,' the King replied, 'until you swear to serve me by bringing me the Book of Silence and aiding in my final magic.'

'You have said that this magic will kill many people; I cannot in good conscience aid you in it.'

'Then I will not accept the sword.' He did not say anything more, but it was plain to both what was implied; while Garth kept the sword, he would be in constant danger of having further death and destruction on his conscience. He faced a choice of two evils, neither clearly the lesser, and both, in fact, quite large.

Garth reached up to his breast and picked at the knot that held the scabbard on his neck. As he had expected, he was unable to work the strands at all.

'Will you not reconsider?' he asked.

'Will you?'

Defeated for the moment, Garth sat back and thought.

It seemed clear that the Forgotten King would not help him; the overman had feared as much. The sword had not obliged him by driving him into a frenzy that the

King would have been forced to quell; a glance over his left shoulder showed that the gem was glowing moderately, yet he felt no particular anger, no great compulsion. The thing was biding its time. Perhaps it knew something of the future and was waiting for something specific; perhaps it was aware of the Forgotten King and had learned that he was able to control it, and so was restraining itself.

Perhaps, should it attempt to wreak havoc in the future, he could contrive to bring it here and threaten the King, so that the old man would be forced to dampen its power in self-defense.

No, that would not work; what need did the King have to defend himself? He was immortal and wanted to die – at least, so he claimed.

That might be bluff, Garth thought, to convince him that there was no point in threatening the old man. Next time the killing fury came, Garth decided, he would make an attempt to find the King and test out his invulnerability again.

For the present, though, there seemed nothing more to be gained here. He rose and left the tavern.

The streets were dark, but torches lit the marketplace directly in front of him on the far side of the cellars of the Baron's destroyed mansion. He paused and looked again at the knot that held the scabbard in place.

It was a very simple, rough knot; he had tied it himself and knew that to be the case. Ordinarily it would have been hardly adequate to hold the sword; normal jarring would have worked it loose in an hour or two. The sword's power, however, could apparently be spread beyond the weapon itself; the knot was tight and solid.

He picked at it again, but could not work the strands loose.

There was an ancient legend about a knot that could not be untied. The story was that after many wise men had tried to undo it, a simple warrior had cut it apart with his knife. If Garth could not untie the scabbard strap while the sword was sheathed, perhaps he could cut it.

He made his way around the cellars and approached the nearest overman he saw. It was Fyrsh, relaxing by a campfire after his supper. He had no objection to loaning Garth his dagger. 'After all,' he said, 'you've already got that sword if you want to start trouble.'

Garth agreed, smiling, and thanked him. Then he found a quiet spot to sit and tried to cut the strap.

It was difficult slipping the blade under the strap at all; where a moment before it had seemed comfortably loose, it was now drawn tight across his chest. Finally, though, he managed to force it in and turned the blade, working it against the leather.

The blade was notched almost immediately, as if meeting steel.

Garth shifted it and tried again, sawing at the leather.

The blade snapped off completely, gashing his chest with the broken edge and cutting a long slit in his tunic before falling to the hard ground with a rattle.

The broken stump was of no use. He returned the pieces to Fyrsh with his sincere apologies and promised to pay for a new one.

It was growing late, and he had no further ideas that could be readily tried. Disgruntled, he set out to find somewhere to sleep. He did not care to be near other people; he was afraid that the sword might make him murder them while they slept.

After much walking, he settled down for the night in the shelter of a relatively intact stretch of the town's wall, midway between the North and East Gates. His sleep was calm and dreamless.

16

The first to arrive at the High King's castle was Karag of Sland, which was somewhat surprising; Sland lay almost two days' ride to the west of Kholis, and Shandiph knew there were other councillors closer at hand.

Furthermore, Karag did not come alone. The Baron of Sland accompanied him, with a party of half a dozen black-clad soldiers.

The presence of the Baron made the arrival a matter of state; the High King was roused and formal presentation arranged. While this went on, Chalkara reported to the Chairman that a ragged stranger dressed in brown and carrying a staff had arrived at the scullery gate, refusing to give his name but insisting that Shandiph had sent for him.

'That's all right,' Shandiph told her as he watched the High King accepting Karag's obeisance. 'That would be Derelind the Hermit; he lives just south of here.'

'Why wouldn't he tell me that?'

'Oh, he's a secretive young fool. Don't mind him.'

Karag was rising now, and the six soldiers were being presented, together with a list of names and the honors they had received. Shandiph wondered how warriors could acquire so many marks of distinction on their records when the kingdom had been at peace for almost three hundred years.

'Shouldn't I find Derelind a guest chamber?'

'I don't know; ask him. He would probably prefer to sleep on the kitchen floor with the lower servants, and we may not have enough rooms for everybody, if we get a good response to the call.'

Chalkara nodded and slipped away.

She was back by the time the soldiers had finished their ritual presentation. Now, by custom, the High King and the Baron would retire to the King's private council chamber for a report on the state of the Barony of Sland, and Shandiph would be able to speak to Karag without the Baron's presence.

'Now, my lord Baron, I would hear how your lands have fared since last we spoke.' The King recited the traditional request slowly and precisely; it was plain to all present that he really didn't care how Sland fared, but was merely fulfilling his obligations. That was no surprise; the current King was perhaps the most worthless to reign in Eramma to date.

Still, the ritual would proceed; to make it look good, the King and the Baron would have to stay in seclusion for at least a quarter of an hour. Shandiph suspected they would do little in that time other than drink a few toasts, but it gave him his chance to speak with Karag.

When the nobles had left the room, Shandiph started across the floor of the throne room. Karag met him halfway. Before Shandiph could begin a polite greeting, Karag snarled at him, 'Have you gone mad, you old fool?'

Shandiph was taken aback. 'What?'

'What in the name of all the gods did you think you were doing, summoning the Council to this castle?'

'This is a matter for the Council to discuss,' Shandiph replied stiffly. Chalkara came up behind him as he spoke.

'So you blithely called us all here, to the castle of the High King at Kholis?'

'Yes, of course. Why not? I was here; as chairman, it is my prerogative to choose the meeting site. Further, Kholis is centrally located and has good roads.'

'Does it mean nothing to you that our little group is supposed to be a secret organization, one whose existence is unknown to the world at large? For three centuries we have guarded that secret, and now you have virtually announced to the High King that there is an organization of wizards meeting here.'

'I have done nothing of the sort. Is that why you came so promptly? To tell me this?'

'Yes, it is; I thought that, if I got here soon enough, I could talk sense to you and convince you to warn the others away. We have ridden night and day since half an hour after I received the summons.'

'And you've brought the Baron of Sland with you.'

'I had to; had I left without telling him, he would have had my head. I told him that I needed to speak with you immediately, and he insisted on accompanying me.'

'And you call me a fool? Do you think he won't suspect that something out of the ordinary required such urgency?'

Chalkara interrupted Karag's sputtered reply. 'Why did he come with you? Did you not tell him this was a matter involving only wizards and their affairs?'

'Yes, I told him; I think that's why he chose to come. He's been taking a great interest in magic lately, even asking if I could teach him a few simple spells.'

'You haven't, have you?' Chalkara asked.

'Of course not! But as you have probably heard, it's unhealthy to deny Barach of Sland anything, however slight. I dared not argue with him about this trip as well.'

'If there is anything that will reveal the nature of this meeting, Karag, it is his presence. The King pays no attention to what happens around him; he cares for nothing but wine, women, and old books. The servants and courtiers can be frightened or bribed into silence. The Baron of Sland, however, is not so easily handled.' Shandiph tried his best to sound stern.

Karag paused for a moment, then said, with no trace of contrition, 'Well, it's done now, and if we're to keep it secret you'll have to turn back all the others. I'm sure that the three of us can handle whatever this problem is by ourselves.'

'The four of us; Derelind the Hermit is downstairs somewhere.'

'Very well, then, the four of us. What is this world-shaking problem? Has someone stolen a love potion somewhere or caught a councillor kissing a baron's daughter?'

'The problem requires a quorum of the Council. An overman has gotten hold of a magic sword, a very powerful one, and has destroyed large parts of two cities. The Seer of Weideth has divined that he is beyond the power of ordinary measures. At the very least he'll require assassination, and we may stand to be even more drastic. Now, Karag of Sland, do you feel I was unjustified in calling the Council together?'

There was a moment of silence.

'Are you sure of the facts?'

'The Seer of Weideth swore to them.'

'Are you sure it was the true Seer?'

'No, but if it were not, Karag, then we have an even worse problem, do we not? The message was an image-sending; if it was not the Seer, then we have an enemy or traitor of unknown purpose and power to deal with.'

'True. What cities were destroyed?'

'Shall we go somewhere more private?'

'Yes, of course. Chalkara?'

'There is my chamber; it has the customary wards upon it.'

'Good.' They retired to her quarters, pausing only to order a servant to send up Derelind, and any other enchanters who might arrive.

When Shandiph and Karag had settled on the velvet cushions in her sitting room, Chalkara found the remains of the golden wine that she and Shandiph had been drinking when the message first arrived and served it out to the three of them. They sipped it, waiting for Derelind.

When the hermit had arrived and refused cushions and wine, preferring to squat on the bare stone between rugs, Karag again asked, 'What two cities were destroyed?'

'Permit me to explain, Derelind. The matter that I have summoned the Council to discuss involves an overman who has obtained a very powerful magic sword. He has already destroyed much of the city of Dûsarra, in western Nekutta, defiling most of its temples, burning the market and much of the surrounding area, and spreading the White Death, a particularly vile sort of plague. Dûsarra being what it is, I think we might forgive him that, but he has continued by laying waste to the border town of Skelleth and murdering its Baron.'

'Murdering?' Derelind inquired.

'He was stabbed in the back, I am told.'

'That would seem to be murder,' Karag agreed. 'What else?'

'He and a force of overmen have occupied Skelleth and are rebuilding it to suit themselves. It appears that they may intend to renew the Racial Wars. I need not remind you that it was those wars that created this Council in the first place; we were sworn to maintain peace by whatever means necessary.'

'Is the High King aware of this invasion?' Derelind asked.

'No.'

'You have not told him?'

'We would prefer to settle the whole matter ourselves. The Seer of Weideth tells us that armies would be of no use against this overman, and what other option would the King have, save to send an army?'

'What, then, do you propose instead?'

'I wish to send either one or more very good assassins,

or to use magic of a level this sword cannot counter,' Shandiph said.

'What magic did you have in mind?' Karag asked.

'You know what our great weapon is, Karag,' Derelind said.

'Yes, and I also know that many people think it a panacea and wish to use it every time the least difficulty arises.'

'You exaggerate, Karag. It has been used only once in the last three centuries,' Derelind said.

'That once was more than enough; were it not for the sorry state of trade in these decadent times, the news of that use would have been a world-wide legend by now.'

'Would that be so harmful?' Chalkara asked.

'Our organization's existence is a secret,' Karag stated slowly and precisely. 'We want to keep it a secret. Only in secret can we continue to maintain peace and to manipulate the governments of the world so that there is no aggressive action taken. Only by acting in secret can we limit the knowledge of the arcane arts and prevent the magical battle that caused such catastrophes in the earlier ages.'

'It seems to me,' Chalkara said, 'that we are getting ahead of ourselves. It is not our place to decide this; it is a matter for a quorum of the Council. I think we can all agree on that.'

'There is no harm,' Derelind said, 'in planning ahead. I suspect that the Council as a whole will, in fact, agree that this situation may require drastic remedies – and quickly. Might I suggest that, as soon as someone with the requisite talents arrives, we should send a magical message to the keeper of the weapon? I know little about the spells involved in controlling it; do they require any preparation time?'

'I'm afraid I don't know either,' Shandiph admitted. 'That has always been left entirely to the keeper.'

'I still think it's a mistake,' Karag said. 'Turning people to stone can't help but attract attention.'

'We are only suggesting sending a message, to have it ready if needed. You know that Shang has orders to stay where he is and to ignore the summons I sent; we can't leave the thing unguarded.'

'All right, then, send a message to Mormoreth. I still think, though, that using the basilisk is a mistake, and I'll vote against it in the Council.'

17

Over the course of the next several days Garth attempted repeatedly to get rid of the sword. In doing so he broke two dozen assorted blades; hurt his jaw in trying to chew through the scabbard strap; burned his hand badly in a candle flame in the hope that sufficient heat or pain might cause the sword to lose its hold; cut the same hand and lost considerable blood in trying to pry his fingers open with a knife – which eventually broke; and acquired several scrapes and bruises in using various blunt instruments to try and pry his fingers from the hilt.

He antagonized several people, both human and overman, by breaking their tools, wasting their time, avoiding their questions, and sometimes by accidentally inflicting minor injuries of the sort that had battered his own hands and chest. He also talked three individuals into burning their hands in varying degrees by trying to handle the sword, which continued to allow no one other than himself to touch it.

His own injuries were of no consequence, however, and in fact scarcely even rated as a nuisance, since every cut, bruise, burn, or scrape healed miraculously overnight. There could be no denying that the sword had its beneficial aspects.

Unfortunately, the injuries received by others were not so obliging, though the burns caused by touching the sword invariably turned out to be less severe than they first appeared and always healed quickly and cleanly.

His attempts to remove the sword were further complicated by the necessity of keeping them secret from Galt; Garth was quite sure that Galt would interfere if he realized that the sword did have a hold on Garth, and that any such interference would do far more harm than good.

Saram was more astute than Galt and quickly figured out the truth of the matter. Garth was able to convince him to say and do nothing about it.

Galt, fortunately, was too busy trying to organize and govern Skelleth and the warrior overmen to pay much attention to Garth – particularly since Garth was specifically excluded from any say in the new government.

Garth was amused by his observation of Skelleth's resurrection. He had plenty of time to play the disinterested observer, since he was the only person of either species not actively involved in it. He had nothing to do with his time except to eat, drink, sleep, think, try to dispose of the sword, and watch the events going on around him.

His amusement derived from the differing styles and results of Galt and Saram. Galt had thrown himself completely into a frenzy of planning and organizing, spending every waking moment hard at work on governing. Any dispute that came before him was given careful and detailed attention and settled logically after much thought and analysis.

Saram, on the other hand, spent as little time as possible in work of any sort; he often joined Garth in doing nothing but watching. He settled disputes by fiat, without discussion, or by vote of whoever happened to be present – assuming disputes ever reached him in the first place, as he had given his horde of ministers to understand that it was their responsibility to keep their people in hand and out of his hair. Only when an argument crossed jurisdictional lines or involved jurisdictional lines did it reach Saram's ear.

Galt's efforts had resulted in very little in the way of concrete accomplishment; he had not managed to set up any permanent housing for his overmen, despite the approach of winter, nor to establish any lower levels of governance that could function without constant supervision.

Saram, on the other hand, had been building houses out of rubble at the rate of almost three a day and had the town's wells cleaned out and a rudimentary distribution set up. His ministers had sifted themselves out into levels of importance; some had resigned, either because their jobs were done or because they felt that they weren't needed. Two had been fired for incompetence and replaced. In short, Saram was the head of a working government.

That was the situation that existed when the messenger from Ordunin arrived.

Garth was sitting on a block of stone in front of the hole where the Baron's cellars had been, the stone walls having been excavated for use in new buildings; he wore his quilted gambeson beneath his tunic to keep out the growing chill in the air. Changing his clothing while the sword retained its grip had proved difficult, but possible. He had exhausted every method he could think of for getting free of the sword's hold that did not involve either travel or giving in to the Forgotten King and was now trying to decide where he should go first – the nearest ocean, to see if salt water might have an effect, or Ordunin, where the Wise Women might be able to suggest a solution. He was no longer particularly concerned about his oath, though he had never been released from it, because it hardly applied to the current situation.

He was beginning to think that, after all, he no longer had much reason for staying in Skelleth. He had declined to accompany Kyrith because he had wanted to deal with the sword, which was then in Skelleth; now, though, the sword was wherever he was, and he could easily carry it to Ordunin and deal with it there. Ordunin was on the ocean, as well, though hardly the closest coast. Furthermore, if he were to travel, he would prefer to do so before winter closed in.

The only thing still keeping him in Skelleth – other than his interest in the rebuilding – was the presence of the Forgotten King, the one person known to be capable of controlling the sword.

There was a possibility that by taking the sword elsewhere it would stop being so complacent and again drive him into a destructive fury; that would be very unfortunate if it happened in Ordunin. But then, it might happen in Skelleth, which would also be unfortunate now that the rebuilding was well under way. His best course might be to head due east to the coast of the Sea of Mori; there were no towns along that route, nothing that he might destroy.

He reached up and pulled the hilt of the sword down so that he could look at the gem. Its glow was faintly visible even in the midday sun, yet he felt no anger nor bloodlust building up. The thing was being subtle, he was sure, planning something, waiting for something, or perhaps affecting him in some new way he hadn't yet detected.

As he stared at the red gem, he heard the rattle of armor and looked up. It came from somewhere behind him, to his right; he turned and saw three overmen approaching, with two men trailing along behind them. One of the overmen was riding a good-sized warbeast.

Garth recognized the humans and the two overmen on foot, but he could not place the mounted figure for a long moment.

As the party drew up near him, he finally realized who it was: Selk, one of the City Council's messengers. He had not been among the sixty volunteers.

This, then, he knew, must be the response to Kyrith's mission to acquaint the Council with the situation.

'Where is the master trader Galt?' the messenger demanded.

'He's in the King's Inn,' Garth replied politely, ignoring the other's imperious tone.

'You, fetch him,' Selk ordered one of the two overmen who had accompanied him. Garth realized that they and the humans must be those who had been posted to guard the North Gate.

The warrior hurried to obey, taking the direct route through the pit; earthen ramps had been built on both sides to aid in removing the stones.

'Have you come alone?' Garth inquired.

'You're Garth, Prince of Ordunin?'

'You know who I am.'

'I wish to be sure.'

'Yes, I am Garth, and you are Selk, son of Zhenk and Valik. Did you come alone?'

'I am here alone.'

'Kyrith did not come with you?'

'I have said I am alone.'

Garth was dismayed by the messenger's surliness; it did not bode well for the message the overman carried. He rose to get a better look at Selk's face. The warbeast growled.

Surprised, Garth looked at it, rather than at its rider.

Like almost every warbeast, it was black; its eyes were green, and its belly-fur white. Its fangs were gleaming white, a sign that it was young and healthy, since the teeth tended to yellow with age. Perhaps, he thought, it still had some of the excitability of cubhood.

Its tail was lashing, and Garth realized that it was looking, not at him, but at the hilt of the sword that protruded up above his left shoulder.

This was something new; none of the warbeasts remaining in Skelleth had reacted to the sword before. He wondered if this beast might have some special sensitivity

191

to magic, or if maybe the sword was doing something new that was perceptible to a warbeast but not to an overman.

Selk also looked at the sword, startled, and said, 'It really does glow!'

It was the first thing he had said that had not been spoken as harshly as possible. Garth hoped that it was a sign that Selk was relaxing somewhat.

'Yes, it glows,' he replied. 'It also burns and does other unpleasant things. Did Kyrith tell you about it?'

'Kyrith said nothing – I mean, she wrote nothing of it in her statement. The others with her, however, did mention it.'

'Did you doubt them?'

Selk did not answer immediately; when he did reply, it was only indirectly. 'I have never encountered magic before.'

'You have now. Be glad that you have not seen much, though; in my experience, most magic is very unpleasant.'

Selk made no reply.

Before Garth had decided on his next remark, Galt and his escort arrived. In addition to the warrior sent after him, he was accompanied by three humans, including Frima, and another overman, a young fellow named Palkh. Garth had seen both the male humans before, but did not know their names.

'Greetings, Selk!' Galt called as he climbed up the ramp from the cellars.

Selk did not reply. Garth thought he glimpsed a trace of worry in Galt's expression at that. For his own part, Garth now suspected that either Selk's news was very bad indeed or that the fellow was simply rude by nature.

When Galt had reached the top of the slope, Selk suddenly spoke, declaiming in a loud voice while he held up a golden rod that represented his authority to speak for the Council:

'Know all present that this is the decision of the City Council of Ordunin! I have been sent here to present this decision, and bear no responsibility for its content. I bear no malice toward any present, nor do I favor them. I speak as I have been commanded.'

Several woman and children who were gathered in the marketplace, trading salvaged household goods among themselves, stopped and turned to listen.

'Whereas it has come to the attention of the Council that the party of overmen of Ordunin under the joint command of the master trader Galt, son of Kant and Filit, and Kyrith, daughter of Dynth and Dharith, and commissioned to negotiate trade agreements with Doran, Baron of Skelleth, has exceeded its authority and committed acts of war against the Barony of Skelleth; and whereas these acts were committed under the direction of the aforementioned Galt and also Garth, Prince of Ordunin, son of Karth and Tarith, and a lord of the Overmen of the Northern Waste, and resulted in unnecessary bloodshed and destruction; therefore, the City Council of Ordunin hereby disavows all responsibility for these actions.'

Selk paused to catch his breath, and Galt started to protest. Garth silenced him with a gesture.

'Furthermore, inasmuch as the members of the party in question may have been unaware of the limits of the authority granted to their commanders, no blame shall be assigned to any person other than the aforementioned Galt, Kyrith and Garth, if those persons immediately remove themselves from the area of Skelleth and return to the Northern Waste. No charges shall be drawn up against these persons.

'Furthermore, the aforementioned Kyrith, by virtue of her avowed reluctance to participate in acts of war, and by virtue of her presence before the Council and arguments presented, is hereby pardoned, conditional upon her continued presence in Ordunin.

'Finally, the Council disavows all claim to any portion of the Kingdom of Eramma, or to any profits that may accrue from acts of war committed against the Kingdom of Eramma, and declares the aforementioned Galt and Garth to be outlaws, this information to be delivered to them as soon as circumstances shall allow.'

Selk stopped speaking, returned the rod to its place beneath his tunic, and sat astride his warbeast, looking down at Galt and Garth. There was a moment of silence.

'They can't do that,' Galt said at last.

Garth was unsure what to say. Palkh said, 'It appears that they have done it, though.'

The women who had heard the announcement suddenly began talking among themselves, discussing this unexpected news.

Garth felt anger growing somewhere within him; he did not bother to look at the red jewel. Whether this anger was wholly his own or not did not seem important.

'Selk,' he said, 'is that your entire message?'

'Yes, that's it, at least so far as you are concerned.'

'What do you mean by that?'

'I am to carry the same message to the High King at Kholis, together with a formal apology.'

Garth had reached the conclusion three days earlier that, through some great good fortune, the High King and the other lords of Eramma were as yet unaware of the sacking of Skelleth. Had they known about it, there would surely have been some sort of reaction by now, such as a formal demand for surrender.

This ignorance was very useful. It gave them time. The King would have to learn eventually, but Garth hoped that the news would be delivered at the right time and under the right circumstances for the maximum advantage of overmankind. Therefore, he did not want this messenger spreading the word prematurely.

'I can't allow that,' he said.

'What?' Selk was plainly astonished.

'Garth, what are you doing?' Galt asked.

'I cannot allow any such message to reach the High King at Kholis at this time,' he said.

'You have no authority to stop me,' Selk answered.

'I need no authority. I am an outlaw, am I not? Dismount, Selk, slowly and carefully, and make no move toward your weapons.'

Selk hesitated.

In a single fluid motion Garth unsheathed the Sword of Bheleu; the red gem was gleaming brightly, and the blade shone silver.

'Dismount, Selk.'

The bystanders, including Galt, were drawing back, unsure what to do. Frima called, 'Garth, is it the sword?'

Without turning his gaze from Selk's face, Garth answered, 'I don't think so. This is really what I think best.'

Selk looked about uncertainly and saw that no one was making any move to aid him. Garth stood ahead of him and to his left, five feet away, the immense broadsword clutched before him in both hands. Selk was not a warrior, but a messenger and a peaceful person, yet he dared not surrender; the Council would hear, and he would lose his position.

He could not fight and he could not surrender. That left flight. Trying to give as little warning as possible, he suddenly shouted the command to run to his mount.

Obediently, the warbeast surged forward; the Sword of Bheleu lashed out with preternatural speed and caught Selk across the chest. Garth had managed at the last instant to turn the blade so that the flat struck the overman, not the edge; the sword had fought the turn, but given in. Therefore Selk was not killed, but he was knocked backward off the beast's back, to lie stunned on the hard ground, his chestplate dented in more than an inch, his chest crossed by a great bruise, and two ribs cracked.

Garth started to lower the sword but found it resisting him; almost immediately he saw why.

The warbeast had been trained to protect its rider. As soon as it realized he was no longer in the saddle, it whirled to face Garth.

Everyone in the marketplace – the women, Frima, Galt, the three men, and the other overmen – immediately fled, amid a chorus of shrieks and shouting, leaving Selk lying on the ground and Garth facing the monstrous creature.

The warbeast roared deafeningly, baring fangs more than three inches in length, and charged toward Garth.

For an instant Garth was certain that he was about to die; he had seen warbeasts in action and knew that an overman was no match for one, regardless of what weapons he might hold. Spears and arrows could not penetrate the natural armor created by thick fur, loose, leathery hide, and layer upon layer of muscle that protected a warbeast's vital organs. A well-wielded sword might manage it, but only by luck; no other creature could move as fast as a fighting warbeast, or dodge with so much skill. A single blow from one of the great padded paws could tear an overman in half.

He forgot all that, though, as the warbeast neared him. He forgot everything except that he held the Sword of Bheleu. It came up in his hands, hissing with flame and moving with blurring speed to meet the warbeast's charge.

The monster leaped upon him, and the blade met it in mid-air, at the base of its throat.

There was a sudden roar of flame, and Garth was smashed backward and down.

He came to a second or so later and found himself

lying on his back on the ground, pinned beneath the immense bulk of a dead warbeast, both his hands still clutching the hilt of the sword. The blade had gone cleanly through the beast, its tip emerging between the shoulders, red with blood.

The air was full of the stench of scorched fur and burned flesh.

Garth found it hard to believe that he was still alive. How could the warbeast have died so quickly? Even had he struck it through the heart, which he had not, it should have lived long enough to tear him apart.

'Garth?' It was Galt's voice that called uncertainly. 'Are you alive?'

'Yes,' he answered. The effort was painful; the wind had been knocked out of him by the creature's impact, and one fang had gashed his cheek in passing.

'Can you move?'

Garth was not sure whether he could or not; he tried, shifting slightly, and discovered that he could not.

'No,' he called, 'I'm pinned here.'

There were sounds, but no further words reached him.

Something occurred to him, and he called, 'Don't let Selk escape!'

'He's not going anywhere,' someone said grimly; Garth thought the voice was human, rather than overman. It was definitely not Galt.

Something else occurred to him, and he looked down at the hilt of the sword. He was unable to raise his head enough to see anything other than black fur; there was no way he could see whether the stone pressing into his belly was glowing.

Cautiously, he removed his left hand from the hilt; it came away easily, as he had expected. Then he tried to open his right hand.

One thumb and one finger came free, but the other

197

thumb and fingers remained in place. The sword had not released its hold.

He lay back, disappointed.

A few minutes later, with much straining, Galt and a party of overmen managed to push the warbeast's carcass off him. He pulled the sword free, wishing he didn't have to, then staggered to his feet, the weapon hanging loose in one hand. The gemstone flickered dimly.

'Thank you,' he said.

'Garth,' Galt demanded, 'why did you do that?'

Garth looked at him. The brief battle had tired him and his entire body ached from the strain of supporting the warbeast's weight and from being slammed against the ground. A stray pebble had cut open the back of his head when he fell, and he felt blood dripping down his back, across immense bruises, as well as running down his cheek.

'Do what?'

'Why did you stop Selk from leaving?'

He stared at Galt in astonishment. Could the trader really be that stupid? 'Galt,' he said, 'what would the High King do upon receiving such a message?'

'I don't know,' Galt answered. 'Send a polite reply, I suppose.'

'Don't you think that he might send an army to recapture Skelleth, once he was aware that we had taken it and that Ordunin would not send any reinforcements to our aid or back us in any way?'

'But he wouldn't have to recapture Skelleth!'

'Why not? We happen to be running it right now.'

'But we're leaving, aren't we? The Council has disowned our occupation; our troops will be going home to take advantage of the amnesty, and we'll either have to go back and plead for pardon or seek refuge somewhere.'

'Galt, I am not leaving. The Council has declared us to be outlaws and renounced all claim to Skelleth. The rightful baron is dead, without heir. We are in control of the barony. It seems to me that we can do quite well for ourselves by staying here in control. If the High King believes us to be here with the approval of the Council and the Lords of the Overmen of the Northern Waste, he will negotiate with us to save bloodshed – I hope – and we can have Saram declared the new Baron, thereby ensuring us of a place here. The Council will not interfere; they have disclaimed the whole affair.'

'I don't understand. What good will it do to stay here and have Saram made Baron? We will still be outlaws in both lands.'

'No, we will not; we will be Erammans, able to establish trade between the two realms. Benefits aside, though, have you considered what will happen to Saram and his ministers if we leave? He will be tried for treason and beheaded for cooperating with us. Would you willingly allow that to happen?'

'I had not considered that. I find myself confused.'

'Are you certain that all our warriors will take advantage of the amnesty? Might some not prefer to remain here, outlawed or not? There are things to be done here and very little to be done in Ordunin. Here they are a powerful elite; in Ordunin they are nothing out of the ordinary.'

'I don't know.'

'Galt, if you wish, you can go home and plead for clemency, but I am staying here and intend to call for volunteers to stay with me. And so long as I stay here, I dare not let Selk deliver his message to the High King. Is that clear?'

'Clear enough. I will have to think this through carefully.'

'In the meanwhile, what will be done with Selk?'

'He's under arrest, more or less; I'll keep him there until I decide.'

Garth nodded; that would do for the present.

Things had changed suddenly, he realized; less than an hour earlier, he had been thinking that he might return to Ordunin. Now he was absolutely refusing to do so.

The difference was in Selk's message. It had not occurred to him that the Council could be stupid enough to throw away its claim to Skelleth. The Council might be sufficiently timid to let Skelleth go for nothing, but Garth was not. He intended to hold it. If he was not to hold it on behalf of Ordunin, then he would hold it on his own behalf. He was sure that he could run it better than the Council could in any case. He found himself almost hoping that Galt would give up, go home, and leave him in charge. He would show the trader how a village should be run.

That was still to be decided, though. He stood and watched as Galt walked off, lost in thought, toward the King's Inn.

Saram appeared from somewhere; he had finally gotten word of the fight. He looked at the dead warbeast and called, 'Find someone who knows how to skin animals! We shouldn't let so fine a hide go to waste. Garth, will warbeasts eat their own kind? We've been running short of meat for them.'

Garth's chain of thought was broken as he tried to recall whether he knew anything about cannibalism among warbeasts.

Resorting to experimentation after the fur had been stripped from the carcass, he and Saram learned that warbeasts had no objection to cannibalism.

When the warbeasts had stripped much of the flesh away, it also became clear how the Sword of Bheleu had killed the monster quickly enough to save Garth's life; the internal organs had all been burned to a fine ash.

18

The first arrival capable of sending a message to Shang was the sorceress Zhinza, an ancient, tiny woman who maintained a small farm a few leagues to the east. Despite her age, she was still cheerful and energetic. She gladly consented to make the attempt when Shandiph explained the situation.

Chalkara obtained the High King's permission to use the castle's highest tower, which Zhinza said would make her sending easier. The topmost chamber, which had been used for storage of old weaponry, was cleared out and furnished with a clean, new mattress and an assortment of cushions and hangings; that done, Zhinza was moved in and left in the privacy she demanded.

The dozen councillors present by this time had expected her to emerge with an answer within the hour; as the minutes crawled by, they became first impatient, then concerned, and finally worried. The minutes became hours, and finally a full day passed, during which Zhinza had had no food or drink.

The more impatient wizards finally convinced Shandiph that something must have gone wrong, that the strain had been too much for the poor old creature; a rescue party was on its way up the stairs of the tower when Zhinza finally emerged.

It was apparent that the sorceress had not slept or rested any more than she had eaten, and Shandiph arranged for her to have a good meal and a few hours rest before reporting her results to the members present.

By the time Zhinza felt sufficiently recovered to tell the gathering Council what had happened, the members in attendance numbered fifteen besides herself, and Shandiph had finally found time to speak with the two astrologers present as well as the one theurgist. He had also, by compiling information brought him regarding the deaths of members, by accepting proxies granted, and by consulting the Council's by-laws, determined that the quorum necessary to conduct business was twenty-one members. A quorum required two-thirds of the total votes, but not all members were equal; he, as chairman, had five votes of his own and several by proxy, while the most junior members had only one. It was also required that a quorum be one of the numbers with mystical properties; twenty-one, being the product of the mystical numbers three and seven, as well as the recognized age of adulthood, met that prerequisite neatly.

No formal action could be taken until five more members arrived; nevertheless, to ease the impatience of many present, Shandiph officially convened the Council of the Most High. With the High King's permission, he had converted an unused gallery into a meeting chamber, complete with warding spells on each door and a row of three long trestle table in the center.

The meeting was to have begun at noon; but as Shandiph had anticipated, it proved impossible to gather the entire group together on schedule. It was a good hour past midday when he finally rose at the end of the first table and called the meeting to order.

The gallery had a southern exposure and high, narrow windows; the sunlight from one of them lit Shandiph from head to foot, from the sweat glistening on his balding scalp to the sterling silver buckles on his black leather sandals. His remaining hair was thin and gray, his face broad and flat. He wore a tunic of black silk worked with silver that was cut to disguise his growing paunch, and soft gray breeches hid his thighs.

'Fellow magicians, seers and scholars, I welcome you

here and hereby convoke the session of the Council of the Most High,' he said. 'We are met to consider a matter that threatens to disrupt the peace of the world, which we are sworn to safeguard. A border has been violated, and magic of great power has been used.'

'We all know that,' Karag of Sland called. 'Get on with it! What has Zhinza got to say?'

'Karag, I want to deal with the necessary formalities, if you don't mind, and get them out of the way. Now, is there anyone present who questions my authority to convene this Council or question that I had sufficient reason to do so in this instance?'

There was a moment of silence; Karag was visibly restraining himself from interrupting again.

'In that case, is there anyone present who does not have a clear understanding of the situation we're here to discuss?'

This time there were muttered words and a few uncertain questioning noises. Shandiph gestured for silence, then began an account of what was known of Garth and the Sword of Bheleu.

'Reliable divinations have determined that this sword is in fact powerful enough that it could be used to defeat any army that Eramma might send against this Garth,' he concluded. 'Therefore, it falls to the Council to deal with this trouble maker and prevent a long and bloody war. We are considering both assassination by ordinary methods and the possibility of using the basilisk to turn this Garth to stone. Other suggestions will be welcome. For the present, though, we asked the sorceress Zhinza to contact Shang in Mormoreth, the keeper of the basilisk, and inquire as to the monster's readiness for use. I now ask Zhinza to report what she has learned.'

He gestured toward the old woman, then sat down, glad to be off his feet.

Zhinza rose, looked around at the gathering, and

cleared her throat. She was at least two inches short of five feet in height, thin, and frail; her face was narrow and wrinkled, her hair long and shining white. She wore a simple unbelted gown of white linen.

'Shang isn't there,' she said.

There was a moment of silent surprise; before anyone could speak, she went on, 'I mean, I can't find him. As a lot of you know, my specialty is the knowledge of other planes of reality and the conveying of messages through them or drawing knowledge and power from them. I think I know as much as anybody about communicating over long distances or through other realms and probably more than any of you here. I used every bit of that knowledge in searching for any trace of Shang. I knew him when he was young and I know the shape of his thoughts and the image of his face. I couldn't find him – not in Mormoreth, not anywhere in Orûn or Derbarok, and not in any of the known planes that he might have been translated into. I think he must be dead. If he's not dead, then he's behind a warding spell the like of which I've never seen or else has gone someplace completely beyond my knowledge. I think he's dead and I wish he had carried a warning spell so we could be sure, but he didn't.'

She paused, and then rushed on before anyone could interrupt, 'And I can't find the basilisk either. After I couldn't find Shang, I looked for the basilisk, and it's not there. I don't know its thoughts, but it has an aura of evil and death that's unmistakable, and there was nothing but the memory of it in the crypts of Mormoreth.'

She looked around defiantly and then abruptly sat down.

There was a moment of babble; then Shandiph rose and silenced the meeting. 'Let us behave calmly and rationally,' he said. 'Now, who wishes to speak? You, Karag, what do you want to say?'

Karag rose, impressive in his red velvet and black leather, his black beard bristling. He was not particularly tall or especially heavy, but he gave the impression of great strength nonetheless, for his every muscle was hard and tense.

'I would like to know,' he announced, 'how reliable this old woman's findings are. I do not deny that she was, in her time, a sorceress of great repute, but she must have lived three-fourths of a century by now, and even the mightiest of us is not immune to the effects of time.'

'I'm eighty-six, but I still know more than you ever will, you strutting idiot!' Zhinza retorted.

Karag looked at her with manifest disdain, and Shandiph rose again. 'Sit down, Karag,' he said. A hand gestured for his attention, and he added, 'Yes, Chalkara, what is it?'

The court wizard to the High King got to her feet; like Shandiph, she stood in the direct light of a window, so that her long red hair and cloth-of-gold gown were as vivid as flame. Karag glared at her, then seated himself, though not before Shandiph had noticed for the first time that she stood slightly taller than Sland's wizard.

'I do not impugn Zhinza's knowledge or power, but the fact remains that we do not know what has become of Shang; as she says, he may be concealed by some warding spell of which we know nothing or hiding in a place of which we know nothing. Or it may be that something has deceived Zhinza, by means we do not know, and Shang and the basilisk remain in Mormoreth, as always. This is a matter that must be investigated immediately, and I suggest that we send someone in person to Mormoreth to inquire there what has become of our great weapon and honored colleague.'

Karag objected. 'If Shang is dead, then there won't be anyone in Mormoreth to ask!'

Without rising, Thetheru of Amag said, 'If Shang is dead, then his killer will be in Mormoreth.'

Karag whirled to face the Amagite and retorted, 'Nonsense! The killer would have fled long ago!'

'We don't even know that there is a killer,' Deriam of Ur-Dormulk interjected. 'Shang may have gotten careless with the basilisk's venom.'

'Shang was never careless,' replied Lord Dor, Baron of Therin – or at least the avatar he had sent to the meeting, since Dor had developed the ability to reproduce himself in identical copies that shared his consciousness.

'Anyone can be careless once,' Deriam insisted.

'Please, councillors!' Shandiph called as argument became general. He was answered, after some shuffling, by silence; Karag seated himself, having risen so as to be able to yell in Thetheru's face more easily. The old sorceress shifted in her chair, and Shandiph asked, 'Is there something you wished to add, Zhinza?'

'There is someone in Mormoreth; I could see that when I looked for Shang and for the basilisk. There are several people, none of whom I could identify in any way, and none of whom were magicians, so that I couldn't communicate with them.'

'There, you see?' Thetheru said; Karag turned toward him, his hand falling to the hilt of the dagger he carried on his belt.

'Silence!' Shandiph bellowed.

When he was satisfied that he had the full attention of those present, he went on, 'It would appear that there are people in Mormoreth, whether or not they are connected with Shang's death. These people may know what became of Shang and of the basilisk. I think that it would, indeed, be a very good idea to send someone to investigate, particularly since we are still five votes short of a quorum to decide matters of importance and can therefore spare the time. I suggest we vote on that, here

206

and now; no quorum is necessary for sending a messenger. All those in favor of sending an investigator to Mormoreth will signify their position by standing.'

With much scraping of chairs, most of the members rose; Shandiph tallied up the votes, to make it official. Zhinza did not stand, nor did Deriam, nor did a blue-clad young woman Shandiph could not immediately place; all others had voted in favor. Karag and Thetheru were glaring at each other, obviously annoyed that they had voted the same way.

'Good,' Shandiph said. 'The next question is who should be sent?'

'With the Chairman's permission,' Derelind the Hermit said, 'I volunteer.'

'Are there any other volunteers?'

There were several, and a disorganized debate ensued. It was finally settled in favor of Derelind when he explained his proposed mode of transportation, which none of the others could equal; he claimed to have learned the languages of winds and birds, and to be able therefore to fly to Mormoreth, carried on the backs of eagles, his weight borne up by the west wind. He estimated the round trip at three days' travel.

Once that was settled, Chalkara suggested that no round trip was necessary to deliver information, since Zhinza should be able to communicate with him while he was still in Mormoreth. Derelind agreed, but asked that no votes for death be taken until he had returned.

When that, too, was settled, Derelind said, 'By your leave, then, I will depart immediately.'

Shandiph replied, 'You may if you choose, but the meeting is not done; we have yet to hear the advice of the astrologers and our theurgist on the nature of the danger that Garth and the Sword of Bheleu present.'

'I will forgo that pleasure.' He bowed his head politely and headed for the door. Deriam released the wards he had placed upon it, and Derelind stepped through, closing the door behind him.

When he had gone, Shandiph announced, 'I will now call on Herina the Stargazer, one of our most learned astrologers and scholars, to tell us what she feels may be relevant in the motions of the stars.'

Herina rose; she wore light blue that contrasted well with her butter-yellow hair. She was plump, but not distressingly so, and age had not yet done any serious damage to her figure or face – certainly no more than had her diet.

'Ah . . . it appears we have the misfortune to be living in evil times. The beginning of a new age is upon us; the familiar Thirteenth Age, which has lasted for three hundred years and is all any of us has known, is over. The Fourteenth Age began approximately a month ago, and I believe that all these events that we are here to discuss relate somehow to its advent. The Fourteenth Age is, according to the priests and scholars as well as to the more orthodox astrologers, to be ruled by the god Bheleu, Lord of Destruction, as signified by the presence of the three wandering stars in the constellation of the Broken Sword. It is therefore believed that this age, which is to last for only thirty years, will be an age of fire and blood, in which the wars that ended with the coming of the Thirteenth Age will return threefold.

'The ancient texts and prophecies include several descriptions of signs, omens, and warnings that will signal the onset of this great destruction. An overman will come out of the east to the city of the dark gods, according to one; this is obviously fulfilled by Garth's visit to Dûsarra. The worshippers of P'hul will honor the servant of Bheleu, says another; this is not confirmed, but it could be interpreted to mean Garth's alleged spreading of the White Death. The others I am familiar with do not appear to have been fulfilled as yet, though. There is mention of

208

a slayer of monsters who shall come out of the north, and of storms of fire, and of various other portents. Since none of these has occurred, as far as I know, I don't believe that too much weight should be given to the seeming fulfillment of one or two of the prophecies. They're quite vague, after all.

'Regarding the Sword of Bheleu, that's not really within my area of expertise, but it seems to fit in with the start of the new age. I have no idea where it came from or what it is capable of.'

She sat down.

Shandiph rose and said, 'We have a second astrologer on hand; Veyel of Nekutta, have you anything to add?'

The old man robed in black shook his head. 'No. She covered the general topic well, and I cannot deal with specifics without casting a proper horoscope of this overman, something I do not have sufficient information to attempt.'

'In that case, I call on Miloshir the Theurgist to inform us regarding the nature of the Sword of Bheleu.'

The theurgist was a middle-aged man wearing white and gold, of nondescript appearance except for his flowing brown hair. He got slowly to his feet, and spoke.

'I am afraid that we may be in serious trouble very soon. As Herina has told us, this is now the Fourteenth Age of the world, ruled by Bheleu, the god of destruction. Bheleu is the second most powerful of the Lords of Dûs, the evil gods, second only to The God Whose Name Is Not Spoken. Among all the gods, only the ineffable Dagha and the gods of life and death are reckoned his superiors, and Bel Vala, god of strength and courage, is his only near-equal. Furthermore, Bheleu is not a god who can be accommodated and lived with, as we have lived with the goddess P'hul for these past three centuries; he demands constant destruction, unlimited death and chaos. Herina said that this age would last for thirty years; my own studies indicate that it will last for only three, since it will take no longer than that for the world to destroy itself utterly under the influence of Bheleu.

'As for the Sword, every god, in his time, uses tools to work his will in our mortal world. Each deity has some token, some powerful magical object, through which his power is channelled and by which he dominates the age given to him. Each token has existed, it is said, since the very beginning of time, when the First Age began, but each remains hidden and powerless until it is found at the proper time and used by the mortal being or beings chosen by the god to wield it.

'I am very much afraid that this overman, Garth, is Bheleu's chosen agent and has already found and begun using the sword that is the god's token. This means that he has at his command, should he learn to use it, the full might of the god and all the supernatural powers and abilities attributed to the god. While I might ordinarily suspect that this overman is a fraud and the sword a fake given a prestigious name – such hoaxes have occurred – I fear that is not the case here. You will recall, some of you, that idols of Bheleu always depict him as an overman, and that, as the astrologer mentioned, this Garth has already fulfilled at least one and probably two or more of the relevant prophecies.

'As the agent of destruction, this Garth – or, if you prefer, the god Bheleu – will be most eager to destroy the forces that help preserve order. The foremost force for order in this decadent world of ours is this very Council. Therefore, we will be one of his prime targets.'

He stopped speaking. Karag asked, 'Then do you say there is nothing that can be done?'

'Oh, no! I never said that. It is entirely possible that Garth can be defeated and much of the havoc he would cause averted. Only three of the gods are so mighty that they cannot be thwarted, and though Bheleu, in this age, is fourth among the gods, he is not one of the three. He can be defeated, his agent destroyed, and his token suppressed. However, any such action must be taken immediately, since the god's power will grow steadily for some time as the new age asserts itself.'

'You are saying, then, that if we do not immediately destroy this overman, he will destroy us?'

'Yes, and the world with us. Exactly.'

Chalkara said, 'You spoke of tokens of all the gods. Could we find these other tokens and use them against this overman?'

'I suppose so, yes. Of course, the tokens of the Arkhein are of very little power and would be of no use at all against the Sword of Bheleu. I believe the tokens of the Lords of Eir may have been destroyed in the Eighth Age, when the balance first shifted in favor of the Lords of Dûs; I certainly know of nothing that would indicate that they still exist. That leaves us only the tokens of the other six dark gods. We already possess one of the six, and I know what the others are, but not where they might be found.'

'We already possess one?'

Miloshir was suddenly hesitant and uncertain. He glanced at Shandiph. 'I have spoken out of turn.'

Shandiph rose again; his knees were growing tired. 'That's all right. Yes, we already possess one; it was the Ring of P'hul that first permitted the Council of the Most High to gain what power we now hold, at the end of the Twelfth Age. It has been kept carefully hidden ever since, because it is far too dangerous to use; it was the Ring which caused the Great Plague that wiped out the Royal Eramman Army and thereby put an end to the Racial Wars before the overmen could be wiped out. It was the Ring that laid waste the Plain of Derbarok. It always did what was asked of it, but never in the way desired; it ended the Racial Wars only by killing the army and

211

ended the war with Orûn only by ruining what both sides fought for.'

'What are the others?'

Miloshir replied, 'The White Stone of Tema, the Black Stone of Andhur Regvos, the Whip of Sai, the Dagger of Aghad, and the Book of Silence are the remaining five.'

'And each of these is as mighty as the Sword of Bheleu, yet we know where none of these potential menaces are?' Karag demanded.

'Oh, no, they are not equally powerful; none of these is the equal of the Sword of Bheleu except the Book of Silence, which holds the fate of the world in its pages.'

'But we know where none of them are?'

'That's right.'

'Where does the basilisk fit into this?' Deriam asked. 'Surely it's the equal of one of these mysterious objects!'

'Ah, there's debate about that. Some say that the basilisk is the true token of The God Whose Name Is Not Spoken, and that the Book of Silence is a lesser item, or a myth, or perhaps the token of Dagha himself.'

'I can readily believe that that thing is the symbol of the death-god. If it is, then we possess two of the tokens, including one mightier than this sword; Garth stands no chance.'

Miloshir looked at Deriam, and then up and down the tables at the thirteen other councillors present. 'I hope you're right,' he said.

19

It was plain that there would be no shortage of fuel in Skelleth that winter; partially burned beams and rafters were plentiful, and charcoal abounded. Nor was building stone lacking, since the ring of ruins provided all that might be needed. It was sound wood, for roofing, flooring, and furniture, that was most sorely missed. Ceilings could be constructed of arched stone and roofs made of thatch, but such work took vast amounts of time, as well as consuming great quantities of stone and requiring elaborate scaffolding.

There were no forests or even groves anywhere in the vicinity; firewood had traditionally been gathered from bushes by those fortunate enough to use wood at all, rather than dried dung. No building had been done in Skelleth since the completion of the Baron's mansion some two hundred years earlier. Prior to that, wood had been shipped in by caravan in great wagons, as had much of the stone and other material.

What wood could be salvaged was used, but the supply ran out when some twenty-odd houses had been erected and before any had been furnished.

There was talk of using the wood, chairs, and tables from the King's Inn, but that was quickly abandoned when it became clear that neither Garth nor the Forgotten King thought much of the idea.

Therefore, Saram decided that it was time to re-establish communication with the south, so that wood could be bought. He said as much to Garth.

Garth had been doing very little since Selk's arrival

and the killing of the warbeast. He had made a half-hearted attempt to cut off his left hand while it held the sword; but as he had expected, the knife blade broke before it had cut deeply, and the wound healed overnight. After that failure, he had spent much of his time sitting and staring at the sword, trying to devise some way to get free of it without giving in to the Forgotten King.

Galt, after due consideration, had decided to stay; he realized that the City Council would almost certainly be willing to put him to death to appease the Erammans. They were unlikely to pardon him, since such an action would look very suspicious once the High King heard of it. Someone had to be the scapegoat, and he and Garth had been chosen.

Of the forty-one other overmen in Skelleth, fourteen had remained; twenty-seven, including all the wounded, had gone home when offered the choice.

Selk was being kept under guard in one of the upstairs rooms of the King's Inn; he remained fairly quiet, but complained at every opportunity that there was something unsettling about the room, something in the air that made his skin crawl. Garth and the others could detect nothing but an extraordinary amount of dust.

The overman guards at the five gates were withdrawn, due to the loss of so many survivors, leaving only humans.

Galt lost interest in governing his remaining party, leaving Saram in virtually complete control of the village. It was under these circumstances that Saram came to ask Garth's opinion about sending an embassy to Kholis.

Garth considered. 'I think,' he said, 'that you may be right. It has been more than a fortnight since the battle, and we have heard nothing from anywhere south of here. I think that we can therefore tell them whatever we choose, and they will accept it. Furthermore, winter will be here soon – already the winds have turned northerly and cold – and the High King will be unable to send an army here without extreme difficulty once the snows begin.'

'I hope he'll have no reason to send an army. I don't intend to tell him that you're an occupying force.'

'That's good; what do you propose to tell him?'

'I've been thinking it over some, and I think this will hold up. I will send a message saying that the Baron, whom everyone knew to be mad, finally went berserk while speaking with a peaceful trading mission and set fire to the village. In the ensuing confusion many died, and much of the town was destroyed. The survivors joined together to rebuild, with the aid of your overmen, when it became clear that it was the Baron's insanity that began the fighting and fires, rather than any legitimate dispute or action of your party. We need not mention that your trade mission consisted of sixty warriors; we need not mention anyone but the sixteen of you still here. I exclude Selk, the seventeenth; he can be another little secret. We will ask for supplies to be sent so that we may survive the winter and for a new Baron of Skelleth to be named; and we will express our continued loyalty to the Kingdom of Eramma. How does that sound?'

'Good, very good; it puts all the responsibility for wrongdoing on the dead Baron.'

'I thought you'd like it.'

'If the King accepts it, then we can present the City Council with a whole new situation and ask them to reconsider.'

'If you want to, yes.'

'Why do you say, "If you want to"? Why should I not want to?'

'It seems to me that your Council isn't very helpful; why not just forget about them?'

'I came here to establish trade between the Northern Waste and Eramma. I intend to establish that trade, whether the others involved want it or not; it will benefit both, whether the rulers have the wit to realize it or not.'

'Oh, I see. Garth – whatever happens, whether you convince your City Council or not – you're welcome to stay here in Skelleth as long as I'm running it.'

'With luck, though, that won't be long; the High King will be sending a new Baron.'

'Ah, that's true. I'd forgotten.' He smiled. 'I'll be able to relax, then, and pay some attention to my wife.'

'Your wife?' Garth was startled.

'Certainly.'

'What wife?'

'Frima, of course.'

'Oh.' Garth considered that. 'Are you two married?'

'More or less. The law says that a marriage is valid if approved by the lord of the region. As acting baron, I'm the local lord, and *I* say we're married. When we get a new Baron I may ask him to confirm it.'

'I see. Congratulations, then.'

Saram studied the overman's face. 'Are you missing your own wives? Perhaps you could send for them.'

'No. My kind is not as prone to loneliness as you humans are.'

'You seem depressed, though.'

'I am depressed, not by the absence of my wives, but by the presence of this sword, and by the stupidity of the Council.'

'Oh. There isn't anything I can do about the Council, other than send my message to Kholis; is there any way I can help you with the sword?'

'I know of none.'

'Let me see if I can pull your fingers free.'

Garth cooperated, and a moment later Saram was stuffing burned fingers in his mouth.

'How can you *hold* that thing?' he muttered.

'I don't have much choice; I have even tried severing my hand, with no success.'

'Shall I try?'

'If you wish, but I warn you, your blade will probably break.'

'I won't try it, then; I like my sword.'

Garth snorted.

'Listen, maybe you can burn the thing out.'

'I don't understand.'

'Maybe you can use up all its power. Then it would be too weak to hold you.'

'I had considered that, but I could think of no way to do so without killing innocent people and destroying property.'

'Why don't you go out on the plain somewhere, where there's no one to kill and nothing to destroy?'

'And what would I do then?'

'Can you direct the sword's power, as you did when it possessed you?'

'I don't know.'

'Can you make it possess you?'

'I have tried without success.'

'Well, I suggest that you go out on the plain, find a nice barren spot, and then try to make the sword burn, as it did when you slew the Baron. Try to burn the earth itself. See what happens.'

Garth thought that over. His mind was not clear, and he could think only slowly and muddily; he knew, vaguely, that this was the sword's doing.

He could think of no objection to Saram's proposal. 'I will try it,' he said.

'Good. I have to go put together that embassy to Kholis,' Saram said, rising, 'but I wish you luck.'

Garth watched him depart, then held up the sword and looked at it. The gem was glowing bright blood-red.

Nothing else he had tried had done any good, and he

couldn't trust the sword to behave itself much longer. He rose, pulled the cloak he had borrowed from Galt more tightly around him with his free hand, and headed toward the West Gate; that direction led to the most desolate stretch of wilderness.

He could feel winter coming; the air felt thin and hard and chilled him, even through the cloak, tunic, gambeson, and his own fur beneath. Skelleth had no autumn in the usual sense, since there were no trees to drop leaves nor late crops to harvest – the hay was brought in late in summer – but it did have a brief period between the warmth of summer and the first snow, and that was what had arrived in the last few days. The only warmth Garth could detect anywhere in the world around him was the heat of the sword's hilt in his hand.

It was oddly comforting. He knew that he should be uneasy about feeling anything positive about the thing's power, but the warmth was welcome nonetheless.

None of the few people he passed on the way out of town paid much attention to him; they had become accustomed to seeing him wandering about the village, hoping to find some means of release from the sword's thrall. Even the guards at the West Gate did nothing more than nod polite greetings.

Out on the open plain, the north wind drove through him; his right flank became so cold that his left seemed warm by contrast. The sword's hilt in his right hand burned like a live coal, but it was a good soothing heat and did not cause him any pain.

He strode on across the wasteland. Skelleth was not considered part of the Northern Waste, but it was still harsh, barren country, little better than his homeland. The few farms that he passed or crossed were empty and silent; the hay had been cut and gathered a month before, and the farmers had taken their crops and their goats and gone to the village to take shelter for the winter when

218

first the north wind blew down from the hills. Only the ice-cutters ventured out on the plains once the snows came, and then only in large groups.

At the end of an hour he had traveled something over four miles, a distance he thought should be sufficient. He stopped and looked around.

The plain lay, bleak and empty, in all directions. To the north, it ended in low hills; to the east, Skelleth was still visible as a line on the horizon; to the south and west, there was nothing else for as far as he could see. He had left the old Yprian Road a hundred yards from the gate, and it was now lost in the distance.

He took the sword in two hands and stood for a moment feeling the warmth that now bathed them both; the left seemed to be thawing, though it had not actually frozen. He concentrated on the heat and let it flow up his arms.

He was not sure at first how to go about what he wanted to do. He recalled that, when he was possessed, he often lifted the sword above his head just prior to performing his magical feats; feeling slightly foolish, he raised the blade up.

Without any conscious volition, his hesitant gesture changed; he thrust the sword powerfully upward, pointing at the sky, until the red gem was directly before his red eyes, its glow as bright and warm as fresh blood. Overhead, the steely gray sky was darkened by wisps of black cloud.

The glowing jewel held his gaze. He stared at it in fascination for a long moment, and the clouds gathered above him. Thunder rumbled in the northern hills.

The sound broke his trance, and he looked upward.

The sky had not been clear when he left the town, but it had shown no threat. Now it was filled with blossoming thunderclouds. There would be a storm long before he could reach the shelter of the village walls.

He still held the sword before him, its point toward the sky; now, involuntarily, he thrust it above his head, crying out, '*Melith!*'

The name was unfamiliar to him; it was answered by a flash of lightning and a low rumble of thunder.

He remembered suddenly that, when he had entered the temple of Bheleu in Dûsarra and first taken the sword, the sky had been full of thunder, and lightning had blasted the broken roof of the temple. Lightning had struck the altar and scattered the bonfire that surrounded it.

Lightning had struck the sword while he held it.

He realized suddenly he was standing on a dead flat plain in a thunderstorm, holding up six feet of bare steel. Lightning had an affinity for metal, as everyone knew, and was drawn as well to the highest objects in reach. Standing thus would ordinarily have verged on suicide.

This was no ordinary sword, however, and he began to wonder if it was an ordinary storm. Was it natural or had the sword summoned it? Had the storm that shattered the temple of Bheleu been natural?

He did not think he cared to try so dangerous a test of the sword's nature as to invite being struck by lightning. Merely because he had survived it once did not mean he could do it again. He yanked the sword down.

It resisted, but obeyed.

Immediately the seething clouds overhead stilled; where it had seemed that the storm would break in seconds and pour a torrent upon him, now the clouds were calm, and it seemed as if there were no storm at all. No lightning flashed. No thunder roared. Even the north wind died away to a breeze.

He recalled Saram's proposed test; would the sword burn the earth? He thrust it out before him, pointing at the ground a dozen feet away.

The gem flared up brightly, and a rumble sounded. At

first he thought that it was fresh thunder, but then the ground heaved up beneath him, rolling under his feet. Staggering to keep his balance, his left hand fell from the hilt, while his right, holding the sword, swung out to his side.

The tremor stopped, and the earth was again as still and solid as ever.

He no longer felt the cold; the warmth of the sword's touch had spread through his body. As he looked at the blade and realized what had just happened, sweat broke out on his forehead.

He could not believe that the sword had caused an earthquake. He took it in both hands, in a reversed grip, and placed the tip on the soil at his feet.

Nothing happened.

He held it in that position, waiting and thinking. He realized that he did not *want* anything to happen. Perhaps that was affecting his experiment. He forced himself to stop denying the sword's power, and instead recited to himself, 'Move, earth, I command it!'

The ground shook, roaring; he saw dust swirl up on all sides.

'Stop!' he cried.

It stopped.

Earthquakes frightened him. The uneasy movement of the most immovable of things upset his view of the way the world should be. Such displays undoubtedly consumed vast amounts of the sword's energy, but he could not bear to continue.

Storms, however, were something he was accustomed to.

He looked at the gem. It was glowing brightly, vividly red.

It could not be limitless, he told himself. It must exhaust itself eventually.

With that thought in his mind, he raised the sword above his head and summoned the storm to him.

The light of the jewel bathed him in crimson, and the blade glowed brilliantly white as the storm broke about him with preternatural fury. A bolt of lightning burned through the air over his head and shattered against the sword, bathing him in a shower of immense blue-white sparks, but he felt nothing but a slight warmth and a mounting joy in the power he wielded.

Another bolt followed the first, though Garth knew that was not natural; and then a third came. He was washed in white fire, and the ground at his feet was burned black.

Lightning continued to pour down upon him while cold rain beat against the plain around him. He stayed dry in the heart of the storm, for the lightning and the heat of the sword boiled away the rain before it could touch him, encircling him in steam and mist.

He discovered that he could steer the lightning away from him and direct it where he chose by pointing with the sword, as he had spread flame in Skelleth. He drew the sword's heat into him and thrust it upward, and the rain turned warm around him; then he sucked it back down and away, and the rain became first sleet, and then hail – though the frozen drops were smaller than natural hailstones.

He called aloud another strange name, '*Kewerro!*' The wind howled down out of the north, and the storm became a snowstorm, then a raging blizzard.

He was drunk and staggering with the power of the sword, and still the gem glowed as brightly as ever, the blade as gleaming white as the moon.

He sent the snow away again, turning the north wind back, and allowed the south wind to bring rain in its place. The sky was black, the sun buried in thunderheads;

only lightning and the light of the sword lessened the gloom.

He drew the storm around him, whipped it into a howling maelstrom, and forced its winds to whirl faster, until his cloak was flapping with a sound like the breaking of stone; still the gem remained undimmed. Maintaining the roaring hurricane, he moved the earth as well, rippling it around him like a lake in a breeze. He pulled the rain from the sky in sheets, in streams, and pounded lightning on the shifting ground, surrounding himself in a halo of crawling electric fire.

Finally, he could stand no more; he fell to his knees. The earth stilled. One hand fell from the sword's hilt; the lightning stopped, and the wind dropped. In the sudden silence after the final thunderclap, he closed his eyes and heard the beating of the rain soften to a gentle patter.

He opened his eyes and looked hopelessly at the sword. His fingers adhered to the hilt as firmly as ever.

The gem glowed fiery red, and he thought he heard mocking laughter, his own voice laughing at his despair.

20

The twenty-first councillor and Derelind's report from Mormoreth arrived almost simultaneously.

It was the Seer of Weideth, uncomfortable on a borrowed horse, who completed the Council's quorum; he arrived late in the evening while a light, chilling drizzle blew down out of the north, and his calls to the castle's gatekeeper went unheeded for fully fifteen minutes, unheard over the hiss of the rain and the mutter of the wind. There was only a single guard posted at the gate after dark and he was huddled well away from the window, drawing what warmth he could from his shuttered lantern and a skin of cheap red wine; finally, though, he heard something worth checking on and peered down to discover the Seer, shivering at the gate, wrapped in an immense gray cloak.

The gatekeeper was an honest man and not inconsiderate; he hurried to his winch and called down an apology as he cranked open the portcullis. That done, he rushed down the tower steps, stumbling in the dark and very nearly sending himself falling head first, and opened the Lesser Portal. In daylight there would have been two other guards to share the task.

'My lord, I am very sorry, truly I am! I had not thought any would be out in such dreary weather!'

The Seer nodded, but did not manage to say anything. His home village was kept perpetually warm and dry by the heat of the neighboring volcanoes, and he was not accustomed to the damp chill of autumn rains.

'I should have known better, though, with all of you folk arriving for these past several days; I don't suppose you're the last, either. I guess the rain caught you already on the road, and you didn't wish to waste money on an inn with the castle so close; I'd do the same myself. It's damnably strange weather for this early in the year, too, my lord – far colder than any year in my memory.'

The Seer looked at the gatekeeper and realized that he was a very lonely man, spending his nights sitting alone at the gate. He was unmarried, with no children, and his most recent woman had left him a few days earlier.

That was not his business, the Seer told himself. His gift sometimes told him more than he wanted to know – and then other times it wouldn't tell him anything. He wished it were more reliable. He didn't particularly care if he were ever a great prophet, but it would be pleasant, he mused, at least to be a competent one, rather than having erratic flashes of insight and foreknowledge.

It was the guard's loneliness, combined with his genuine contrition, that had brought on his little speech. He would go on talking until he got an answer.

'Oh, I'm all right,' the Seer managed. 'You mustn't trouble yourself.'

'That's kind of you, my lord. Is there anything I can do for you?'

'Where can I put my horse?'

The gatekeeper replied with directions to the stable, instructions on whom to rouse and how, and warnings against trusting the worthless grooms.

'Thank you,' the Seer replied. He rode on as directed, before the man could begin another speech.

At the stable, he obtained directions to a hall where he might find someone who would know where he was supposed to be; following them, he got lost briefly in the maze of stone corridors. Eventually, though, by asking whomever he chanced to meet, he found his way to the upper gallery where the Council was gathering.

Chalkara noticed him as he reached the top of the

stairs and recognized him immediately from his sending. 'Greetings, O Seer,' she said. 'I hadn't known you were here. When did you arrive?'

The Seer held out a flap of his cloak so that she could see that it was still wet and answered, 'Just now. What's going on?'

A stranger in a gaudy robe of purple velvet pushed past him and entered the gallery as Chalkara answered, 'It's rather complicated to explain, and the meeting is about to start. Why don't you just come in, sit down, and warm up? If you have any questions, ask them as they come up.'

Confused, the Seer let Chalkara shove him through the door. There were chairs inside, arranged around a row of three long tables; he was tired, and sank into one gratefully.

The room was lighted by several dozen candles in hanging chandeliers and standing candelabra, and a dozen or so men and women were already seated around the tables. Others were arriving as he took this in. Shandiph was seated at the head of the table he had chosen; none of the others were immediately recognizable. There was a tiny old woman seated at Shandiph's right.

A stout man not quite into middle age seated himself at the Seer's right and remarked without preamble, 'You're wet.'

'It's raining,' he answered.

'Have you just arrived, then?'

'Yes.'

'Who are you?'

'I am the Seer of Weideth.'

'Ah, then it's you who started all this!'

'I suppose it is. Who are you, then?'

'You don't know me? I am Deriam of Ur-Dormulk, and probably the only wizard here who knows what he's doing.' He gestured to take in the entire assembly.

226

The Seer decided that he didn't care for Deriam of Ur-Dormulk. He was trying to think of a polite way to break off the conversation when Shandiph rose and broke it off for him by calling the meeting to order.

'I see that we now have the necessary numbers,' he said when the entire group was seated and silent, 'counting Derelind. With this quorum, then, we are constituted an official gathering of the Council of the Most High, empowered to take action on behalf of the entire membership. I think that you will all agree shortly that some action must be taken, and quickly.'

He paused dramatically, and someone in his audience snorted derisively. Shandiph ignored it.

'We have just received word, through the offices of the sorceress Zhinza, from Derelind the Hermit, who was earlier sent to the city of Mormoreth in Orûn to ascertain the status of our comrade Shang and the basilisk which had been placed in his keeping. I now yield to Zhinza, so that she may give Derelind's message herself.' He gestured toward the ancient woman and then sank into his chair.

Zhinza rose and proclaimed, 'Shang is dead. I was right.'

Deriam muttered something into his beard.

'Tell them what Derelind said,' Shandiph reminded her.

'Derelind said,' she went on, 'that he arrived safely and found that Mormoreth is now inhabited by the bandit tribe that formerly roamed the Plain of Derbarok. Being a wizard, he was easily able to convince the bandits to talk to him and tell him how this came about. They claim the city was given to them as a gift by the person who killed Shang, as a blood-price for several tribesmen he killed as well.'

'All right, woman, who was it killed him?' Karag demanded.

227

'Shang was killed by an overman named Garth.'

There was a moment of stunned silence as this news sank in.

'What about the basilisk?' someone called.

There was a hush as Zhinza looked about for the speaker and failed to locate her. Finally, addressing the group at large, she said, 'Garth took it with him.'

The ensuing silence was brief and followed by a babble of many voices. Shandiph let it go on for several minutes before demanding order be restored.

'You mean,' Karag of Sland said, when he was reasonably sure he could be heard, 'that our greatest weapon has fallen into the hands of the enemy even before we have begun to fight him?'

'That would appear to be the case,' Shandiph said. 'Before we begin debate, however, I would like to have all the available information laid out. We are fortunate in that Kala of Mara thought to bring with her a good scrying glass. At my request, she has been studying this overman. At this time, I would like to ask her what she has learned.'

Kala was a young woman in a simple brown robe; she stood and said, 'I haven't learned much, I'm afraid. It's very hard to use the glass on Garth of Ordunin; the sword resists the presence of all other magic, and he is never apart from the sword.'

'Have you seen the basilisk?' asked Thetheru.

'No, I haven't. I haven't seen any trace of it anywhere in Skelleth. I don't know what happened to it, but I don't think it's there.'

'That's good,' Deriam said.

'What I have seen, though, is enough to frighten me badly. I cannot look at Garth directly; the sword will not allow it. When I attempt to force it, it retaliates by filling my crystal with its own hideous light, so that I can see nothing. I haven't the strength of will to fight it. However,

I have watched the village of Skelleth and places around the overman. There have of late been several great storms in that area, as well as earthquakes; they have had snow and hail, as well as the rain and sleet that might be expected in this season, and winds sufficient to tear apart thatched roofs. I have glimpsed lightning storms that lighted the night sky as if it were day. I think that Garth is somehow using the sword to create or summon these storms.'

'You say that you haven't been able to watch the overman himself?' Karag asked.

'No, I haven't. I have also been unable to see inside the local tavern he frequents, whether he is there or not; I have no idea what this might mean.'

'These storms,' Karag asked. 'Are you sure he's causing them? I've never heard of any such magic.'

'I am not certain, but they are like no natural storms I have ever seen.'

There was a moment of silence; then Thetheru of Amag said quietly, 'Do we have any chance of stopping such power?'

'He has already taken our greatest weapon,' Herina the Stargazer observed.

'Well, no,' Shandiph said, 'he hasn't really.'

There was another moment of silence; then Miloshir the Theurgist asked, 'Are you referring to the Ring of P'hul?'

'Among other things, yes.'

The Seer was confused. He had never heard of the Ring of P'hul. He looked about for Chalkara, but she was seated well down the table on the opposite side.

'What other things?' Karag demanded.

Shandiph sighed. 'I was afraid this would happen sometime. A need was bound to arise.'

'What in the name of the seven Lords of Eir are you talking about?' someone asked. The Seer was surprised to see that it was Chalkara; he would have guessed that she was privy to all the Chairman's secrets.

'Have none of you ever wondered at how little power our magic has? Haven't you all heard the tales of the great magicks used in the wars of the Twelfth Age and wondered what became of them?'

The other magicians were all staring at Shandiph now.

'They're just stories,' someone said.

'No, I'm afraid they aren't.'

'You mean that Llarimuir the Great really did move mountains? That he created the overmen on a whim? That Quellimour raised a city overnight and then sent it sailing in the clouds?' Karag's voice was openly sarcastic.

'Yes, they probably did just what you say,' Shandiph replied mildly.

'Then what happened?' Miloshir asked.

'It was at the end of the Twelfth Age,' Shandiph explained. 'The world had been in a constant state of war for over a thousand years, probably more than two thousand – the wars destroyed all the records, so we can't be sure. The wizards of that age fought in those wars, using all the magic at their command; reading their descriptions, I find it miraculous that anyone survived at all. The seers and oracles helped by giving military counsel to the generals and warlords.'

'But that's forbidden!' the Seer burst out.

'It is now, yes; it wasn't then. As I was saying, magicks mightier than any we can imagine were common and were employed without any compunction, not only in genuine wars, but in looting and pillaging at whim. The wizards themselves were among the most feared of the warlords. It was only the balance of power, the fact that each side could recruit and use equal amounts of magic, that kept wars going – and it was probably that balance that kept most of the population alive. Each

230

wizard, you see, defended his subjects, and there were protective spells as powerful as the destructive spells.

'At any rate, this continued throughout the Twelfth Age; but about three centuries ago, the surviving wizards grew tired of the constant conflict and gathered in council to arrange a peace. That was the beginning of the Council of the Most High. You've all probably heard that the wizards were advisors to the warlords, and some were, but most were the warlords themselves. It was agreed that all wars would stop at once, whether the other lords wanted them to or not; the Ring of P'hul was used to end the Orûnian War and the Racial Wars, and lesser magicks dealt with the lesser conflicts. It was then decided, when it was seen what the Ring and the other spells had done, that such powers were too dangerous to keep in use, and they were sealed away in a spot known only to the first Chairman of the Council.'

'And I suppose the secret has been passed on from chairman to chairman, down to you?' Karag said.

'No, not exactly; not the secret itself, but only the means of obtaining it. I didn't know until an hour ago where the great magicks were, only that a certain spell would inform me. I used it when I first heard Derelind's message, before calling this meeting. The old magicks, those that survived, are in the crypts beneath Ur-Dormulk.'

'They are?' Deriam exclaimed.

'Yes, they are,' Shandiph replied.

'What of it?' Karag asked.

'Comrades, I think we could debate on this for hours or even days, but Miloshir tells us that time is precious, that the overman draws greater power from the Sword of Bheleu with every passing moment. Therefore, I would like to put this proposal to an immediate vote: that we should without any further delay send a party to Ur-Dormulk to acquire these ancient powers, whatever they

231

may include, and then use them to end the threat posed by Garth of Ordunin and the Sword of Bheleu, thereby averting the coming Age of Destruction. If the vote does not show a clear consensus, I will open debate, but I hope that it won't be necessary.'

It wasn't. There were three dissenting voices, for a total of only four votes.

21

For three days Garth had tried to burn out the sword's power with storms and earthquakes, but had succeeded only in exhausting himself and disrupting the reconstruction of Skelleth. Finally, when the gem still glowed as brightly as ever at the end of the third day, he admitted defeat.

At least, he admitted temporary defeat; he had not yet abandoned hope, but only convinced himself that he could not exhaust the sword in such displays. He suspected that he might manage to free himself by allowing the sword a surfeit of killing, but that was not a method he cared to employ; it was to avoid unnecessary killing that he wanted to dispose of the thing.

He spent the following day sitting in the King's Inn, drinking and talking with Saram. The reconstruction was continuing, but only slowly; the cold had made work difficult, and materials were running low – stone excepted. The embassy had been sent to Kholis as planned. The petrified thief had been set up in the center of the marketplace on an elaborate pedestal of stone blocks from the Baron's dungeon. Galt, Garth, and the other overmen considered this to be a mistake, but Saram and Frima insisted that the pitiful figure was appropriate and admirable.

Another petrified villager had been found in a ruin nearby; apparently someone had had the misfortune to look out a window while the basilisk was being moved through the streets. This figure was not to become a public statue; even had it not broken in half when the house it was in collapsed in flames around it, it was much less attractive. The person in question had been a plump matron, bent over to peer around a shutter.

No one had known that this second petrification had occurred until the rubble had been cleared from the house. The victim had been a recluse, little liked by those who knew her at all. Garth still thought it odd that her absence could have gone unnoticed for the intervening months.

'I had hoped,' he remarked to Saram, 'that the death of the basilisk would remove the spell that it had cast upon its victims.'

'It would seem that magic is not as transitory as some tales would have it,' Saram replied.

'I suppose that if it were, then Shang's death would have ended the usefulness of his charms, and thereby freed the basilisk from my control.'

'And if that had happened, you might be a statue now yourself.'

'But on the other hand, these two innocents would not.'

'Oh, you can't be sure; what if the basilisk had begun roaming, once freed, and eventually reached Skelleth?'

'That seems extremely unlikely.'

'Yes, it does. But then, the very existence of such a creature seems unlikely.'

'It does, doesn't it? Everything that's happened to me since I first came south seems unlikely. One strange event has followed another, almost as if they were planned.'

'Perhaps they were.'

'Perhaps they were, but by whom and how? Is it all a scheme of the Forgotten King's contrivance? If so, how did he influence me to ask the Wise Women of Ordunin the questions that would send me to him in the first place? If not he, then who? Have I become a pawn of the god of destruction? Is there some other power manipulating us all?'

'Perhaps it's fate, or destiny.'

'The Wise Women mentioned fate when last I spoke with them, fate and chance; I have never believed in fate, but only in chance.'

'Yet now you say that events don't appear to be shaped by chance. That would seem to leave fate, if your oracle's words were complete.'

'They probably weren't.'

'You don't trust these women?'

'They're overwomen, actually, despite their name, and I am not sure whether I trust them or not.'

'Perhaps you should go and speak with them again, and settle the matter once and for all. They might know how you can be freed of the sword.'

'They might, at that. They are, however, in Ordunin, where I am now an outlaw.'

'Do you know of any other oracles?'

'I'm not sure; I once met a seer, of sorts, and of course there is the Forgotten King, who knows more than he should. There was also a priest in Dûsarra who was said to have special knowledge. None of these are even as trustworthy as the Wise Women.'

'I would say, then, that you would be well-advised to return to Ordunin, outlaw or not, and speak with your oracle. If you travel by night and stay clear of the city, can you not manage it?'

'Probably. I will think about it.'

He did think about it and by morning he had resolved to make the attempt.

Unfortunately, by morning the winter snows had begun, blowing down from the northern hills. This storm was wholly natural, but fierce enough that he decided travel would be foolhardy. He would wait it out, he told himself.

It was only after two days of tedium, sitting in the King's Inn worrying about the warbeasts' food supply –

five of eleven, including Koros, had stayed in Skelleth when the others had returned to Ordunin – that it occurred to him that, if the sword could create storms, it might be able to control natural ones as well.

It could. He ripped the storm into tattered shreds of cloud and sputtering gusts of wind in ten minutes of concentration.

A foot of wet snow lay on the ground, but he thought Koros could handle that without undue difficulty. He set about gathering supplies.

With the ground under snow, game would be scarce along the way, and foraging difficult; furthermore, he did not dare to visit his home, which meant that he needed supplies for a round trip. Saram was reluctant to part with so much of the village's meager provisions.

Garth also wanted another sword, a more ordinary blade that he could use without worrying about whether he was controlling it or it was controlling him, a knife for skinning and dressing whatever game he might find, an axe to cut firewood, and various other tools that were in short supply in Skelleth. His friendship with Saram did not provide unlimited credit, and he found himself spending part of the Aghadite gold to purchase what he needed.

It took another two days before he felt himself properly equipped; but at last, one morning, he mounted his warbeast and rode out the North Gate toward the hills that marked the border of the Northern Waste.

22

The party sent to Ur-Dormulk consisted of Deriam, since he knew his own city better than anyone else; Shandiph, since he alone could use the spell that would show them the way to the crypt that held what they sought; Karag, who insisted upon accompanying them; and Thetheru of Amag, who refused to remain behind if Karag went. The four rode the finest horses in the High King's stable; Chalkara, with the aid of a subtle spell, acquired retroactive approval for this from the King an hour or so after the quartet had slipped quietly out.

The stealth was considered necessary because of the presence of the Baron of Sland. He had already protested the existence of secret meetings of wizards in the High King's castle and tried to force Karag to tell him what was under discussion. Only the presence of the other wizards had kept him from resorting to violence.

Two of his six soldiers had vanished since their arrival, and Karag suspected that the Baron was keeping his own secrets. His men did not desert; they did not dare.

Therefore, the four wizards had begun their journey an hour before dawn, while the Baron and his men slept. A simple spell of drowsiness kept the gatekeeper from noticing their departure.

Once out of the castle, they rode night and day, using invigorating spells to keep their horses alive and moving. Such travel was hard on the older two, Shandiph and Deriam, but did not seem to bother Karag at all – and Thetheru concealed his own fatigue rather than admit that Karag was more fit. Ordinarily, each would have avoided the use of so much magic so quickly, but with such a threat hanging over them and such a promise of greater power before them, it seemed foolish to worry about conserving relatively trivial resources.

They were slowed by the necessity of crossing the Great River, which they reached early in the second day, but they nevertheless managed to arrive at the gates of Ur-Dormulk by the sunset following their ferry ride.

It then became necessary to conceal their haste, and they struggled to appear as if nothing unusual were taking place – as if the four of them had decided on a casual visit to Deriam's home. They received curious glances from pedestrians as they made their way through the streets, while Karag and Thetheru displayed their own curiosity in studying the city around them. Shandiph and Deriam were both natives of Ur-Dormulk, though Shandiph had left it as a child to become a wanderer, and they were accustomed to its peculiarities; but the other two had never before seen it.

The entire city was built of stone and was so ancient that the stone had been worn and weathered on even the newest buildings. The older structures did not have a single sharp corner remaining, and some resembled mounds or natural rock formations as much as they resembled anything man-made. The streets were all paved with great slabs of stone, yet there were grooves worn in them where countless cart wheels had passed, and wider, shallower depressions where the majority of the foot traffic had gone.

Deriam's home was a tall, narrow house on a busy avenue, of no special distinction save that there were gaps in its ancient granite walls where softer stones used as trim had been weathered away completely.

'We'll have to hide the horses,' Deriam said as he dismounted at his door.

'Why?' Karag asked.

'There are no horses in Ur-Dormulk,' Shandiph

replied. 'It was probably a mistake even riding them past the gate.'

'What will happen if we just leave them here?' Thetheru asked.

'I don't know,' Shandiph said.

'They'll probably be stolen,' Deriam said.

'Then put a warding spell on them,' Karag suggested. 'Shandiph, you're good at that.'

'I'm tired, Karag.'

'It's a good thought,' Deriam said.

'Then you do it,' Shandiph replied.

Thetheru objected. 'I think we should just hide them.'

'We're wasting time,' Deriam said. 'Shandiph, put a ward on them and let's get on with it. You're outvoted, Thetheru.'

Wearily, Shandiph assented, and cast a simple ward on the horses. The four then left them tied to the door handle while they entered the house.

'If we're in such a hurry,' Thetheru asked, 'why are we here instead of going directly to the crypts?'

'We *are* going directly to the crypts,' Deriam said. 'They can be reached through my cellars. There are easily a hundred entrances, and this is the one I know best. The crypts of Ur-Dormulk are a true marvel, you see; they extend . . .'

'Shut up, Deriam, we haven't got time for that,' Shandiph said, made irritable by fatigue.

Offended, Deriam made no reply, but instead pulled a bell rope and called for his servants.

'You do well for yourself,' Karag remarked. 'I have no servants to wait on me.'

'Ur-Dormulk is a rich city,' Deriam replied. 'And besides, I was not so foolish as to become a servant myself. I do not work for the Overlord here, but on my own behalf.'

'I doubt that you suffer from your lack, Karag,' Shandiph remarked. 'After all, you have the run of the Baron of Sland's castle and staff, don't you?'

'More or less,' Karag admitted. 'I can command the household workers, but have no authority over the guards.'

The conversation was cut off by the arrival of Deriam's retainers. He sent one to fetch food and drink, another to bring the keys to the cellars, and the third and last to take a polite greeting to the Overlord and tell him that his faithful Deriam had returned but was resting from the journey and not to be disturbed.

The three vanished without comment on their various errands, and the four wizards settled down to await the promised meal. 'We shouldn't take the time,' Shandiph said, 'but I'm hungry.'

'Yes, and cold and thirsty as well,' Thetheru added.

While waiting, the newcomers looked over Deriam's parlor. It was lush to the point of ostentation, with thick patterned carpets overlapping to cover every inch of floor, rich tapestries covering every wall, and ornate carved frames around every door and window. The furnishings included a myriad of cushions of silk and velvet and an assortment of tables, chairs, pedestals, statuettes, display shelves, bric-à-brac, and general clutter, every item made of costly materials and showing elaborate workmanship. A few of the cushions had old stains on them, and one carving of a handsome young couple was chipped through the woman's arm.

When the servant he had sent for the keys delivered them, Deriam sent the youth after as many lanterns and torches as could be found in the house. 'We'll need light in the crypts,' he explained, 'and there's no sense in wasting magic.'

The food, when it arrived, consisted of a plate of fruit, nuts, and cakes; the drink was a decanter of yellow wine and a steaming pitcher of a brownish liquid Karag and Thetheru did not recognize.

'A discovery of my own,' Deriam explained with an air of patently false modesty. 'It's an infusion of herbs and spices in boiling water and it's really quite invigorating. Try it.'

Karag refused the unfamiliar brew and confined himself to cakes and wine; Thetheru took a cup of the steaming concoction and an assortment of fruit and pronounced both to be good.

Both wine and herbal brew were warming and felt so good to the weary travelers that they made no effort to silence Deriam when he began a long description of the history of the crypts.

'They aren't exactly crypts in the usual sense of burial vaults or areas for underground storage,' he said. 'They're actually another city that used to stand on this same site. Ur-Dormulk, you see, is the most ancient city in all the world and has stood for longer than any records have existed. It was once called Stur-dar-Malik, which means "City of the Old Ones" in the language of the time. Even then it was old. The most learned scholars in the city, who are of course the wisest and most learned in the world, say that there must once have been a great catastrophe that destroyed much of the city, and the survivors built the new city upon the ruins without bothering to excavate them. The old cellars and passages were forgotten for centuries, until finally someone broke into them while digging a new wine cellar. That was, I have heard, in the Eleventh Age, about four thousand years ago. Since then they have been explored and extended and elaborated, until now they are so complex that no man living knows them all – and I personally doubt that anyone ever did. They reach under every corner of the city and extend out beyond the walls for miles in every direction, as well as continuing quite deeply down into the earth. There are said to be many strange and wondrous things in them, and there are tales of men and women who have become lost down there only to be preserved by the unnatural powers that lurk in the darkness, to wander about forever.'

'That's a cheering thought,' Thetheru said.

'Oh, it's just a legend,' Shandiph replied.

'We thought that the great old magicks were just a legend,' Thetheru returned.

'If the crypts are so extensive, how can we hope to find these magicks we seek?' Karag asked.

'There are signs,' Shandiph replied.

'Signs? You mean that these carefully hidden things, too dangerous to leave where they might be misused, can be found by following signposts?'

'Not exactly. The signs can only be read by means of an enchanted glass.'

'Where do we find this glass, then?'

Shandiph reached down to a pouch on his belt. 'It's right here,' he answered.

'Let me see it,' Karag asked.

'Not yet,' Shandiph replied.

Karag started to protest, then caught sight of Thetheru's smile and thought better of it.

They finished their repast in silence. As Deriam drank the last of the wine, his servant reappeared with a double armful of prepared torches and with four lanterns.

The torches were distributed evenly among the four wizards. Karag suggested that Deriam's servant accompany them, but Deriam overruled the notion immediately. 'That is beyond their duties,' he explained.

'Besides, we want to keep the whole thing secret,' Shandiph added.

Accordingly, the servants stayed where they were, while the wizards made their way through Deriam's kitchen and down the stairs into his wine cellars. From there they descended another flight into a fruit cellar, where a trap door opened to reveal a ladder leading down into utter darkness. The light of the lanterns did not reach the bottom.

With the torches bundled on their backs, the four descended, Karag first, followed by Deriam, Shandiph, and Thetheru. The ladder swayed beneath their weight but did not break or fall. After what seemed an incredibly long time, they finally came in sight of the bottom.

When they stepped from the ladder, they found themselves on a flagstone floor buried in a thick layer of dust. At Shandiph's suggestion they lit one torch apiece to provide additional light.

They were in an immense chamber of stone; their footsteps echoed from the bare walls, which even the light of torches and lanterns combined revealed only as vague and distant patches amid the all-encompassing darkness. Three of the four stared about in uneasy surprise at the room's extent; Deriam remarked casually, 'I haven't been down here in a long, long time; I'd forgotten just how big it is.'

'Where's the door to the crypts?' Karag asked.

'We are *in* the crypts, Karag,' Deriam replied. 'This chamber has a dozen doors opening on various rooms and passages.'

'Which way do we go?' Thetheru asked.

'I haven't any idea,' Deriam answered.

Shandiph carefully placed his torch and lantern on the stone floor and fumbled with the pouch on his belt. He brought out a small sphere of yellow glass and held it up to his eye.

After a long moment he said, 'I see nothing.'

'What do we do now?' Thetheru asked.

'Pick a direction at random,' Karag suggested.

Deriam shrugged, and led the party to the wall of the

243

room, choosing his route by walking forward in the direction he happened to be facing.

The wall was bare stone and faintly dusty.

'Now,' Deriam said, 'I propose that we walk along the wall until we find one of the signs Shandiph mentioned.'

No one objected, and the foursome moved along the wall.

Almost immediately, they came to an open doorway; Deriam looked at Shandiph, who shook his head. They moved on.

A second doorway was passed, and a corner of the room. At the third doorway Shandiph asked, 'Does the pentacle above the door mean anything?'

'What pentacle?' Thetheru asked, holding up his lantern. The stone lintel was blank.

'I think we've found it,' Karag replied.

Shandiph lowered the glass from his eye and stared at the lintel in puzzlement. 'I still see the pentacle, though,' he said. 'Don't you see it?'

'There is nothing there, Shandiph,' Karag replied.

'We see nothing but bare stone,' Deriam added.

Shandiph looked at the glass, then back at the stone. 'I thought I had to look through it,' he said. 'It appears I was wrong.' With a shrug, he led the way through the door and into the passage beyond.

The passage was more of the dull gray stone, huge blocks of it stacked together without mortar, forming a corridor ten feet wide and twelve feet high. It sloped downward for a hundred yards or so and then ended in a T-shaped intersection. Karag had moved into the lead and now stopped, unsure which way to turn.

'The pentagram is on the left,' Shandiph said as he came up. Karag immediately turned left, and the party advanced.

Following Shandiph's directions, the foursome made their way deeper and deeper into the crypts, through corridors and rooms that ranged from mere cubicles to vast caverns, up and down ramps and stairs, across bridges that spanned seemingly bottomless chasms, and past doors of wood, iron, and brass that stood ajar or were tightly sealed, with no discernible pattern. The first torches burned down to uselessness and were discarded, and the lanterns dimmed and died as they wound onward. There was no light save what they carried, and the only sounds were their own footsteps, their own breath, and occasionally the distant dripping of water. In one room they found a spot where drops of water fell and saw that it ran from the tip of a five-inch stalactite clinging to the low ceiling, to land with the smallest of splashes on a stubby projection from the floor. The chamber they were in was not a natural cave, but man-made; the water came through a crack between the stones of the ceiling.

The second set of torches died, and the third was lit; Deriam began complaining of the stupidity Shandiph had displayed in not bringing food and drink. Karag came to the Chairman's defense, pointing out that he had no way of knowing how long the search would take, while Thetheru remained silent. When Deriam demanded that the Amagite choose a side, he ended the argument by saying, 'I'm too busy trying to remember our route.'

'I hadn't thought of that,' Deriam said after a moment of silence.

'I've been too busy finding our way forward,' Shandiph said.

'Can you lead us back out?' Karag asked.

'I'm not sure,' Thetheru admitted.

'Maybe we should turn back. Do we even know what we're looking for?' Deriam asked. 'How will we know these wonders when we find them? Have they really survived for three hundred years in this damp darkness?'

'Darkness wouldn't hurt anything,' Karag retorted.

'But we don't even know what we're looking for,' Thetheru said.

'I assume that we'll find a few chests somewhere,' Shandiph said, 'and perhaps a shelf of books.'

'I hope so,' Deriam answered.

They were discarding the last of the fourth set of torches when Shandiph, who had moved on ahead while Karag lit the new torch from the stub of his old one, called out, 'I've found something.'

'What is it?' Karag called.

'This door has the pentagram sign on it, and another pentagram inside the first.'

'Is it open?'

'No. It's locked.'

The other three came up to join him and found that the Chairman was standing before a large oaken door bound in rusty iron; he was pulling and pushing at the great iron handle. The door did not move.

'Whatever we're looking for must be in there,' Karag said.

'How do we get in?' Deriam asked.

'Break it down,' Karag suggested.

Shandiph and Deriam looked at each other; Deriam shrugged. 'Let him try; he's the strongest of us.'

The other three stepped back, and Karag took a short run toward the door, slamming his shoulder against it.

Immediately, he was flung back against the far wall of the corridor in a shower of pure white sparks.

He lay stunned on the dusty stone. Thetheru said unnecessarily, 'It must have a warding spell on it.'

'I never saw a ward like that,' Deriam replied. He was blinking, trying to help his eyes readjust to the dim yellow torchlight after the vivid brilliance of the sparks.

Shandiph looked at the door for a moment and then said, 'I suppose they wanted to be sure that no one who just happened along could get in. We are the rightful heirs, though, so there must be some way we can annull the wards.'

'There was no mention of this in your directions?'

'No. You have to understand, I know very little more than you do. When I became Chairman I was given the seal of office and a box of charms, and taught a spell that would tell me what each charm was for when the need arose; that spell told me that the yellow glass would show me the way through the crypts, but it said nothing of this door.'

'Did you bring the other charms?'

'No. That shouldn't matter, though; I know what almost all of them do. Besides, if one was needed here, the spell should have told me before I left Kholis.'

'Perhaps the spell has become muddled over the years.'

'Aal and Amera, I hope not!'

'Is there some hidden instruction in the pentacle, perhaps?' Thetheru asked.

Karag was climbing to his feet once again. He said nothing, but stood unsteadily, staring at the door.

'Did you bring any magic besides the yellow glass?' Deriam asked Shandiph.

Before the Chairman could answer, Karag said, 'I can see the pentagram now.'

'What?' The others turned toward him in surprise.

'I can see the pentagram. But you said there was another pentagram within it, Shandiph, and it's not a pentagram, it's the Council seal.'

'Is it?' Shandiph also stared at the door; to him it still appeared to be a pentacle inside a pentacle. A possibility occurred to him, and he reached inside the neck of his tunic to pull forth the golden medallion that he, as Chairman of the Council of the Most High, wore at all times. He placed it against the center of the pentagram and announced, 'I am Shandiph, heir to Hemmaron,

Chairman of the Council of the Most High, chief among the wise and first among equals!'

Nothing happened.

In desperation, Shandiph reached out and pushed once more at the iron handle. The door swung open.

The chamber beyond was utterly black, and the light of the torches did not penetrate. The four wizards stared into it for a long moment, none daring to step into the unnatural darkness.

'I think that magic is called for,' Deriam said at last.

Shandiph nodded. '*Hoi, khiri! I'a anagarosye t'aryo ansuyen, o mi alekye i zhure Leuk!*' he called. '*Hear me, spirits! I am an agent of the lords of demons, and with this talisman I invoke Leuk!*'

The room was suddenly flooded with golden light, and the four stared in astonishment.

The chamber was perhaps thirty feet wide, but so long that its far end could not be seen in the conjured light. The walls were lined with shelves of books, row after row of chests, hundreds of pegs from which hung amulets and talismans of every sort, and racks which held sceptres, staves, orbs, jewels, swords, daggers, cups, plates, goblets, spears, stones, carvings, statues, sacks, pouches, jars, phials, and a hundred other implements and objects. More chests were lined up down the center of the room. Many objects glowed or glittered, and soft rustlings could be heard.

Directly before them stood an immense reading stand carved of some dark, rich wood, which held a great blackbound book.

Everything was brightly and clearly lighted for fifty yards of the room's length, but without shadows and with no apparent source of light.

'How did you do that?' Thetheru asked Shandiph.

'You mean the light? I learned a little theurgy years ago; it's a simple invocation. If you mean the door, I

248

didn't do anything except what you saw. It must have been ensorcelled to recognize the seal of office.'

'What *is* all this stuff?' Karag demanded, astonished.

Shandiph shrugged. 'How should I know?' He stepped forward and looked at the lone book on the stand. 'I think that this must be here where we see it for a reason.' He opened the book at random and let the front cover fall back against the stand.

Pages flipped over without his touch; when they stopped, he read aloud, 'This book is the true compendium of all arcane knowledge gathered in this room, compiled to guide those who come after us in the use of our arts.'

'Useful,' Deriam remarked.

'How can one volume explain all this?' Thetheru asked, gesturing at the thousands of books and tens of thousands of other objects.

Pages turned, and Shandiph read, 'This book has been enchanted and will answer your every question. Speak, and you shall be answered; ask, and you shall know, that the glory of the Council of the Most High may be reborn upon the earth.' He smiled. 'So much for secrecy,' he said. 'It appears that our predecessors didn't expect it to last forever.'

'Shandiph,' Deriam said, 'this is all too much for me. What are all these things? This is far more than I had imagined we would find.'

A single page turned, and Shandiph read, 'Gathered before you is every magical spell and power known to our members at the end of this Twelfth Age, save those thought too minor to waste space upon, and those that have been withheld by the power of the gods or reserved for the continued use of the Council's master.'

'I think this is more than we can handle,' Thetheru said. 'I think we should contact the rest of the Council before we go any further.'

A thick sheaf of pages flung itself over with an audible thump, and Thetheru looked at in surprise. 'I didn't ask a question,' he said.

'The Greater Spell of Summoning has been embodied for your use in spheres of red crystal, stored in the first chest on your left,' Shandiph read. 'The shattering of one of these crystals in the heart of a well-drawn pentagram will bring you instantly whomsoever you shall name aloud while the smoke is thick.'

'The thing dares to advise us!' Karag exclaimed.

'We should use it, though,' Thetheru said. 'Where is chalk for a pentagram?'

A page riffled over, but Shandiph did not bother to read what it said, as Deriam announced, 'There is already a pentagram here, on the floor, inlaid in gold.'

The other three looked, and Deriam was correct; a thin layer of dust had hidden the golden star.

Shandiph was already on the way to the chest indicated by the book by the time Karag and Thetheru had convinced themselves of the pentagram's reality. He opened it and found that a dozen identical spheres of red crystal, each the size of a clenched fist, were arrayed in a tray at one end. The rest of the chest held an assortment of other fascinating devices, but he resolved to leave those for later. He picked out a single red globe and, with a careful toss, flung it into the center of the pentagram. It shattered spectacularly when it hit the floor, and an impossibly thick cloud of red smoke billowed forth.

'Chalkara of Kholis, Derelind the Hermit, Miloshir the Theurgist, Herina the Stargazer, Veyel of Nekutta, the sorceress Zhinza, the mage Ranendin, the Baron Dor of Therin, Kala of Mara, Sharatha of Ilnan,' he recited quickly.

The smoke continued to roll outward in a solid, spreading mass, with no sign of thinning; Shandiph continued his listing. 'Kubal of Tadumuri, Haladar of Mara, Sherek the Thaumaturge!' He was beginning to have trouble remembering which other councillors had been at Kholis. 'Amarda the Blood Drinker! Linder the Nightwalker!'

Vague shapes were becoming visible in the seething red cloud, which had reached out far enough to surround the original party of four. 'The Seer of Weideth!' Shandiph added. There were still one or two others, he knew. 'The wizard Alagar . . .' Were there still more?

The smoke showed the first signs of dispersing, and it occurred to him that he need not restrict himself to those who had attended the meetings. He remembered one more who had been at Kholis, though, and named him first, saying, 'Phamakh the Wise!'

Abruptly the red fog thinned and vanished, and the room was suddenly crowded. Every person he had named was present, jammed together in the area around the golden pentagram; all were looking about themselves with varying mixtures of surprise and fear.

Shandiph realized that he had missed an opportunity to settle Shang's fate definitely once and for all by summoning him as well; or he might have called for someone who could provide a firsthand account of recent events in Dûsarra. He considered using another crystal but decided against it.

There was a sudden babble of voices as the new arrivals all began to talk at once; the only question that was decipherable in the confusion of noise was one that was repeated by several speakers, though the pages of the guidebook riffled wildly in trying to answer every startled query.

'Where are we?' was the one question that could be understood.

'Fellow councillors!' Shandiph called. 'Your attention, please!'

The questions ceased, the book's pages lay still, and the entire group turned to face him.

'You are in the vault where our ancestors placed much of their magic for safekeeping; you were brought here by an ancient spell because we felt that the unexpected wealth of this lost magic was more than we four could handle by ourselves. If you will look around you, you will see that there is far more here than was anticipated; every single thing in this chamber is magical, it appears, and every book here contains arcane knowledge. As may be determined by the ease with which you were brought here, using a single, simple device – beware that you don't step on those shards of glass – much of this magic is extremely potent by our standards. We thought that all of you should have some say in the management of this treasure trove.'

'*You* thought so, Shandiph, you and Thetheru,' Karag said. 'We four were appointed as representatives, and I see no need to waste time in further debate. We were sent to find powerful weapons to use against the overman Garth, and there are undoubtedly powerful weapons here around us. I say that we should find them, using that guidebook, and then go and deal with this overman and his magic sword before he becomes any more dangerous than he already is.'

There were a few calls of support from the gathered crowd and several shouted questions; once again, the guidebook tossed pages back and forth, attempting to answer them all at once.

'Shandiph, where are we? Where is this vault?' someone called over the general din. Shandiph looked for the speaker and tried to call an answer.

Deriam and Thetheru were each beset by two or three of their comrades demanding explanations; most of the others crowded around Shandiph, barraging him with questions and opinions. Karag, too, drew his share of attention; the wizard Alagar and Kubal of Tadumuri, both old friends, came toward him. One or two individuals wandered off down the long room, looking at the thousands of trinkets and talismans.

Karag saw an opportunity in this complete disorganization and made his way to the reading stand, where he asked in a low voice,'What are the most powerful weapons in this chamber, and where are they to be found?'

Alagar and Kubal watched with him, saying nothing, as the pages turned and revealed a long list – much too long to be of use.

'Which of these are the three mightiest and most effective?' he asked.

Two pages flipped back, and Karag read, 'The Ring of P'hul, on the Chairman's ring finger, the Great Staff of Power, first in the third rack of staves on the right-hand wall, and the Blood-Sword of Hishan of Darbul, fifth in the second rack of blades on the right-hand wall.'

'We can't use the Ring,' Alagar whispered.

'You both intend to join me, then?'

'Yes, of course,' Kubal replied. 'These fools will be arguing for hours. They'll thank us when it's done.'

'True enough. All right, book, what is the fourth most powerful among the weapons here?'

The book turned a few pages. 'The Sword of Koros,' Kubal read. 'I'll take that.'

'I'll take the other sword,' Alagar said.

'And I'll take the staff,' Karag agreed

'Karag, what are you doing?' Shandiph called. He had finally noticed that the other was using the guidebook.

'I thought that the book might be able to advise us on how to proceed.'

'Has it?'

'No, not yet; give it a few more minutes.'

'Well . . .' Shandiph was uncertain. Karag was impetuous, he knew, but usually meant well. Several of the newcomers had given him news that directly concerned Karag, but he was distracted by another question about the guidebook's working before he could tell Karag. He decided to trust Karag for the moment and to wait before telling him that his secret departure from the High King's castle had led to a dispute between the King and the Baron of Sland. Chalkara said that the Baron had accused the King of kidnapping Karag to deprive the Baron of his services. There was a great deal of acrimonious talk going on, though no action had yet been taken.

While Karag and Shandiph spoke, Alagar had been using the book; when Karag looked down again it was to find complete instructions for the use of the three weapons chosen. He read through them quickly, as did Alagar and Kubal.

Shandiph remained distracted; the Baron of Therin had been conjured in his true person, rather than the simulacrum that had come to Kholis, and was therefore able to relay information. The disappearance of the other magicians was creating quite a stir, and Dor's other self, together with Sindolmer of Therin, who had arrived after the foursome had left and therefore been excluded from Shandiph's listing, were trying to calm matters. The coincidence that both the apparent survivors were from Therin did not make their task easier.

Deriam had become entangled in a debate concerning the nature and origin of the crypts, and Thetheru was explaining the red crystal spheres to Sharatha and Miloshir. No one paid any attention to Karag, Alagar, and Kubal.

'What is the quickest means by which we three may be transported with our chosen weapons, to wherever we may find Garth of Ordunin?'

Karag read the answer, and then closed the book.

'It is yours, Shandiph, to do with as you please,' he called.

'Thank you, Karag. I'll want to speak with you in a moment.'

'You have no objection if we look around, do you?'

'No, not if you're careful.' Shandiph was too busy to be really suspicious; he was trying to answer questions about the vault room even as he asked his own about the Baron of Sland and affairs at the High King's castle.

Moving casually, so as not to draw attention, Karag and his two comrades gathered their chosen weapons, ignoring the questions and comments of the other wizards. When they were armed, Karag opened the first chest on the right and took out a blue crystal sphere very much like the red one that had summoned the majority of the Council.

At that point it became impossible to hide their actions and intentions any longer, and Kubal and Alagar, brandishing their swords, ordered that the pentagram be cleared.

Startled, the other councillors obeyed.

The three stood in the center of the golden star, and Karag announced, 'We are going to do what must be done, without wasting any more time. We go to face Garth of Ordunin!' With that, he dropped the blue sphere.

It exploded in a cloud of bright blue smoke; when the smoke cleared instants later, the three wizards were gone.

23

As Koros reached the top of the first low ridge, Garth turned for a final look at Skelleth. The town's silhouette was subtly changed from the last time he had seen it from this spot, when he had ridden down from Ordunin with his little trading party; a few of the old rooftops were gone, lost to the fires he had spread, and not rebuilt. None of the new structures were high enough to be seen from this distance.

The snow, too, changed the outline, blurring the lines and bleaching the surfaces to an even white that made the shadows stand out more sharply.

When last he had ridden the Wasteland Road, he had been accompanied by Larth, Galt, and Tand; now Galt was an outlaw and Tand had not yet returned from the Yprian Coast. He wondered what had become of his double-cousin Larth; he had not been among the sixty volunteers. He was probably living safe at home, going about his business as always, never questioning the wisdom of the City Council.

Garth turned his gaze forward once again, then cast a quick glimpse over his left shoulder. The sword's gem was glowing more brightly than usual, he thought. He wondered why. Was it pleased to be leaving Skelleth?

There was little he could do about its glow; there was no guarantee that turning back toward Skelleth would make any difference, and he was determined to speak with the Wise Women of Ordunin.

He looked at the road before him – or rather, at the ground ahead of him. He could not be sure that Koros was actually following the Wasteland Road; the snow made it impossible to see where the road lay. He was heading in the right direction and knew the landmarks; he was not concerned about becoming lost.

There was a dip, and then a second low ridge ahead; after that, the road veered to the right somewhat, to follow the lay of the land and to avoid the steeper slopes. The snow was smooth and unbroken; no one had passed this way of late.

There was a curious bluish mist hanging in the air above the second ridge; as he watched it seemed to thicken.

It was definitely unnatural, he decided, as Koros reached the bottom of the slope. It was a small cloud now, and an utterly impossible shade of blue.

Then, abruptly, the haze was gone, and three men stood atop the ridge looking down at him.

He leaned forward and spoke a quiet word in the warbeast's ear; the beast stopped dead.

He studied the three men. One was tall and thin, with light brown hair, and carried a strange curved sword; he wore a thin, gray cloak that flapped open in the breeze, revealing richly embroidered garments underneath. The second was of average size for a human, with thick black hair and beard, and wrapped in a heavy black cloak; he carried a staff of carved wood trimmed with bright metal. The last was large, with a dark complexion and very short, very black hair – and no beard, which struck Garth as odd indeed. He had never seen an adult male human without any beard at all. This last man wore no cloak, but a tunic of black leather trimmed with silver and breeches also of black leather; he carried a cross-hilted broadsword.

The third man fascinated Garth; aside from his beard-lessness, this was the second human he had seen with skin as dark as an overman's, or nearly so. The first had been the wizard Shang, in the city of Mormoreth, who

257

had been even darker than this newcomer or than Garth himself.

Judging by the manner of their appearance, at least one of these three was evidently a magician of some sort; Garth wondered whether wizards had some special predilection toward dark skin. Or perhaps there was a land somewhere inhabited by dark-skinned humans, whence many wizards came.

The three men were looking about them, as if unsure where they were and why they were there; Garth watched without moving.

Then the tallest of the three, the one with the curved sword, pointed at him. Garth could not hear his words over the intervening distance, but there was no doubt he was calling his comrades' attention to the overman and warbeast.

Garth had no reason to believe the strangers to be hostile, but he found his right hand reaching up toward the hilt of the Sword of Bheleu. He stopped it and considered.

The sword obviously wanted to be drawn, as he had made no conscious decision to move his hand toward it and would have preferred to use his more ordinary blade. The thing had demonstrated in the past that it wanted to protect him and keep him alive for its own reasons – but it had also demonstrated an incredible bloodlust and eagerness to kill anyone within reach.

These strangers were obviously here by magic; the only explanation for that blue smoke was magic, even if it had been nothing but a means of covering their appearance over the top of the rise, and Garth thought it more likely that the smoke itself had somehow materialized them from thin air. The three men might be wielding the magic themselves, or might be innocent victims – but would innocent victims be carrying drawn swords? And that staff that the center one carried looked very much like a magical device of some sort.

The only defenses Garth had against magic were the feeble natural resistance of magically created species such as overmen and warbeasts to other magicks, and the much more powerful magic of the Sword of Bheleu.

He decided that his own survival was more important than any danger these three strangers might face from the sword. After all, they were in the Northern Waste, which was overman territory; the accepted border ran along the top of the first ridge. As invading enemies, their deaths would be acceptable. Garth drew the great sword.

He hoped that there would be no deaths.

The man with the staff was moving; he drew a circle in the snow around himself and his companions with the metal-shod tip as Garth watched, and then held the staff horizontally before him, gripped in both hands.

This looked more and more like magic at work, Garth thought; he lifted his own magical weapon in both hands.

The black-bearded man was speaking now, calling out words that reached Garth despite the fifty yards and wind between.

'*Yahai Eknissa eknissaye!*'

Garth knew that Eknissa was the goddess of fire, and assumed that what he heard was an invocation of some sort; he did not recognize the other two words. He had little time to worry about them before being distracted by their result.

A wall of flame had sprung up from the circle the staff had drawn in the snow, and was spreading outward with incredible speed. It roared up from the snow, melting it instantly as it marched, and reached a height of ten feet or more. Even before it came within twenty yards, Garth could feel its heat.

He raised the sword and summoned a storm to blow

out the flames or drive them back toward their creator. He had had considerable practice in summoning storms in his attempts to burn out the sword's power.

The wind rose to a howling gale immediately, and clouds gathered overhead; the flames grew taller, and their advance slowed – but only slightly. Garth watched in dismay as they continued to approach.

The clouds were not yet thick enough to summon lightning, so he could not blast the wizard's staff – and there was no guarantee that that would stop the wall of fire; the death of the basilisk had not reversed the petrification of its victims.

The flames were within a dozen feet when he finally allowed the sword to act on its own. It had been tugging at him, but he had resisted it; he did not trust the thing. Now, with the heat beating against him as if he stood opposite the bellows in a blacksmith's forge, he let it have its way.

It twisted in his grip and pointed directly at the advancing barrier. The snow erupted into a second sheet of flame.

For a few seconds Garth did not understand how the sword hoped to save him by starting its own fire; then he saw that the ring had stopped expanding. It could not pass the new fire his sword had started.

The sword's fire spread; when it met the stalled ring, it vanished with a great roaring rush of hot air – and with it, several yards of the wall of flame vanished as well.

With the mystic circle broken, the remaining flames sank down and became nothing but flickering natural fires; when the sparse damp grass that had been under the snow was burned, they died into sputtering remnants, then went out completely, leaving charred earth behind.

The snow was gone and the ground blackened in a broad circle around the three human enchanters, and the heat had melted much of the ground cover well past

Garth's own position, but the circle where the wizards stood was still untouched, their feet sunk past their ankles in snow. Garth could not see their faces clearly over the fifty yards distance, but he was sure that they were surprised by the failure of their attack.

Koros growled, and Garth allowed the warbeast to advance. It stopped of its own volition when it reached the edge of the scorched area; the ground was still hot and its paws were sensitive.

There was no need to risk the warbeast, Garth decided; as long as it remained within earshot, he could summon it if he needed it. He prepared to dismount and then stopped, one foot out of the stirrup.

The central wizard was wielding his staff again. Holding it as he had before, he called aloud, *'Yahai Sneg ghyemye, yahai Srig srigye!'*

The final word Garth recognized; it meant 'cold.'

He had no desire to waste time fighting off one assault after another; he raised the sword and cried aloud his own invocation. *'Melith!'*

Lightning flashed overhead, and thunder exploded deafeningly. He realized he had forgotten to direct the lightning; it had struck nothing. He was still inexperienced at wielding magic.

He had seen no new ring appear when the wizard spoke his spell, but the air about him was suddenly cold, much colder than it had been before the humans had appeared, colder than it had any right to be so early in the season. He ignored it and willed another bolt of lightning into existence; it struck with a blinding brilliance and earth-shaking roar at the feet of the three strangers.

'That was a warning!' he bellowed, slackening the gale he had conjured so that he could be heard. 'Annoy me no further!'

'Surrender yourself and your sword, and we will let you live!' shouted back the man with the staff.

261

Garth began to consider whether he might, in fact, be wise to surrender or at least to inquire about exact terms, but then dropped the idea as a rush of anger flooded through him. He was dimly aware that it was the sword's doing, but that did not give him the power to resist it.

'I am Bheleu!' he screamed. 'I surrender to no one!'

The storm roared into redoubled frenzy, and twin lightning bolts bracketed the three wizards. Garth swept the sword through the air above his head, leaving a trail of flame glowing in the air. With a word he sent Koros charging toward them, though his left foot was still out of the stirrup.

He was within a few yards before the wizards could manage any reaction beyond cringing in fear; but before he could strike at them, the central human raised the staff again. This time his invocation was in everyday speech, not archaic phrasing, as he called, 'By all the gods, help!'

The staff suddenly blazed with light and Garth was himself again, free of Bheleu's control, though the sword still flamed in his hands. He held the sword in one hand while he used the other to slap Koros on the neck, turning its charge aside before it trampled the wizard into the little patch of snow at his feet. He called for the warbeast to halt.

The other two wizards had turned and fled as the warbeast approached, but the man with the staff had stood his ground.

'Yield, Garth of Ordunin!' he cried.

'Don't be a fool,' Garth replied. 'You're no danger to me; why should I yield? Who are you, anyway?'

'I am Karag of Sland, and I hold the Great Staff of Power, lost these three centuries!'

Garth looked the man over carefully and decided that even Karag wasn't entirely sure if he was bluffing.

Whatever this staff was, Garth guessed that he hadn't had it long.

'Why did you attack me?'

'You have taken the Sword of Bheleu and destroyed Dûsarra and Skelleth with it; you must be stopped before you usher in the true Age of Destruction!'

Garth was grateful that the man's desperate invocation had apparently had the unintentional effect of freeing him temporarily from the sword's control. He might, he thought, be able to settle this peacefully.

'I don't want an age of destruction any more than you do,' he replied mildly. 'If that staff is as powerful as the sword, though, what do you have to worry about?' As he spoke he tested his hands, and discovered that though his mind might be free, his fingers were not. He regretted that; he had hoped that this over-eager wizard might have solved all his problems for him without meaning to.

His conversation was interrupted abruptly by the return of the tall, brown-haired human, who came lurching back out of the surrounding storm. With a hysterical scream of 'Die, monster!' he swung his strange, curved sword at Garth's waist – mounted as Garth was, his neck was well out of the man's reach.

With one hand, without thinking about it, Garth brought the Sword of Bheleu around to fend off the attack. The two blades met in a spitting shower of red and white sparks; then the wizard's sword exploded into glittering shards that stitched red gashes across the man's face and chest. Garth was unharmed. He felt a twinge of annoyance and then a renewed surge of fury; the sword was winning out over whatever had restrained it.

He lifted the blade to the sky and lightning blazed down around him, wrapping him in blue-white fire for a brief instant and then jumping to the broken hilt of the Blood-Sword of Hishan of Darbul – though Garth did not know that was its name. The tall human staggered, his mouth open as if to scream, though all sound was lost in the booming torrent of thunder; the blood boiled from the wizard's wounds, and he fell in a charred heap at the warbeast's feet.

The fit of rage passed and, hoping that this death might serve him, Garth tried again to drop the sword. It still held him.

He did not even notice that he was in the center of a blazing pyre; there had been so many pyrotechnic displays in the last few minutes that he had lost track of them. Koros growled, and he looked up from the glowing red jewel.

He was surrounded by flame, but he felt no heat and remained unharmed; something held it back, protecting both him and his mount.

He waved the sword, and the flames parted before him. He found himself looking at the man who called himself Karag of Sland; the man stood, the staff in his hands and the blood draining from his face, directly in front of the warbeast and its rider.

Then suddenly, red mist swirled out of nowhere and wrapped around the wizard. There was nothing Garth could do in time to stop it, other than slaying the man where he stood, which he chose not to do. He looked around and saw that a similar fog was appearing around the other two wizards, both the live one who was still fleeing some two hundred yards away, and the smoldering corpse.

As he watched, the red stuff vanished again, taking the three humans with it. He had almost expected that to happen.

He gazed around at the area of blackened earth which had now frozen hard, pocked with small craters where lightning bolts had struck. The central circle of snow was mostly a puddle. A few glittering fragments of sword were visible, and a few traces of bright blood.

264

New snow would come and cover the signs, he knew; but, come spring, it would be months before anything grew here. It was only a minor work of destruction and a single death, but still he sighed. It seemed that even when the sword did not force him to destroy of its own volition, other forces drove him to destroy in self-defense.

No, he corrected himself, most of this destruction was not his doing, but that of the wizards. He was simply the focus for it. The death, though, was his doing; he regretted that.

This was a new complication in his life. He wondered whether it justified changing his plan to consult the Wise Women. If wizards were to pop out of nowhere everywhere he went, he could hardly keep a visit to Ordunin a secret.

He would move on slowly, he decided; if there were further attacks, he would turn back.

That decided, he took a moment to get his foot securely back in the stirrup and urged Koros forward.

24

The councillors all stared in horror at the charred corpse that had appeared on the edge of the pentagram, almost ignoring Karag and Kubal.

'What happened?' Shandiph asked at last.

'He can control lightning,' Karag answered. He was shaking, the staff that was still clutched in his hands fluttering like a bird's wing.

'How did you survive, then?'

'I don't know. Kubal fled, and I tried to ward him off with the staff. I think it worked, at least temporarily.'

'Then the sword is not unbeatably powerful!' someone exclaimed.

Karag shook his head. 'I have never seen so much power. I don't mean just the sword, but the staff as well. It felt like a live thing in my hands. Without the magicks in this room, we wouldn't have a chance. He made a storm from nothing with a single gesture, and directed the lightning wherever he chose; the sword burned and spat fire. The staff made a wall of flame that consumed everything it touched, until he turned it back with the sword's flame. He rides a great black monster with fangs as long as my fingers.'

Kubal nodded agreement. 'I didn't know what we were doing; I didn't know he could be so powerful. I didn't believe Kala when she said that he could summon storms.'

'The three of you were all acting stupidly,' Shandiph said. 'The essence of magic is not power, but subtlety and deception, and poor Alagar paid for your rashness in not thinking of that. As additional folly, you alerted the overman.'

'He is no wizard, though,' the Baron of Therin said. 'He won't know how to defend himself against us. Karag made a natural mistake in thinking that three wizards could handle him, magic sword or no.'

'I do not say that they underestimated the overman, but that they underestimated the sword,' Shandiph replied. 'We need to use subtler methods, methods that the sword cannot counter directly.'

'What do you have in mind?' Chalkara asked.

Shandiph replied by crossing to the guidebook, opening it, and asking, 'Are there magicks in this chamber that can kill a foe from afar?'

The book turned to a page very near the front, which said, in large, ornate runes, simply, 'YES.'

'What are the dozen most effective that can be used without great preparation, how do they work, and where can they be found?'

Pages turned, revealing a list.

'Kala, ready your scrying glass, so that we can see what happens.'

'I don't have my glass; it was left in Kholis.'

Disconcerted, Shandiph admitted, 'I hadn't thought of that.'

'There must be a scrying glass here somewhere,' Chalkara said. 'Ask the book.'

A glass was found and given to Kala; she wandered several yards down the room and found a suitable spot to work in.

The magical light Shandiph had conjured was beginning to fade, which suited her well; it was easier to use a glass in dim light. She attempted to summon up Garth's image, and found it impossible. The sword's power still blocked her.

She said as much to the others, who had gathered together most of the devices and spellbooks the guidebook had listed as necessary for the dozen death-spells.

267

'I forgot about that entirely,' Shandiph said. 'I suppose we'll just have to try these, and then go there and see.'

'If he resists other magic as well as he resists a scrying spell, I think we had best go prepared for battle.'

'I fear you're right,' Shandiph agreed. 'Let me ask the book what other weapons we might take.'

'I already asked that,' Karag said. He was beginning to regain his composure. 'We took three of the four most powerful – the Great Staff of Power, the Sword of Koros, and something the book called the Blood-Sword of Hishan of Darbul. The book said it was the third most powerful weapon here, after the Staff and the Ring of P'hul, but the Sword of Bheleu shattered it instantly.'

There was a glum silence in response to this news.

After a pause, Shandiph asked, 'Book, what would you recommend we use against the Sword of Bheleu?'

The page revealed bore a single sentence, which Chalkara read aloud over Shandiph's shoulder. 'There is no power in the Council's possession that can withstand the Sword of Bheleu.'

'You say there is nothing we can do?'

With a thump, pages turned back to reveal the single ornate word.

'Is there no power that can defeat the wielder of the sword?' Chalkara asked.

'There are two; the Book of Silence and the King in Yellow,' Shandiph read.

'Who is the King in Yellow?' Thetheru asked.

A single page turned, and Shandiph said, 'I knew this already. It says, "the immortal high priest of Death".'

'Where can we find him?' Chalkara asked.

No pages turned, but Shandiph replied, 'We don't want to find him; he would be worse than the overman. He is the agent of Death as Garth is the agent of Bheleu.'

'Then what of the Book of Silence?' called someone from the back of the little crowd.

'Do you know why it's called the Book of Silence?' Miloshir replied. 'To speak aloud a single word written therein will kill anyone but its rightful owner.'

There was a somber silence. Herina spoke up at last. 'We could draw lots, and the loser would use the Book . . .'

'No, it won't work. The loser would die before completing the spell. It would take one of us for each word of the spell, and I have no idea how long the incantation we want might be.'

'Can we find the rightful owner and ask his aid?'

'The Book belongs to the King in Yellow.'

'It would seem we are defeated before we have begun,' Derelind said.

'We must *try*, at the very least,' Veyel replied.

'We must and we will. We will try each of these twelve spells the book led us to. It may be that the book is not infallible and has overestimated the power of the sword; it may be that Garth is not yet fully attuned to the sword's power. We still have a chance.'

'Attuned?' Karag snorted. 'The overman can summon storms from a clear sky and steer the lightning! How much more control over the sword's magic can he possess?'

'Much more, Karag. The sword's power is virtually limitless.'

Kubal shuddered at that.

The discussion broke down after that into several groups of two or three, each working on one or two of the long-range spells. One by one, the death-spells were worked, amid strange chants, evil-smelling smoke, eerie lights, and other by-products of magic. The golden light vanished completely, and lanterns were found to replace it. Several of the councillors had become hungry, and Deriam used the book to locate a bottomless purse that could be made to produce an unlimited supply of biscuits and cakes and a wine flask that never ran dry.

'This is a very useful thing,' he remarked as he gulped down the red wine, 'though it's hardly a great vintage. I wonder why it was sealed away here?'

Shandiph was watching the last death-spell being worked, which involved an elaborate dance with a very sharp knife. Chalkara was the dancer. He answered absentmindedly, 'Someone must have thought it was dangerous.'

'How could a wine flask be dangerous?'

'Oh, easily enough, I think.'

'How?'

'You could drown someone, I suppose,' Amarda the Blood-Drinker suggested, 'or flood out a place.' She was nursing cuts on her palms from the spell she had helped with and licking off the blood with disconcerting relish. Deriam glanced at her, then quickly looked away again.

'I hadn't thought of that,' he admitted.

At that moment the Baron of Therin distracted Shandiph from the dance. 'I have news from Kholis,' he said.

The Chairman turned and asked, 'What is it?'

'An embassy from Skelleth has arrived and is at this moment speaking with the High King; my other self has just entered the audience chamber to hear what they have to say.'

'What are they saying?'

Dor paused for a moment, as if listening, then answered, 'They say that Skelleth has been burned and many of its people slain as a result of the dead Baron's madness. They say that a peaceful trade mission of overmen was attacked by the Baron's guards without cause, and the ensuing battle ended with the guardsmen and the Baron all dead, and many others as well.'

'That is not what the Seer of Weideth said had happened.'

Dor shrugged. 'The ambassador is undoubtedly lying. Now he is explaining that the overmen stayed to aid in

270

the rebuilding, and that a man named Saram, once a lieutenant in the Baron's guard, organized the survivors.'

Shandiph glanced at where Chalkara was whirling, her knife glinting in the lantern light, and then looked about. 'Where is the Seer?'

The man from Weideth made his presence known from somewhere behind the Chairman.

'Ah, there you are. Can you say anything of the truth or falsehood of what Lord Dor is telling us?'

'Lord Dor speaks the truth as he knows it, my lord; but of course, that is to be expected, and says nothing about the truthfulness of the ambassador from Skelleth. I cannot know what is true at secondhand, like this.'

'You said that the Baron of Skelleth was murdered.'

'Oh, yes, he was! I tested that by three separate divinations; he was stabbed from behind without warning, by the Sword of Bheleu, while unarmed.'

'Then this ambassador is lying.'

'Yes, I suppose so.'

'What is he saying now, Dor?'

'He is explaining that Skelleth hasn't enough wood or food to last the winter and asking that the High King send aid and name a new baron, so that the town will flourish as before, despite this unfortunate incident.'

'Skelleth hasn't flourished in two hundred years!' Deriam said.

'True enough,' Dor agreed. 'I merely repeat what I hear.'

'Now what's happening?'

'Barach of Sland has interrupted the ambassador's speech; he says that the man is obviously a lying blackguard, and asks that the High King send him to Skelleth to learn the truth of the matter.'

'The Baron of Sland *wants* to go to Skelleth?' Thetheru was plainly astonished. He could not imagine anyone wanting to go to such a place.

'That's no surprise,' Karag replied. 'He has always liked the idea of acquiring a second barony, and was rather annoyed when Skelleth went to someone else – when was it? – twenty-three, twenty-four years ago.'

'Even if we do dispose of the overman, it appears that we may have to settle other matters regarding Skelleth,' Shandiph observed.

'I would say so,' Dor agreed. 'The High King has just said that he sees no reason to disbelieve the ambassador and will send what aid he can. He is naming this man Saram as the new Baron of Skelleth, pending his formal presentation at Kholis for confirmation. Barach is raging mad. He's storming out now, calling for his men.'

'We will have to patch up this quarrel when time allows,' Shandiph said.

'Shouldn't we see to it immediately, before anyone does anything foolish?' Deriam asked.

'No,' Shandiph answered, 'I think we should tend to what we've begun first and deal with the overman. He's the more dangerous problem.' He gestured at Chalkara, who was nearing the end of her ritual. 'If these spells have worked, any of them, we should be in plenty of time. If they haven't, then it's all the more important that we handle Garth immediately.'

Chalkara completed her dance with a final flourish and flung the dagger to the floor between her feet. According to the book that contained the spell, the blade was supposed to penetrate any floor, even stone, easily and draw blood. The blood would be that of the intended victim.

The knife struck, ringing, and stuck into the stone floor as intended, but only the tip had penetrated; no blood flowed.

'I don't think it worked,' Kubal said.

'It may be that the overman was already dead,' Derelind said. 'After all, we have tried to kill him a dozen

272

times over. We have burned him, choked him, stabbed him, flayed him, smothered him, poisoned him, and sent birds to tear him to pieces.'

'I hope that's it,' Shandiph said. He leaned on the reading stand and asked the guidebook, 'Is Garth of Ordunin dead?'

Pages turned, and he read aloud. 'This book is not a true oracle, and answers only questions about magic and arcane information known to the Council of the Most High at the close of the Twelfth Age.'

'Try your scrying glass, Kala,' someone said.

There was a general chorus of agreement, and Kala withdrew into the darkness with a single candle she had found. The candle came from a chest of similar candles, each of which the book said held a minor fire-elemental; this was supposed to allow it to burn for several days before being consumed.

The others spoke quietly among themselves for several minutes while Kala struggled with her glass. Most consciously did not look at her, but Karag could not resist; he watched and saw the crystal globe glowing a vivid red.

Then Zhinza, who stood nearest Kala, remarked, 'I smell cooking meat.' An instant later Kala cried out and dropped the sphere. It exploded, and goblets of semi-molten glass spattered in every direction.

Most of the councillors were unhurt, since Kala had stayed well away from the crowd, but Zhinza and Kala received several cuts and burns, and a glowing shard had cut open Sherek's arm. Derelind used the guidebook to locate a healing spell, which Chalkara applied.

The spell stopped the cuts from bleeding and eased most of the burns, but did nothing for Kala's scorched palms.

When that emergency had been dealt with, the twenty councillors looked at one another in the lantern light, each waiting for someone else to speak, until at last

273

Chalkara said, 'Now what? The overman is still alive, or else Kala's glass would not have exploded. None of our spells touched him, apparently. What do we do now?'

Shandiph, for once, had no reply; it was Karag who finally answered slowly, 'I think I have an idea.'

25

Garth was considering his situation as he rode northeastward along the narrow valley.

He was beginning to doubt that he would find any way out of his dilemma. It looked very much as if the only way to free himself of the Sword of Bheleu was to swear to serve the Forgotten King. After all, he knew that the King was someone unique and uniquely powerful; it might well be that there was nothing and no one else who could control the sword. The three wizards had certainly not given it much of a fight.

If it did finally come down to a choice between the King and the sword, he was unsure which he preferred. Either choice would lead to several unwanted deaths; he knew that he could not hope to restrain the sword forever, and the old man admitted that his great magic would kill many people besides himself.

Of course, the Forgotten King's spell would be a single event, while the sword was an ongoing problem. Furthermore, it was possible that Garth would not live long enough to fetch the mysterious book the King wanted. The book might have been destroyed or irrevocably lost long ago.

If it came down to a simple final choice, then, Garth would choose to serve the Forgotten King again, although he was not happy with that decision, since he did not like or trust the old man. He felt that the King was manipulating him, controlling him as if he were a mere beast of burden, to be ordered about or coerced into obedience when it proved reluctant.

Even that, though, was preferable to being possessed

outright by the sword's malevolent power, whatever it was.

He might never find the Book of Silence. His oath to the Forgotten King might lead to nothing. He could not believe, however, that possession of the sword would lead to nothing.

He might somehow contrive to avoid delivering the book, if he did find it. If he worded his oath carefully, he might manage that – or if he broke his oath . . . He stopped his chain of thought abruptly at that point, and looked at that idea.

No overman, it was said, had ever broken a sworn oath, in all the thousand years since the species first came to exist. Garth certainly had not, though he had taken advantage of poor wording on occasion and events beyond his control had sometimes betrayed him.

To break an oath was said to be an offense against the gods – not just whatever gods one might swear by, but any others that might be listening. Garth would once have dismissed this as superstitious human nonsense; now that he was no longer firm in his atheism, he considered it, but dismissed it eventually, anyway. Surely the gods had better things to do than to interfere in mortal affairs over mere words.

Furthermore, he had already defied and offended several gods – Tema, Aghad, Andhur Regvos, Sai, and even The God Whose Name Is Not Spoken. He had defiled their temples and slain their priests, yet no harm had befallen him as a result. He did not need to worry about offending gods, he was quite certain.

But to break an oath would be to destroy his own honor, his family's honor, and the honor of his clan and of his entire species. Never again would anyone trust him, nor would he deserve trust. He would be outcast forever from Ordunin and all the Northern Waste, a disgraced exile. That is, this would be so if it became known that he had broken his word.

Even if it did not become common knowledge, though, *he* would know. His honor would be gone. He would be nothing; he would be no true overman. He would be no better than the lowest human in the alleys of Skelleth.

Ordinarily, he would never even have considered such an action. When the only other choices he faced involved nothing but widespread death, however, he had to consider the possibility. He owed it to the innocents that he might be consigning to death. Was his personal honor worth more than their lives?

Tradition said it was; the legends and tales he had heard in his youth said that nothing was more important than honor. There were stories of overmen and even humans who had died rather than be dishonored, who had allowed family and friends to die, who had slain friends and comrades, all in the name of honor.

It was still too early to be so pessimistic, he told himself. He would first ask the Wise Women what he could do to free himself of the sword. If they told him that only the Forgotten King could free him, then he would swear the oath – and most probably, he would keep it. He could not go against all he had been taught.

He hoped, though, that Ao would tell him of another way in which he could be free.

He studied the hills to his left; he was nearing the point at which the road turned northward again, leading over the next few ridges into a much wider valley, beyond which he would have to cross another, higher range of hills – a range that came much closer to being mountains.

The snow hid the details of the ground, but he was fairly certain he recognized an irregular peak ahead. His turn was just to the nearer side of that.

The sun was low in the west. He would have to consider making camp soon; the daylight had faded sufficiently for

277

the glow of the sword's gem to be visible without turning his head. It seemed to be flickering oddly.

It had been a very strange day. First the three wizards had appeared and then vanished after a brief battle; then later a flock of ravens – unusual in itself, since in his experience ravens tended to be solitary – had swooped down within inches of him before veering off and fleeing, in what he suspected was an omen of some sort. He had felt a series of minor discomforts, which he thought might be unpleasant side-effects of the sword's hold on him; there had been a brief choking, a slight fever, and various prickings and pricklings. Each time the sword's glow had brightened briefly. Each had passed quickly, however, without harming him.

Koros growled faintly, and Garth looked carefully at the surrounding terrain. A faint blue mist was forming ahead of him.

He called a command, and Koros stopped.

The blue fog thickened into a sphere of solid smoke and then spread out to either side. Garth watched and saw vague figures within it.

The smoke continued to spread, and Garth realized that he was not going to be facing three wizards this time, but a small army. Already he could see at least a dozen humans.

Then suddenly the smoke cleared, and he had no time to count his attackers. Without knowing how it came to be there, he saw that the great broadsword was in his hand, and a ball of orange fire was coming directly toward him.

The sword moved in his hands, and the ball was consumed by a greater burst of flame.

More attacks were coming at him, several at once; there was a drifting black smoke, another ball of fire, and a shimmering transparent something that slid down the air toward him. The sword blazed into white flame in his hands and twisted to meet each one.

Overhead clouds gathered. Thunder rumbled in the distance.

A dark exultation grew within him with each threat he met and countered; when he sent a fourth fireball bouncing back toward its creator and skewered a whimpering batlike thing, he could contain it no longer and burst into roaring laughter. Lightning spilled across the sky above him, and thunder blended with his mirth.

Still the attacks came; the staff that he had fought earlier was sending wave after wave of flame toward him, while other magic tore the air around him and shook the ground beneath his feet.

He laughed again. Didn't these fools know who and what he was? As ravens dove out of the sky at him, to be incinerated by the sword's fire, he bellowed, 'I am Bheleu, god of destruction! Death and desolation follow me as hounds; cities are sundered at my touch, and the earth itself shattered! Who are you that dare to affront me thus?'

His warbeast was shifting beneath him; the unnatural assault had upset it. With a wave of the sword he absorbed its consciousness into his own, making its body a part of him.

'I am Shandiph, Master of Demons, Chairman of the Council of the Most High!' someone answered him; the words were almost lost amid the roar of flame and thunder. 'We have come to take the Sword of Bheleu from you, Garth, and thereby prevent the Age of Destruction!'

'Garth?' The overman-thing laughed, and the warbeast growled. 'I am Bheleu, fool! Garth is nothing. Garth is my tool and nothing more. He was born that I might live through him. My time is come at last, and nothing can prevent it!'

'You are Garth of Ordunin, an overman who had the misfortune to acquire a sword you could not control, and we are here to take it from you!'

Garth heard the wizard's words, somewhere beneath the conscious self that called itself Bheleu. He struggled to regain control of his body; the god did not even notice.

'I am Bheleu, the destroyer, and I will destroy you all!'

The wind screamed, and the entire world seemed to vanish in a blinding flash of blue-white light. When Garth could see again, Bheleu's hold on him seemed weaker. He looked around and saw that there had been some sort of immense discharge of energy; several wizards were down, injured or dead.

He struggled again to regain control, vaguely aware that around him the surviving wizards were shouting, screaming, and crying.

The outside world vanished again, this time in blackness. He was floating somewhere in infinite empty darkness, and before him was a vague outline of a figure.

It opened baleful red eyes and spoke to him in his own voice, magnified somehow so that it resounded from the very bones of his skull.

'Garth, why do you resist me?'

Confused, uncertain what was happening, Garth did not answer.

'It does you no good to defy me, Garth. You are my chosen vehicle. I created you in my own image, formed you from conception to birth, shaped your body to house me. You are destined to wield my sword and wreak my will. I have waited since the beginning of time for my age of dominion, and you cannot deny it to me. You will serve me, willingly in the joy of power and destruction, or unwillingly in bondage, for the thirty years I am to rule. The choice is yours. Do you still defy me?'

Garth stared in horror, unable to answer. He had caught a glimpse of the thing's face.

'*I have been benevolent so far. I have refrained from destruction on your behalf and allowed you to waste time in useless attempts to free yourself from my power. You still resist, and thus I have deigned to speak to you. I could smash your will and force you to submit, and I will do so if you do not cooperate, but I would prefer to have you savor my triumph with me. You are my chosen; do not make me destroy you.*'

'I . . . I must think,' Garth replied, stalling for time.

'*I give you until dawn.*'

The blackness vanished and the world returned, but Garth could still see, in the back of his mind, the red eyes of the god.

They were his own eyes. As Bheleu had said, Garth was created in his image. The god had Garth's face, distorted somehow into an insane thing of terror.

The wizards were still attacking him, despite the carnage they had suffered. Eldritch flashes of light and color sparked up on every side, and a shimmering golden pentagram had formed in the air around him. The thing was of no consequence; pentacles could bind demons, but not gods.

One of the humans had crept up behind him, and he saw from the corner of his eye that it was the dark-skinned wizard, flinging a blue crystal sphere at him; he swung the sword to meet it in mid-air. It shattered, and blue smoke poured out.

'Twenty leagues due north of Lagur!' someone called, his voice cracking.

The blue smoke expanded and began to wrap itself around Garth. He laughed and blasted the smoke away with a twitch of his blade.

'You sought to dump me in mid-ocean?' He laughed again; he was a mix of both selves, Garth's consciousness with Bheleu's power and knowledge – which he needed

281

to carry on the fight. 'Is that the best you can do?' he asked mockingly.

Kubal, still standing where he had crept to fling the teleporting crystal, stared up at the overman. Karag's scheme had not worked. The overman had resisted the spell. Half the councillors were dead already, and the overman was laughing.

Kubal fainted.

Bheleu laughed and brought the sword around, intending to incinerate the unconscious wizard.

Garth fought him. The man had battled to prevent destruction; Garth could do no less. There was no need to kill him.

The sword wavered.

'Perhaps I was too generous. I may not wait until dawn,' a voice within Garth said. He alone heard and understood the words.

Bheleu was threatening him. The god did not care to be thwarted. He wanted to kill this feckless wizard here and now, regardless of Garth's reluctance and his avowed intention of allowing Garth freedom to choose his fate.

Garth realized that he could not give in to the god; his choice was no choice at all. He could fight and have his own personality destroyed, or he could acquiesce and cooperate – which would require him to act in a manner alien to him, taking pleasure in killing, surrounding himself with death and chaos. If he chose that course, he would no longer be himself any more than if he forced Bheleu to blot his consciousness out of existence. He had a choice of quick destruction, or slow, subtle, but equally sure destruction.

He had to free himself of the god's domination, and he had to act immediately. Bheleu had given him until dawn, so that was the maximum he could hope for, but it was plain his time might be even shorter; the god did not seem to feel any obligation to live up to his offer, should Garth continue to resist in the interim.

He wished he had never left Skelleth; he might be able to call upon the Forgotten King and surrender to him before Bheleu could prevent it. Here, in the wilderness, he appeared to be doomed.

In despair, he chose to proclaim his defiance rather than yield willingly. There was always a chance that some miracle would save him. He called, in the same voice Bheleu had used, 'I would rather serve the Forgotten King and Death himself!'

The sword turned and pointed at Kubal's prostrate form, but before it could spit forth its flame, a bony hand reached up and grabbed the overman's wrist.

'Swear, Garth,' the familiar hideous voice said, plainly audible in a sudden silence that descended upon the battlefield.

Garth stared at the hand and the tattered yellow cowl that flapped in the dying wind. He swallowed and realized he could detect no trace of Bheleu's influence upon him. The fire in the sword was dying away, the red gem's glow dimming.

The gem went black.

Garth remembered that the old man had always seemed to know more than he should. He must have known what was happening here. It was nevertheless a mystery how he had appeared, unscathed, in the midst of the battle, at exactly the right moment. Garth realized that there were still attackers on all sides and said, 'The wizards . . .'

'They will not harm us,' the Forgotten King replied. 'Swear that you will fetch me the Book of Silence.'

Garth looked down at Kubal. He knew nothing about the man, save that he was a wizard who had come to halt the Age of Bheleu. He would die if Garth did not swear the oath asked of him.

All the wizards would die and hundreds more in time.

Bheleu had said that his age would last for thirty years. Garth had not thought of it in those terms; he had thought of the duration of the sword's control as indefinite and vague. Thirty years was definite, and far longer than anything he had thought about.

Thirty years with no control of his own actions – thirty years of killing anyone who opposed him, rightly or wrongly – thirty years of aimless, wanton destruction and death! Garth could not face that. Anything was better than that. He had killed too often already, ended too many lives that were not his to end.

He would not give in to either destruction or death; he would not betray himself and others in that way.

'I swear,' he said, 'that if you tell me where it can be found, I will bring you the Book of Silence.'

'After you bring it, you will aid me in the magic for which I require it. Swear!'

'I will aid in your magic.'

The old man's other hand reached up and plucked the great sword casually from Garth's numbed fingers. 'I will keep this,' he said, 'as a token of your good faith.'

The words stung, but Garth nodded. He looked around at the wizards.

They stood, motionless, about him.

The Forgotten King held up the Sword of Bheleu and said, 'I send you to your homes.'

Blue mist gathered around each of the living wizards, thickened, and then vanished, taking them with it and leaving several corpses strewn across the valley, sprawled on the blasted earth. The snow had been melted away for well over a hundred yards in every direction.

'Won't they just return?' Garth asked.

'No. They have the war between Sland and Kholis to keep them busy, and they have been sealed away from the old magicks.'

Garth had no idea what the old man was referring to.

He gazed about regretfully at the dead. They had brought matters to a head sooner than he had wished; he had never had the chance to ask the Wise Women whether he had another course of action available. He was free of the sword now, but at a price to himself that seemed terrible indeed.

He had sworn an oath he had no intention of fulfilling; his honor was gone.

26

Haggat put down his new scrying glass and stared at it thoughtfully. He was not entirely pleased with the course events had followed, but it would do. The Council of the Most High had suffered badly, though it was not destroyed. The overman Garth yet lived, but he no longer possessed the Sword of Bheleu and could therefore be dealt with by the cult's ordinary methods. That was all satisfactory.

The yellow-garbed figure might be a problem, however. Haggat did not know who or what he was, but he obviously controlled considerable power, judging by the ease with which he had taken the sword from Garth and apparently rendered it harmless. The scrying glass would not show him directly, any more than it had been able to show Garth while the sword's power shielded him, but Haggat caught glimpses while watching Garth's slow journey back to Skelleth. The man in yellow tatters had walked at his side the entire distance and occasionally come partially into view. His face had never been visible at all, not even for the briefest of glimpses. He carried the sword as if it weighed nothing and seemed unbothered by cold or fatigue from the long walk – though it was hard to be sure from such fleeting images.

He probably wasn't anybody important, Haggat decided finally. He was some obscure wizard who had chanced upon a spell that could control the sword, at a guess. He was nothing to worry about.

Anyway, it was Garth who concerned the cult. The death of the former high priest had yet to be avenged. Something would have to be done about that.

* * *

Shandiph was a wanderer and had no true home of his own; he materialized in Chalkara's chambers in Kholis, side by side with the court wizard, and then collapsed on to the rug. He had survived the great blast, but his injuries were serious. He had remained upright, casting spells, only through force of will.

Chalkara was unhurt; she bent over him and tended to his injuries as best she could, while shouting for the servants.

'Where are the others?' he managed to ask.

'I don't know,' she replied. 'That . . . that whatever-it-was said it was sending us home; perhaps the others are in their own homes now.'

'They aren't all dead?'

'No, no. They're not. I saw that many still lived.'

'That's good.' His head fell back on the cushion she had slid beneath it.

'Shandi . . . who *was* that? How could he do all that?'

'I think it was the King in Yellow,' Shandiph answered.

'He has the sword now.'

Shandiph shook his head slightly. 'He can't use it. Only the god's chosen one can use it.'

'Then it's all over?'

He nodded, weakly.

A servant appeared in the doorway, staring in astonishment.

'Don't just stand there,' Chalkara snapped. 'Go and find a physician.'

The girl nodded and vanished, her running footsteps echoing in the stone corridor.

Chalkara remained, kneeling over Shandiph's body, praying to the Lords of Eir that he wouldn't die.

There was shouting outside his door; Karag dropped the last splintered fragment of the Great Staff and worked the latch.

287

Servants and guardsmen were hurrying past; he reached out a soot-blackened hand and stopped a rushing housemaid.

'What's happening?' he croaked.

'Oh, my lord wizard, you're back!'

'Yes, I'm back. What's going on?'

'The Baron has just returned from Kholis, my lord, and they say he's angrier than anyone has ever seen him! The High King has again denied him the Barony of Skelleth, he says, and kidnapped his wizard – he means you! Oh, you had better go and see him at once!'

Karag nodded. 'I will go immediately.' He released the woman's arm, and she ran off.

He looked down at himself. He was filthy, his cloak was in tatters, but he was unhurt; the staff had protected him. Then that great burst of light had shattered the staff, and he had been certain he was about to die. He remembered that.

Kubal had crept up behind the overman, as his plan called for, while Chalkara drew the pentagram, and he had used the transporting spell, but it hadn't worked; the sword had absorbed it somehow. The overman had laughed; Karag remembered that with painful clarity. The overman had laughed at his scheme.

Then there had been a stranger in a ragged yellow cloak at the overman's side, taking the sword from him – and then he was here, in his own room.

It didn't seem to make much sense.

There was more shouting somewhere, and he decided against taking time to clean himself up. The Baron would be mad enough with him as it was. He joined the hurrying crowd in the passageway and made his way down to the great hall.

As he walked in the door, the Baron, standing on the dais, immediately caught sight of him.

'There you are, traitor! Have you returned to beg my forgiveness?'

'What have I done, my lord? How did I come here?' He had decided instantly upon his approach; he would claim to remember nothing of the last few days. Let the Baron think he had been kidnapped.

The Baron glared at him for a long moment, then said, 'All right, I will accept you back, and you will tell me later what became of you. Right now I have more important matters to attend to. I have abrogated the covenant and declared war upon the Baron of Kholis, who calls himself King. My men are preparing to march even now, and the messengers I sent back from the false king's castle have had siege engines built. You, wizard, will aid me in this war with your spells.'

Karag stared up at his master in dismay.

Garth sat quietly at the Forgotten King's table in the King's Inn, staring at his mug of ale. He and the old man had travelled all night and half the following morning to return to Skelleth, and Garth had then slept away the rest of the day. When he awoke, the King was back in his corner as if nothing had happened. There was no sign of the sword.

Garth had gotten his ale and seated himself, but neither had spoken.

Finally, the overman said, 'It would seem that the Age of Destruction is averted; what does that do to the reckoning of time?'

'Lessened, not averted,' the old man replied.

'Only lessened?'

'Yes. Already the Kingdom of Eramma is destroyed by civil war.'

'It is?'

The old man nodded.

Garth wondered at that. He saw no sign of any war

and no news of one had reached him since his return to Skelleth. Still, he knew that the Forgotten King had knowledge beyond the ordinary.

'That's unfortunate. Wars are wasteful and unnecessary.'

The King did not reply.

There was a moment of silence, and then Garth asked, 'Who were those wizards? Why did they attack me?'

'The Council of the Most High, as they call themselves, is sworn to preserve peace,' the old man answered.

'Will they stop the war, then?'

'They will try and fail.'

'Might they not attack me again – or you?'

'No. They have no magic powerful enough and are scattered and weakened.'

'They seemed powerful to me.'

'They drew upon the vault where their ancestors stored away much of their power. I have sealed the vault against them.'

'Might they be able to stop the war, if they had this old magic?'

The Forgotten King shrugged.

Garth sipped his ale, then asked, 'When will you send me after the Book of Silence?'

'When I remember where it is.'

'When you remember? Then you knew once?'

The King nodded.

Garth sipped ale again, and asked, 'Have you any idea how long it will take you to remember?'

The King replied, 'I know that it was I who moved the book from its place in Dûsarra, because no one save you and I can carry it and live. That is all I know. I may recall where I left it tomorrow, or not for thirty years. Until I do, do not bother me. You are free to do as you please, so long as you do not leave Skelleth for any extended period of time, until I remember. Now go away.'

Garth kept his face impassive as he picked up his mug and moved to another table. When he was sure that the old man could not see him, he allowed himself a bitter smile.

The King had made an unusually long speech and an unusually careless one. He had failed to say what an extended period of time was, and Garth found no problem in thinking a year or two would not be excessive. The old man himself had freed Garth from much of the restraint his oath would have placed upon him; no one need know he was forsworn for some time yet.

Anything might happen before the Forgotten King remembered; he might die, Garth might die, or the oath might be renounced. Garth's false semblance of honor might be retained for years, perhaps even for the rest of his life.

He knew it to be a false semblance, for he had given his oath in bad faith. He gulped down the rest of his ale and signed to the innkeeper for another.

He wondered whether there might not be a higher honor in sacrificing his name and good word for the lives of others.

No, he told himself, he would not delude himself with such false excuses.

The innkeeper approached with a fresh mug, but before he could place it on the table a sudden loud noise drew the attention of both overman and servitor. There was a burst of shouting and much rattling and thumping somewhere outside the King's Inn.

After a moment of ongoing racket, the unmistakable roar of a warbeast sounded, and the taverner dropped the mug in surprise, denting the pewter vessel and spattering cold ale across the floor and Garth's legs. The overman paid no attention; he shoved back his chair, rose, and strode to the door to see what was happening, while

291

behind him the innkeeper wiped at the floor with his apron.

Garth had a moment of fear that a new battle had begun and that Skelleth was perhaps to be destroyed all over again. Could the King have been wrong about the wizards? Were they attacking anew?

He dismissed such pessimistic thoughts almost immediately; the sounds were not those of battle, nor of any destructive magic he had yet encountered. There was a cheerful note to the shouting.

He paused in the doorway and looked out. Directly before him was the dark hole where the Baron's mansion had stood, but beyond it the marketplace was bright with torches and crowded with people and animals. The sun had been down for the better part of an hour, so this gathering was no ordinary trading.

There were men, women, and overmen in the market, as well as several warbeasts and oxen. Most of the people, of whatever species, appeared to be clustered about a pair of warbeasts and a small group of overmen.

Curious, and with nothing to prevent him from doing as he pleased, he marched down the ramp into the cellar pits, across the floor, and up the opposite slope toward the square. As he emerged, he spotted Saram in the midst of the mob, looking about wildly; Frima was near him, and Galt was approaching from the opposite direction.

Garth looked over the central grouping; with a start, he recognized the warbeasts and one of the overmen. Tand and his party had returned.

The apprentice trader looked exhausted, and at least one of his companions wore a bloody bandage. Behind him, Garth realized for the first time, were several overmen he had never seen before, wearing strange and outlandish attire – bright cloaks, enamelled armor, flaring helmets. Most of them stood quite tall, taller than Garth or most other overmen of the Northern Waste. There were men as well, dressed similarly, and the oxen he had noticed before he now realized formed a line, drawing carts and wagons.

Tand's mission to the Yprian Coast had obviously been successful; he had brought back a full caravan. Garth's bitter gloom dissipated in pleased surprise; he had held little real hope for Tand's errand after his own plans had been shattered by the Sword of Bheleu, the City Council's disavowal of his actions, and the disastrous battles with the wizards. He had somehow assumed, after all that, that nothing could ever go right again.

Saram had spotted him and was calling and waving; Garth could not make out any words over the general hubbub, but it was plain that Saram wanted to speak with him. Accordingly, he shoved his way into the crowd, bellowing, 'Make way! Make way!'

Boots alternately sticking and sliding in the snow and mud underfoot, Garth finally managed to come within earshot of the acting Baron of Skelleth.

'Garth!' Saram called. 'Do you have any money?'

'What?'

It was Tand who replied. 'These people have brought stocks of food, furs, and other goods, but they demand to see payment before they will allow any to be unloaded. There is nothing in Skelleth they wish to trade for; I promised them gold, told them that Ordunin was rich in gold.'

'Aye!' a new voice said in a harsh and alien accent. 'The lad said there was gold to be had!'

'There is!' Garth called back. He turned back toward the King's Inn and bellowed at the top of his lungs, 'Ho! Koros!'

He had left the warbeast in an alley at one side of the Inn; there were still too few buildings under roof in Skelleth to permit the stables to be used for mere beasts rather than homeless humans. Koros answered with an audible growl and emerged into the light of the market's torches.

Garth called again, and the monstrous beast trotted forward. Disdaining the earthen ramps, it leaped down into the cellar pits and then out again on the market side and made its way across the square toward its master.

The crowd parted before it, and it walked in silent majesty down a broad aisle to Garth's side.

He took a sack from behind the saddle and pulled out a handful of Aghadite coins that glittered rich yellow in the firelight.

Somewhere someone in the crowd applauded loudly, and the faces of the Yprians, half-hidden beneath their curious helmets, broke into smiles.

'You see?' Tand said with perceptible relief. 'I did not lie.'

'You did not lie, little one,' agreed the Yprian spokesman. 'Let the bargaining begin!'

Garth lost track of what was happening for several minutes as the crowd gathered around the ox-drawn wagons with much loud talking. He made his way nearer; the presence of Koros at his heel meant that he need not fight the throng, which parted before the warbeast's fangs like snow before flame.

When he reached the caravan, he saw that the villagers were unloading grain, furs, and other goods from the wagons, with Yprian humans keeping careful tally of what was taken, and the Yprian overmen overseeing the operation, making certain that everything went smoothly and no pilferage occurred. As each cart or wagon was emptied of what the people of Skelleth wanted, the man who had been watching it brought the listing of what had been taken and what was left to the group by the warbeasts where Tand, Saram, and several Yprians took note and added the items to their own listings. Galt had made his way in from the other side of the crowd and was watching with evident interest.

Frima was shut out, being far too short to see above the shoulders of the traders; she came over, eyes shining in the torchlight, to speak to Garth.

'Isn't it wonderful?' she exclaimed.

'It is, indeed,' Garth agreed.

'There's enough here to last half the winter!'

Garth could not help wondering aloud, 'But what of the other half?'

'Oh, don't worry! We'll manage something! Saram won't let Skelleth starve.'

Garth noted where she put her trust. 'You seem pleased with Saram's company,' he remarked.

'Oh, I love him! He's so kind and gentle! Thank you, Garth, for rescuing me from Dûsarra and bringing me here!'

Garth found himself amused by her shift in loyalties, but before he could reply, Saram, Tand, and an Yprian suddenly drowned out other conversation, debating the value of Yprian wine in belligerent shouts. Saram, quickly outmatched by the superhuman bellowings of the two overmen, dropped out and tried to settle grain prices with another of the caravan's attendants.

Galt noticed Garth's presence and came over to speak. When the debate died suddenly with Tand's concession that even such a poor vintage was worth a pennyweight of gold for every twenty skins to a starving village, Galt remarked, 'We are doing well. Our gold buys here seven times what it bought in Lagur.'

'Fortunate indeed, since my supply is not unlimited; Tand has just sworn away half a pound of gold on wine and spices, if I heard right.'

'Yours is not the only gold in Skelleth; we'll take up a collection when time permits. And do not think Tand wastes the gold; we can send some of Saram's people to

Ordunin with those wineskins and spice jars and bring you at least triple your money. You've got the trade you wanted, Garth.'

Garth nodded and watched.

Half an hour later the trading was finished; the Yprian oxcarts were mostly empty, and Garth's gold was approximately halved. Skelleth's people were scattering to wherever they currently made their homes, makeshift for most, permanent for a lucky few; the food and goods purchased were being stored in one of the new houses, under the supervision of several of Saram's ministers, for later distribution, save for furs and warm clothing that had been handed out to the old, the ill-clad, and the children of the village. The Yprians themselves made camp in the market, where they could keep a good eye on their profits and their remaining goods. Garth, Tand, Galt, Saram, and Frima gathered in the King's Inn for a round of drinks to celebrate the evening's events before retiring.

There was much congratulation of Tand and his fellows, and the apprentice trader remarked in reply, 'It was mostly luck; they were eager to trade. In fact their leader, Fargan, tells me he's planning a second expedition, to be made with sledges instead of wagons, now that the snows have come.'

'We can use it,' Saram said. 'And we'll want to buy some of those sledges, or build our own, and send them up to Ordunin, Galt tells me.'

'There would be a fine profit in it,' Galt agreed.

'I might send a party to Ur-Dormulk as well,' Saram mused.

No one answered him; they were all tired and thirsty and preferred to drink.

Garth leaned back in his chair, which creaked warningly beneath his weight, and sipped wine. He smiled to himself.

False oath or no, and whatever the state of his personal honor, there was no denying that he had done at least some good here. The gold he had brought from the temple of Aghad and the knowledge of overmen on the Yprian Coast acquired in Dûsarra had saved Skelleth from starvation. The trade he had sought was at last a reality, and Ordunin would be free of Lagur's monopoly. He was himself free of the Sword of Bheleu. His enemies were defeated, and the Baron of Skelleth dead.

Things might be better, but for the present they would do.

Glossary of Gods Mentioned in the Text

(There are four classes of deity in Eramman theology. Dagha is in an unnamed class by himself, above all others. The other major gods are divided into the seven Lords of Eir, or beneficent gods, and the seven Lords of Dûs, or dark gods. Finally, there are innumerable Arkhein, or minor gods, who are neither wholly good nor wholly evil, but cover a broad range between. This glossary is arranged alphabetically, disregarding these distinctions and the elaborate hierarchy within each group, but each god's listing specifies in which of the categories he belongs.)

AAL: Reckoned either second or third of the Lords of Eir, Aal is the god of growth and fertility; he is worshipped widely, being the special favorite of farmers and pregnant women.

AGHAD: Fourth among the Lords of Dûs, Aghad is the god of hatred, loathing, fear, betrayal, and most other actively negative emotions. He is widely sworn by, but worshipped only by his relatively small cult.

AMERA: Goddess of the day, Amera is seventh and last among the Lords of Eir. She is worshipped widely nevertheless and revered as the mother of the sun.

ANDHUR: One of the two aspects of Andhur Regvos, sixth Lord of Dûs, Andhur is god of darkness. He is extremely unpopular.

ANDHUR REGVOS: See ANDHUR and REGVOS.

AYVI: First of the Lords of Eir, Ayvi is the god of life and conception. Since he is ruler only of the creation of life, and not its preservation or improvement, he is prayed to only by would-be parents and breeders of livestock. His name is rarely used; like his dark counterpart, The God Whose Name Is Not Spoken, he is usually referred to by description rather than by name, e.g., Life, the Life-God, the Birth-God (inaccurate but common), the First God.

BEL VALA: God of strength and preservation, Bel Vala is rated either second or third among the Lords of Eir. He is a favorite god of soldiers and warriors, and supposed to be of particular aid if prayed to in times of dire stress.

BHELEU: God of chaos and destruction, ranked second among the Lords of Dûs. Bheleu is worshipped only by a very few people since Garth's killing of his Dûsarran cultists, mostly the more deranged and violent lords and warriors.

DAGHA: In a class by himself/herself/itself, Dagha is the god of time and the creator of the Lords of Eir and Dûs. Dagha is the only deity not assigned a gender, though he is customarily referred to in the masculine form for the sake of convenience. Believed to be above all mundane concerns, Dagha is not worshipped or prayed to.

DÛS, LORDS OF: The dark gods: Tema, Andhur Regvos, Sai, Aghad, P'hul, Bheleu, and The God Whose Name Is Not Spoken.

EIR, LORDS OF: The gods of light: Amera, Leuk, Gau, Pria, Bel Vala, Aal, and Ayvi.

EKNISSA: Arkhein goddess of fire, worshipped mostly by barbaric tribesmen.

ERAMMA: The Arkhein earth-mother goddess, for whom the Kingdom of Eramma was named, since the kingdom's founders intended it to take in all the world – a goal that it never came close to achieving. The worship of Eramma is considered old-fashioned, but still lingers among farming folk.

GAU: Fifth among the Lords of Eir, Gau is goddess of

joy and pleasure in all its forms, including eating, sex, and strong drink, as well as the less earthly delights of humor and good company. Worshipped everywhere, in various and sundry ways.

GOD WHOSE NAME IS NOT SPOKEN, THE: This term is used to refer to the first of the Lords of Dûs, the god of death. He does have a name, known to a very few, but it is popularly believed that any person speaking the name aloud will die instantly. He is sometimes referred to simply as Death. He is not worshipped, but shunned everywhere, feared even by the caretakers of his temple in Dûsarra. Various circumlocutions are used to avoid mentioning him; he is known as the Final God, the Death-God, and other such things.

KEWERRO: A very ancient god identified with storms and the north wind. Placatory sacrifices are common, but he has no real worshippers.

KOROS: Arkhein god of war, strife and battle, often considered to be Bheleu's son and servant. Worshipped by the more fanatical soldiers and warriors.

LEUK: Sixth of the Lords of Eir, Leuk is the god of light, color, and insight.

MELITH: Arkhein goddess of lightning.

MORI: Arkhein god of the sea, worshipped by sailors everywhere. The Sea of Mori is believed to be the god's particular home.

P'HUL: The third among the Lords of Dûs, P'hul is the goddess of decay, disease, and age. She is worshipped only by her small cult in Dûsarra, but is widely prayed to in hopes of warding off her touch.

PRIA: Fourth among the Lords of Eir, Pria is the goddess of love, friendship, and peace, and of beneficial emotions generally, the exact opposite and counterpart to Aghad. She is one of the most popular deities.

REGVOS: The more popular of the two aspects of Andhur

Regvos, sixth Lord of Dûs, Regvos is the god of blindness, ignorance, stupidity, and folly.

SAI: Fifth among the Lords of Dûs, Sai is the goddess of pain and suffering. Where her brother Aghad dominates the actively negative emotions, Sai is the ruler of the passively negative: despair, sorrow, acquiescence, masochism. She is secretly worshipped by those with a sadistic streak throughout the world, since physical pain is within her province.

SAVEL SKAI: Arkhein god of the sun; the name means 'the bright shining one.' Popular to swear by, but not seriously worshipped by civilized people.

SNEG: Sneg is the god of winter, one of the four Arkhein falling into the subcategory of Yaroi, or gods of the seasons. He is worshipped only by those who depend upon him, such as ice-cutters.

SRIG: Arkhein god of cold, usually closely associated with Sneg.

TEMA: Seventh of the Lords of Dûs, Tema is the goddess of the night and its creatures. She is the patroness of most of the population of Dûsarra and much of the rest of Nekutta as well.

WEIDA: Arkhein goddess of wisdom, Weida is worshipped by scholars and seers everywhere.

The world's greatest science fiction authors now available in paperback from Grafton Books

Brian W Aldiss

Helliconia Spring	£2.95	☐
Helliconia Summer	£2.50	☐
Helliconia Winter	£2.95	☐
New Arrivals, Old Encounters	£1.95	☐
Frankenstein Unbound	£1.95	☐
Moreau's Other Island	£1.95	☐
Last Orders	£1.95	☐
Galaxies Like Grains of Sand	£1.95	☐
The Dark Light Years	£1.95	☐
Barefoot in the Head	£1.95	☐
Space, Time and Nathaniel	£1.95	☐
Starswarm	£1.95	☐
Hothouse	£1.95	☐
Cryptozoic	£1.95	☐
Earthworks	£1.95	☐
Brothers of the Head	£1.95	☐
Moment of Eclipse	£1.95	☐
Greybeard	£1.95	☐
Enemies of the System	£1.95	☐
Seasons in Flight	£1.95	☐

General Fiction

The Malacia Tapestry	£1.95	☐

Brian Aldiss with Harry Harrison (Editors)

Farewell Fantastic Venus!	£1.95	☐

To order direct from the publisher just tick the titles you want and fill in the order form.

SF781

All these books are available at your local bookshop or newsagent, or can be ordered direct from the publisher.

To order direct from the publishers just tick the titles you want and fill in the form below.

Name _____

Address _____

_____

Send to:
Grafton Cash Sales
PO Box 11, Falmouth, Cornwall TR10 9EN.

Please enclose remittance to the value of the cover price plus:

UK 60p for the first book, 25p for the second book plus 15p per copy for each additional book ordered to a maximum charge of £1.90.

BFPO 60p for the first book, 25p for the second book plus 15p per copy for the next 7 books, thereafter 9p per book.

Overseas including Eire £1.25 for the first book, 75p for second book and 28p for each additional book.

Grafton Books reserve the right to show new retail prices on covers, which may differ from those previously advertised in the text or elsewhere.